D1236877

The Sorcery Code

Dima Zales

♠ Mozaika Publications ♠

www.dimazales.com

Published by Mozaika Publications, an imprint of Mozaika LLC.

www.mozaikallc.com

e-ISBN: 978-0-9883913-8-3
ISBN: 978-0-9883913-9-0

DEDICATION

I would like to dedicate *The Sorcery Code* to my wife. Without Anna, this book would not have been possible. I am the luckiest husband in the world. I am also grateful to our families and friends, both in New York and Florida, for being so supportive of our dream.

I want to give special thanks to our beta readers (Tanya, Erika, Fern, and Kelly) and all the bloggers who are reviewing the book. And last but not least, our readers!

Koldun

Sanderson

Mariner

Lenten

Monsir

Pesta

Ruark

Dania

Ganir

Turingrad

Dini

Blaise

Furak

Kelvin

Alania

Gina

Neumanngrad

Augusta

CHAPTER ONE

※ BLAISE ※

There was a naked woman on the floor of Blaise's study.

A beautiful naked woman.

Stunned, Blaise stared at the gorgeous creature who just appeared out of thin air. She was looking around with a bewildered expression on her face, apparently as shocked to be there as he was to be seeing her. Her wavy blond hair streamed down her back, partially covering a body that appeared to be perfection itself. Blaise tried not to think about that body and to focus on the situation instead.

A woman. A *She*, not an *It*. Blaise could hardly believe it. Could it be? Could this girl be the object?

She was sitting with her legs folded underneath her, propping herself up with one slim arm. There was something awkward about that pose, as though she didn't know what to do with her own limbs. In general, despite the curves that marked her a fully grown woman, there was a child-like innocence in the way she sat there, completely unselfconscious and totally unaware of her own appeal.

Clearing his throat, Blaise tried to think of what to say. In his wildest dreams, he couldn't have imagined this kind of outcome to the project that had consumed his entire life for the past several months.

Hearing the sound, she turned her head to look at him, and Blaise found himself staring into a pair of unusually clear blue eyes.

She blinked, then cocked her head to the side, studying him with visible curiosity. Blaise wondered what she was seeing. He hadn't seen the light of day in weeks, and he wouldn't be surprised if he looked like a mad sorcerer at this point. There was probably a week's worth of stubble covering his face, and he knew his dark hair was unbrushed and sticking out in every direction. If he'd known he would be facing a beautiful woman today, he would've done a grooming spell in the morning.

"Who am I?" she asked, startling Blaise. Her voice was soft and feminine, as alluring as the rest of her. "What is this place?"

"You don't know?" Blaise was glad he finally managed to string together a semi-coherent sentence. "You don't know who you are or where you are?"

She shook her head. "No."

Blaise swallowed. "I see."

"What am I?" she asked again, staring at him with

those incredible eyes.

"Well," Blaise said slowly, "if you're not some cruel prankster or a figment of my imagination, then it's somewhat difficult to explain . . ."

She was watching his mouth as he spoke, and when he stopped, she looked up again, meeting his gaze. "It's strange," she said, "hearing words this way. These are the first real words I've heard."

Blaise felt a chill go down his spine. Getting up from his chair, he began to pace, trying to keep his eyes off her nude body. He had been expecting *something* to appear. A magical object, a thing. He just hadn't known what form that thing would take. A mirror, perhaps, or a lamp. Maybe even something as unusual as the Life Capture Sphere that sat on his desk like a large round diamond.

But a person? A female person at that?

To be fair, he *had been* trying to make the object intelligent, to ensure it would have the ability to comprehend human language and convert it into the code. Maybe he shouldn't be so surprised that the intelligence he invoked took on a human shape.

A beautiful, feminine, sensual shape.

Focus, Blaise, focus.

"Why are you walking like that?" She slowly got to her feet, her movements uncertain and strangely clumsy. "Should I be walking too? Is that how people talk to each other?"

Blaise stopped in front of her, doing his best to keep his eyes above her neck. "I'm sorry. I'm not accustomed to naked women in my study."

She ran her hands down her body, as though trying to feel it for the first time. Whatever her intent, Blaise found the gesture extremely erotic.

"Is something wrong with the way I look?" she asked. It was such a typical feminine concern that Blaise had to stifle a smile.

"Quite the opposite," he assured her. "You look unimaginably good." So good, in fact, that he was having trouble concentrating on anything but her delicate curves. She was of medium height, and so perfectly proportioned that she could've been used as a sculptor's template.

"Why do I look this way?" A small frown creased her smooth forehead. "What am I?" That last part seemed to be puzzling her the most.

Blaise took a deep breath, trying to calm his racing pulse. "I think I can try to venture a guess, but before I do, I want to give you some clothing. Please wait here—I'll be right back."

And without waiting for her answer, he hurried out of the room.

* * *

Leaving his study, Blaise briskly walked to the other end of his house, to 'her room' as he still thought about the half-empty chamber. This was where Augusta used to keep her things when they were together—a time that now seemed like ages ago. Despite that, entering the dusty room was just as painful now as it had been two years ago. Parting with the woman he'd been with for eight years—the woman he'd been about to marry—had not been easy.

Trying to keep his mind on the task at hand, Blaise approached the closet and surveyed its contents. As he'd hoped, there were a few dozen dresses hanging there. Beautiful long dresses made of silk and velvet, Augusta's favorite materials. Only sorcerers—the upper echelon of their society—could afford such luxury. The regular people were far too poor to wear anything but rough homespun cloth. It made Blaise sick when he thought about it, the terrible inequality that still permeated every aspect of life in Koldun.

He and Augusta had always argued about that, he remembered. She had never shared his concern about the commoners; instead, she enjoyed the status quo and all the privileges that came with being a respected sorcerer. If Blaise recalled correctly, she'd worn a different dress every day of her life, flaunting her wealth without shame.

Well, at least the dresses she left at his house would come in handy now. Grabbing one of them—a blue silk concoction that undoubtedly cost a fortune—and a pair of finely made black velvet slippers, Blaise exited the room, leaving behind layers of dust and bitter memories.

He ran into the naked being on his way back. She was standing near the entrance of his study, looking at a painting his brother Louie had made. It was of a village in Blaise's territory, and the scene it depicted was an idyllic one—a festival after a big harvest. Laughing, rosy-cheeked peasants were dancing with each other, a traveling harpist playing in the background. Blaise liked looking at that painting. It reminded him that his subjects had good times too, that their lives were not solely work.

The girl also seemed to like looking at it—and touching it. Her fingers were stroking the frame as though trying to learn its texture. Her nude body looked just as magnificent from the back as it did from the front, and Blaise again found his thoughts straying in inappropriate directions.

"Here," he said gruffly, entering the study and putting the dress and the shoes down on the dusty couch. "Please put these on." For the first time since Louie's death, he was cognizant of the state of his house—and ashamed of it. Augusta's room was not the only one covered with dust. Even here, where he spent most of his time, the air was musty and stale.

Esther and Maya had repeatedly offered to come over and clean, but he'd refused, not wanting to see anyone. Not even the two peasant women who had been like mothers to him. After the debacle with Louie, all he'd wanted was to be left alone, to hide away from the rest of the world. As far as the other sorcerers were concerned, he was a pariah, an outcast, and that was fine with Blaise. He hated them all now too. Sometimes he thought the bitterness would consume him—and it probably would have, if it hadn't been for his work.

And now the outcome of that work was lifting the

dress and studying it curiously, still as naked as a newborn baby. "How do I put it on?" she asked, looking up at him.

Blaise blinked. He'd had practice taking dresses off women, but putting them on? Still, he probably knew more about clothes than the mysterious being standing in front of him. Taking the dress from her hands, he unlaced the back and held it out to her. "Here. Step into it and pull it up, making sure that your arms go into the sleeves." Then he turned away, doing his best to control his reaction to her beauty.

He heard some fumbling.

"I might need a little help," she said.

Turning back, Blaise was relieved to see that all she needed help with was tying the lace on the back. She had already figured out how to put on the shoes. The dress fit her surprisingly well; she and Augusta had to be of similar size, though this girl appeared more delicate somehow. "Lift your hair," he told her, and she did, holding the long blond locks with unconscious grace. He quickly laced the dress and stepped back, needing to put a little distance between them.

She turned to face him, and their eyes met. Blaise couldn't help but notice the cool intelligence reflected in her gaze. She might not know anything yet, but she was learning fast—and functioning incredibly well, if what he suspected about her origin was true.

For a few seconds, they just looked at each other, sharing a comfortable silence. She didn't appear to be in a rush to speak. Instead, she studied him, her eyes roaming over his face, his body. She seemed to find him as fascinating as he found her. And no wonder—Blaise was probably the first human she'd encountered.

Finally, she broke the silence. "Can we talk now?"

"Yes." Blaise smiled. "We can, and we should." Walking over to the couch area, he sat down on one of the lounge chairs next to the small round table. The woman followed his example, taking a seat in the chair opposite him.

"I'm afraid we're going to have to work out the answers to your many questions together," Blaise told her, and she nodded.

"I want to understand," she said. "What am I?"

Blaise took a deep breath. "Let me start at the beginning," he said, racking his brain for the best way to go about this. "You see, I have been searching for a long time for a way to make magic more accessible for the commoners—"

"Is it not accessible currently?" she asked, looking at him intently. He could tell she was extremely curious about anything and everything, absorbing her surroundings and every word he said like a sponge.

"No, it's not. Right now, magic is only possible for a select few—those who have the right predisposition in terms of how analytical and mathematically inclined their minds are. Even those lucky few have to study very hard to be able to cast spells of any complexity."

She nodded as though it made sense to her. "All right. So what does it have to do with me?"

"Everything," Blaise said. "You see, it all started with Lenard the Great. He's the one who first learned how to tap into the Spell Realm—"

"The Spell Realm?"

"Yes. The Spell Realm is what we call the place where spells are formed—the place that enables us to do magic. We don't know much about it because we live in the Physical Realm—what we think of as the real world." Blaise paused to see if the woman had any questions. He imagined it must all be overwhelming for her.

She cocked her head to the side. "All right. Please continue."

"Some two hundred and seventy years ago, Lenard the Great invented the first oral spells—a way for us to interact with the Spell Realm and change the reality of the Physical Realm. These spells were extremely difficult to get right because they involved a specialized arcane language. It had to be spoken and planned very exactly to get the desired result. It wasn't until recently that a simpler magical language and an easier way to do spells was invented."

"Who invented it?" the woman asked, looking intrigued.

"Well, Augusta and I did, actually," Blaise admitted. "She's my former fiancée. We are what you would call sorcerers—those who have the aptitude for the study of magic. Augusta created a magical object called the Interpreter Stone, and I came up with a simpler magical language to go along with it. So now, instead of reciting a difficult verbal spell, a sorcerer can use the simpler language to write his spell on cards and feed it to the stone."

She blinked. "I see."

"Our work was supposed to change society for the better," Blaise continued, trying to keep the bitterness out of his voice. "Or at least that's what I had hoped. I thought an easier way to do magic would enable more people to do it, but it didn't turn out that way. The powerful sorcerer class got even more powerful—and even more averse to sharing their knowledge with the common people."

"Is that bad?" she asked, regarding him with her clear blue gaze.

"It depends on whom you ask," Blaise said, thinking of Augusta's casual disregard for the peasants. "I think it's terrible, but I'm in the minority. Most sorcerers like the status quo. They have wealth and power, and they don't mind that their subjects live in abject poverty."

"But you do," she said perceptively.

"I do," Blaise confirmed. "And when I left the Sorcerer Council a year ago, I decided to do something about it. You see, I wanted to create a magical object that would understand our normal spoken language—an object that anyone could use. This way, a regular person could do magic. They would just say what they needed, and the object would make it happen."

Her eyes widened, and Blaise could see the

dawning comprehension on her face. "Are you saying—?"

"Yes," he said, staring at her. "I believe I succeeded in creating that object. I think you are the result of my work."

They sat there in silence for a few moments.

"I must have the wrong understanding of the word 'object'," she finally said.

"You probably don't. The chair you sit on is a regular object. If you'll look out the window, you'll see a chaise in the yard. That's a magical object; it can fly. Objects are inanimate. I expected you to be something like a talking mirror, but you are something else entirely."

She frowned a little. "If you created me, does that mean you are my father?"

"No," Blaise denied immediately, everything inside him rejecting that idea. "I am most certainly not your father." Somehow it was important to make sure she did not think of him that way. *Look at where my mind is going again*, he chided himself.

She continued looking confused, so Blaise tried to explain further. "I think it might make more sense to say that I created the basic design for an intelligence—and made sure it had some knowledge to build on—but from there, you must have created yourself."

He could see a spark of recognition in her gaze. Something about that statement resonated with her, so she had to know more than it seemed at first.

"Can you tell me anything about yourself?" Blaise

asked, studying the beautiful creature in front of him. "For starters, what do you call yourself?"

"I don't call myself anything," she said. "What do *you* call yourself?"

"I am Blaise, son of Dasbraw. You would just call me Blaise."

"Blaise," she said slowly, as though tasting his name. Her voice was soft and sensual, innocently seductive. It made Blaise painfully aware that it had been two years since he had been this close to a woman.

"Yes, that's right," he managed to say calmly. "And we should come up with a name for you as well."

"Do you have any ideas?" she asked curiously.

"Well, my grandmother's name was Galina. Would you like to honor my family by taking her name? You can be Galina, daughter of the Spell Realm. I would call you 'Gala' for short." The indomitable old lady had been nothing like the girl sitting in front of him, yet something about the bright intelligence on this woman's face reminded him of her. He smiled fondly at the memories.

"Gala," she tried saying. He could see that she liked it because she smiled back at him, showing even white teeth. The smile lit her entire face, making her glow.

"Yes." Blaise couldn't tear his eyes away from her luminous beauty. "Gala. It suits you."

"Gala," she repeated softly. "Gala. Yes, I agree. It does suit me. But you said that I am daughter of the

Spell Realm. Is that my mother or father?" She gave him a hopeful look.

Blaise shook his head. "Not in the traditional sense, no. The Spell Realm is where you developed into what you are now. Do you know anything about the place?" He paused, looking at his unexpected creation. "In general, how much do you recall before you showed up here, on the floor of my study?"

CHAPTER TWO

✳ AUGUSTA ✳

Augusta slid out of bed and smiled seductively at her lover, enjoying the heated gleam in his eyes as she bent down to pick up her magenta-colored dress from the floor. The beautifully made garment had only one small rip in it—nothing that she wouldn't be able to fix with a simple verbal spell. Her clothes rarely survived her visits to Barson's house intact; if there was one thing she enjoyed about the leader of the Sorcerer Guard, it was the rough, urgent hunger with which he always greeted her arrival.

"Is it already time to go?" he asked, propping himself up on one elbow to watch her get dressed.

"Aren't your men waiting for you?" Augusta wriggled into the dress and reached up to gather her long brown hair into a smooth knot at the back of her neck.

"Let them wait." He sounded arrogant, as usual.

Augusta liked that about Barson—the unshakable confidence that permeated everything he did. He might not be a sorcerer, but he wielded quite a bit of power as the leader of the elite military force that kept law and order in their society.

"The rebels won't wait, though," Augusta reminded him. "We need to intercept them before they get any closer to Turingrad."

"We?" His thick eyebrows arched in surprise. With his short dark hair and olive-toned skin, he was one of the most attractive men she knew—with the possible exception of her former fiancé.

No, don't think about Blaise now. "Oh yes," Augusta said nonchalantly. "Did I forget to mention that I'm coming with you?"

Barson sat up in bed, the muscles in his large frame flexing and rippling with each movement. "You know you did," he growled, but Augusta could tell he was pleased with this development. He had been trying to get her to spend more time with him, to get their relationship out in the open, and Augusta thought it might be time to start giving in a little.

After her painful breakup with Blaise two years ago, all she'd wanted was an uncomplicated affair—an arrangement of mutual desire and nothing more. Her eight-year relationship with Blaise had ended six months before their wedding was to take place, and at the time, she didn't know if she would ever be able to trust another man again. She'd thought that all she needed was a bed companion, a warm body to make her forget the emptiness within—and she'd chosen the Captain of the Guard for that role.

To her surprise, what started off as a simple dalliance grew and evolved. Over time, Augusta found herself both liking and admiring her new lover. He was not an intellectual, like Blaise, but he was quite intelligent in his own way—and she found that she enjoyed his company outside of the bedroom as well. As a result, when she'd heard about the rebellion in the north, she decided it was the perfect opportunity to witness Barson in action, doing what he did best—protecting their way of life and keeping the peasants in check.

Getting up, he pulled on his armor and turned to face her. "Did the Council ask you to come with us?"

"No," Augusta reassured him. "I'm coming of my own initiative." It would be an insult to the Guard if the Council thought them incapable of quelling a minor uprising and asked her to aid them. She was accompanying them solely because she wanted to spend some time with Barson—and because she wanted to see the rebels crushed like the vermin they were.

"In that case," he said, his dark eyes glittering with anticipation, "let's go."

* * *

Augusta rode beside Barson, feeling the rhythmic movements of the horse beneath her. She could see the curious looks she was getting from the other soldiers, but she didn't care. As a sorceress of the

Council, she was used to the attention; she even craved it on some level.

It was strange riding an actual living horse. She had gotten used to the flying chaise—her recent invention that had revolutionized travel for sorcerers—and she couldn't remember the last time she'd gone somewhere the old-fashioned way. The only reason why she was doing so now was because Barson refused to get on the chaise with her while on duty, and she didn't want to hover in the air above the guards all by herself.

"How many rebels are there?" she asked Barson, surprised that there were only about fifty men accompanying them.

"Ganir said there were about three hundred," Barson replied, and Augusta wrinkled her nose at the mention of the Council Leader's name. Ganir appeared to have his spies everywhere these days. Under the guise of protecting the Council, the old sorcerer seemed to be growing more and more powerful every day, a development that bothered Augusta. She had always gotten a sense that the old man didn't like her, and she didn't want to think about what could happen if he decided to turn on her for any reason.

Bringing her attention back to the subject at hand, she gave Barson a questioning look. "And you took only fifty guards?"

He chuckled. "Only fifty? That's probably twenty too many. Any one of my men is worth at least ten of these peasants." Then he added, more seriously,

"Besides, given the unrest everywhere, I thought it best not to leave Turingrad and the Tower unprotected without a good reason—and believe me, three hundred peasants are not a good reason."

Augusta grinned at him, again charmed by his arrogance. "Right, of course. Plus you've got me." Sorcerers rarely used their magic against the common population, but they could certainly do so, particularly if they were in danger. Augusta had no doubt that she could subdue all the rebels singlehandedly, but that wasn't her job. That's what the soldiers were for.

This little rebellion, like so many others in the past couple of years, was no doubt motivated by the drought. It was an unfortunate occurrence, and Augusta could understand the peasants' unhappiness with ruined crops and high food prices—but that didn't make it acceptable for them to march on Turingrad like Ganir claimed they were doing.

The north of Koldun—where these rebels were coming from—was particularly hard-hit. Augusta's own territory was further south, but even her subjects were grumbling about the lack of food. They wouldn't dare do any rioting, of course, but Augusta was not oblivious to the fact that they were unhappy. For almost two years, the rain had been sparse, and grain was becoming increasingly difficult to obtain. Augusta did her best to purchase whatever grain was available and send it to her people, but the ungrateful wretches still complained.

"Who's ruling over the territory of the rebels? Is it

Jandison or Moriner?" she asked, wondering which sorcerer couldn't control his own peasants.

"Jandison."

Jandison. Well, that explained it, Augusta thought. Despite his advanced age and position on the Council, Jandison was considered to be something of a weakling. He was good at teleportation (admittedly, a useful skill) and not much else. How he had ended up on the Council—a ruling body consisting of the most powerful sorcerers—Augusta would never understand.

"Some of his peasants ran off to the mountains," Barson said, looking annoyed with the situation. "And some decided to riot. It's a mess over there."

"To the mountains?" Augusta couldn't suppress her shock. The mountains surrounded the land of Koldun, serving as a natural barrier against the fierce storms that raged beyond them. Only the most intrepid explorers ever ventured out there, given the unpredictable weather and proximity to the dangerous ocean. And these peasants actually went there?

"Yes," Barson confirmed. "At least twenty of them from Jandison's northernmost village fled there."

"They must be suicidal," Augusta said, shaking her head. "Who in their right mind would do something like that?"

"Someone desperate and hungry, I would imagine." Her lover gave her an ironic look. "You don't know hunger, do you?"

"No," Augusta admitted. Most sorcerers only ate

for pleasure; spells to sustain the body's energy were simple to do—and were one of the first things parents taught their children. Augusta had mastered those spells at the age of three, and she'd never felt hungry since.

Barson smiled in response and reached over to squeeze her knee with his large callused hand.

CHAPTER THREE

※ GALA ※

Gala stared at the tall, broad-shouldered man who was her creator, trying to figure out the best way to answer his question. She found it difficult to focus, her senses overwhelmed by being here, in this place Blaise called the Physical Realm. Her body was reacting to the different stimuli in strange and unpredictable ways, her mind attempting to process all the images, sounds, and smells so she could understand everything.

One particularly strong distraction was Blaise himself. She couldn't stop looking at him because he was unlike anything she had seen before. Something about the angular symmetry of his face appealed to her, resonating with her in a way she didn't fully comprehend. She liked everything about it, from the blue color of his eyes to the darkness of the stubble shadowing his firm jaw. She wondered if it would be acceptable to reach out and touch his hair—those short, almost-black locks that looked so different from her own pale strands.

First, though, she wanted to answer his question. Concentrating, she thought back to *before*, to what had happened prior to her experiencing reality for the first time. "I remember realizing that I exist," she said slowly, trying to put into words the strange sensations at the beginning.

"You mean you existed for a time without realizing it?" he asked, his dark eyebrows coming together slightly. Gala thought that expression likely meant confusion because her own eyebrows did the same thing when she didn't understand something.

"It's like there were two ways I existed," she tried to explain. "One way would just happen. This went on longer. When I say I realized that I exist—that's when this other part of me first realized that I am *me*. These parts are not separate; in fact, they are the same thing. There is a strange looping arrangement between the two parts that I don't fully understand and don't know how to put into words—"

"I think I do understand," he said, leaning forward and staring at her intently. "You became self-aware. At first, you existed on a subconscious level, and then, at some critical threshold, you achieved a conscious state of being." He appeared excited, Gala thought, somehow finding the right word to describe her creator's emotional state.

"What is the difference between a conscious and a subconscious state?" she asked, hungering for more information.

"In a human being, the subconscious parts of the mind are in charge of things like breathing or the heart beating," he said, his eyes gleaming brightly. "When I run, my subconscious figures out the complex trajectories of how my limbs move. Some sorcerers also think dreams form in that part of our minds."

"I am not a human being," Gala said, looking at him. That much she knew now. She was something different, and she needed to learn what that something was.

He smiled—an expression that made his face even more fascinating to her. "No," he said softly, "you're not. But you definitely seem like one to me."

"But that was not your intention, right?"

"Right," he confirmed. "However, the parts of you that I designed are based on how I theorized human minds might work. Lenard the Great is the one who first discovered the conscious-subconscious dynamic, and I've always been fascinated by his work. I've done spells on people that gave me insight into their states of being, and that was my framework for you. Additionally, I had some help from Lenard's writings. The spell that created you was supposed to make an interconnected structure of nodes—nodes that can learn. Billions and billions of nodes in the Spell Realm, all magically connected together—"

How interesting, Gala thought, observing the way his face became more animated as he spoke.

"And then, once I performed the spell," he

continued, "I sent dozens of Life Captures to the Spell Realm, as many Life Captures as I could get my hands on—"

"Life Captures?" The term didn't make sense to Gala.

Blaise nodded, his expression darkening for some reason. "Yes. Life Captures are an example of a magical object. A sorcerer named Ganir recently invented these things. It's a little hard to explain what they are. Basically, when you take a Life Capture, you see what someone else saw, you smell what they smelled, and you think you are them for the duration of the spell. You have to experience it to truly understand."

"I think I do understand," Gala said, thinking back to the strange experiences she'd had prior to coming here. "This probably explains my visions."

"Your visions?"

"I think I saw glimpses of the Physical Realm," Gala told him, "and it was like I was in them." The memories were not pleasant; for the longest time, she'd felt lost, not knowing that she was living other people's lives.

"Of course." His eyes widened with understanding. "I should've realized that once your mind was sufficiently developed, you would simply experience the Life Captures like we do—except that you had never been in the real world and probably had no idea what was happening to you. I'm sorry about that. It must've been terribly confusing for you."

Gala shrugged, a gesture she'd seen used once or twice in her visions. She had deduced that it indicated uncertainty. She wasn't sure how she felt about the Life Captures. Seeing the world through them had definitely been confusing, but she *had* gained a lot of knowledge about the Physical Realm that way. There was still a lot she didn't know, of course, but she was not nearly as lost now as she would've been otherwise.

Blaise smiled at her, and she thought again how much she liked his smile. Such a simple thing, just lips curving upwards and a flash of white teeth, and yet it had an effect on her, warming her on the inside and making her want to smile back at him in return. So she did, mimicking his expression. His eyes gleamed brighter, and Gala sensed that she'd done the right thing, that she'd pleased him in some way.

"So what was the Spell Realm itself like?" he asked, still looking at her with that smile. "I can't even imagine what it must be like there . . ." His voice trailed off, and Gala understood that he was hoping she'd tell him about it.

She thought about it, trying to figure out the best way to explain. "It's very . . . different," she finally said. "I don't really know how to describe it to you. There wasn't a lot of time between visions, and when I wasn't experiencing the visions, I couldn't use human senses. It's like there were flashes of light, sound, taste, and smell, but they were coming at me in some other way. I was never able to process them fully before I would get absorbed in another vision.

And then I was pulled here—"

"Pulled here?"

"Yes, that's what it felt like," Gala said. "It was like something pulled me here, into this place you're calling the Physical Realm." She paused for a second. "Pulled me to you."

CHAPTER FOUR

※ BLAISE ※

Pulled to him. She had been pulled to him.

It must've been that last spell he performed that brought Gala to his study, Blaise realized. He had been trying to do a physical manifestation of the magical object, and instead he'd ended up bringing Gala here, to the Physical Realm.

She was looking at him with her large blue eyes, studying him with that odd mixture of childlike curiosity and sharp intelligence. Blaise wondered what she was thinking. Did she have the same emotions as a regular human being? Did she even understand the concept of emotions? Her reactions seemed to indicate that she did. She had smiled in response to his smile, so, at the very least, she knew facial expressions.

"I want to see it," she said suddenly, leaning

forward. "Blaise, I want to experience more of this world. I want to learn about this place. Can you show it to me, please?"

"Of course," Blaise said, getting up. He had a million more questions for her, but she was probably even more eager for knowledge than he was. "Let me start by showing you my house."

He began the tour upstairs, where his study and the bedrooms were located. Gala trailed in his wake, listening attentively as he explained the purpose of each room. Everything seemed to fascinate her, from the closet filled with Augusta's dresses to the glazed windows in Blaise's bedroom.

Approaching one particularly large window, she climbed onto the windowsill and stared outside, pressing her nose against the glass. Blaise couldn't help smiling at that, charmed by the picture she presented.

"What is out there?" she asked, turning her head to look at him. "I want to go down there."

"It's my gardens," Blaise explained, coming closer to help her climb down from the windowsill. "We can go there next."

Reaching up, he took her hand and carefully guided her down. Her hand was small and warm within his grasp, and Blaise again marveled at the striking beauty of his creation . . . and at the strength of his own reaction to her. He hadn't been this attracted to a woman in a long time, not since Augusta—

No, don't think about her, he told himself, feeling

the familiar ache in his chest. The fact that his former fiancée still occupied his thoughts to such extent made him furious. After the way she had betrayed him, he had done his best to erase her from memory, but it was not that easy.

He had known Augusta for over a decade, having met her in the Academy when they were both lowly acolytes. He'd always thought she was beautiful, with her dark, sultry looks, but it wasn't until they began working together on the Interpreter Stone that he found himself falling for her. Young and ambitious, they had seemed like the perfect match, even if they didn't always see eye-to-eye on certain matters. For years, their passion—both for their work and for each other—had been enough to bridge their differences, and it wasn't until Louie's trial that Blaise had found out just how deep the divide between them truly was.

"Here, come with me," he said, forcing himself to release Gala's hand. "Let's go downstairs."

They walked down the stairs and out through the long hallway. Gala kept touching everything along the way, running her fingers over each new surface she encountered.

Finally, they were outside.

"These are my gardens," Blaise said, pointing at the wide green expanse in front of them. "They are a little overgrown at this point—"

"They are beautiful," Gala said slowly, turning in a circle. The look on her face was almost rapturous. "Oh, your Physical Realm is so beautiful, Blaise . . ."

"Yes," Blaise murmured, mesmerized by her. "You're right, it is." Blinking, he forced himself to look away, to stare at something other than her gorgeous features.

She laughed joyously, drawing his gaze back to her, and he saw that she was reaching for a bright-colored butterfly sitting on a white flower. She did feel emotions, he realized, seeing her face glowing with happiness and excitement.

He tried to view the familiar surroundings as Gala must be seeing them, and he had to admit that the gardens had a certain wild beauty to them. His mother had been excellent with plants, judiciously using spells to promote the growth of flowers and fruit trees, and Blaise could still see traces of her magic everywhere.

"Would you like to see something interesting?" he asked impulsively, wanting to see more of that radiant joy on Gala's face.

"Yes," she said immediately. "Please."

"Then watch," Blaise said, and began a simple verbal spell. Holding out his hand, he concentrated on manipulating the particles of light, directing them to gather above his upturned palm. Each word, each sentence that he spoke, was part of the intricate code that enabled him to do sorcery. When he was satisfied that the logic and instructions of the spell were correct, he used the Interpreter Spell—a complex litany that every verbal spell required at the end—to transmit everything to the Spell Realm. And then he waited.

A few seconds later, the air above his outstretched palm began to shimmer, and a bright, shiny shape began to take place. Before long, there was a rose made entirely of light hovering a couple of inches above his hand.

"It's so beautiful," Gala breathed, watching his little demonstration with a look of awe on her perfect face. Reaching out, she touched the rose, her fingers passing right through the cluster of light.

Blaise grinned, glad that he had been able to impress her with something so simple. Given her origins, she would likely be able to do the same and more.

Much, much more, he thought, trying to imagine how powerful someone born in the Spell Realm could be. It was a little too soon to start exploring Gala's abilities, but Blaise had a feeling they would be unlike anything the world had ever seen.

* * *

After Gala got her fill of the gardens, Blaise took her back inside the house.

"I want to learn more," she said when they entered the hallway. "Blaise, I want to learn everything. Can you help me?"

He considered her request. He could give her more Life Captures and let her experience the world that way, or he could try introducing her to books. There was a possibility she might understand written language, as well as the spoken one, since some of the Life Captures he'd sent to the Spell Realm—the Life Captures that helped build her existing knowledge base—were from reading teachers.

He decided to go with the second option for now, to let her learn the old-fashioned way at first. As interesting as it was to immerse oneself into other people's lives, there was still no substitute for the structure of a good book. "Why don't we head to my library?" he suggested. "I want to see if you're able to read."

Gala nodded eagerly, and he led her into the musty room that housed his books. Interspersed with the heavy old tomes, he could see some of Augusta's books, including a couple of romances his former lover had enjoyed in her spare time. "Here," he said, picking up one of them and handing it to Gala, "try reading this."

What she did next seemed very odd to him. She slowly looked over the first page. Then she quickly glanced at the next. And then she started flipping pages with increasing speed, until she was turning them so fast it looked like she was just riffling through the book.

When she was done, Blaise stared at her in astonishment. "Did you just read and understand that whole book?"

"Yes."

Unable to believe his ears, Blaise took the book from her and opened it to a random page, glancing down to quickly skim a couple of paragraphs. "What was the name of the main hero?"

"Ludvig."

"And what happened when he told his wife about Lura?"

"Jurila screamed, lashing out at her husband with her riding crop. Her dark eyes flashed with fire and fury, and her beautiful features were distorted by anger. Ludvig tried to calm her, fearing what she could do—"

"Wait a minute," Blaise said incredulously, listening to her recite the paragraph he'd just read. "Did you just memorize the whole book?"

Gala shrugged. "I think so. It was interesting, but I would like more. Much more."

Shaking his head in amazement, Blaise reached for another book, this one a thick tome covering the history of scientific advancements from the time of the Sorcery Enlightenment to the modern era. Dense and comprehensive, it was required reading for students at the Academy of Sorcery. Handing it to Gala, he said, "Try this one. It might be a bit more challenging."

She took the book and started flipping through it. Within two minutes, she was done.

When she looked up at him, her face was glowing. "Blaise, this is so interesting," she exclaimed. "I can't believe so little was known before Lenard the Great came along. He discovered all these things about nature and how the mind works, not to mention the Spell Realm—"

Blaise nodded, smiling despite his shock. "Yes, he was a genius. And his students continued his work.

That's what the Enlightenment was about. Lenard and the sorcerers who followed in his footsteps shed light on our world, on the nature and mathematics of reality, on human psychology and physics—"

"Oh, I would've loved to meet him," Gala breathed, her eyes huge with excitement. "He reminds me of you . . ."

"Of me?" Blaise couldn't help laughing at that. "I'm very flattered, but I could never live up to Lenard's achievements."

Gala tilted her head to the side, looking thoughtful. "I don't know about that," she said. "You did create me, after all."

"That's true." Blaise had to concede that point. "I'm sure Lenard would've loved to meet you as well. It's too bad he disappeared over two centuries ago. His achievements live on, however, in all these books." He gestured around the room.

She turned to look at the bookshelves and walked up to one of them, gently running her fingers over the dusty book spines.

"If you'd like to read more, my entire library is yours," Blaise offered, seeing how she appeared to be drawn to the books. "It's not as comprehensive as what you'd find in the Tower, but it should occupy even you for a bit."

"I'll start with more romances, I think," she said, turning her head to flash him a dazzling smile. "That first book was more difficult for me."

"You found the romance more difficult?"

"Of course," she said seriously. "The second book

made so much sense, and it flowed so easily, but the romance was more challenging. I didn't fully understand all aspects of those people's actions."

Blaise stared at her. "I see. Well, read whatever you want. My library is at your disposal."

Gala grinned at him, as eager as a child, and dove into another book, flipping through it with the same inhuman speed.

Taking a deep, calming breath, Blaise decided to leave her to it and quietly exited the library.

He needed some time to himself to figure out what happened and to think about what to do next.

* * *

Entering his study, Blaise sat down at his desk and pricked his finger, starting a Life Capture session out of habit. He always recorded himself at work these days, just in case he had some kind of a revelation and needed to relive it later.

Of course, he wasn't expecting to have any kind of revelation about Gala right now. What happened today was so incredible, he could barely begin to process it.

He had created a magical being. A super-intelligent magical being with potential for unimaginable powers.

A being who was also the most beautiful woman Blaise had ever seen.

In hindsight, the fact that Gala took on a human shape made perfect sense. Blaise had been striving to create a mind that was similar to a human's—a mind that could understand regular spoken language and convert it into the sorcery code directly, without having to use any kind of magical objects or spells. He should've considered the possibility that a mind like that would take on a human appearance.

But he hadn't, focusing instead only on the idea that an intelligent object created in the Spell Realm could be used by anyone, regardless of their aptitude for sorcery. An object like that—particularly if made in large quantities—would've been a game changer, forever altering the class dynamics in their society and completing the process started by the Enlightenment.

Gala was not the object he'd meant to create, but it didn't matter. She was something else—something even more wonderful.

His brother Louie would've been proud, Blaise thought, reaching for his journal.

CHAPTER FIVE

※ AUGUSTA ※

The sun was beginning to set, and Barson issued the order to stop for the night. Augusta gladly dismounted and stretched, her body aching from unaccustomed exercise. She would have to do a healing spell on herself later; otherwise, she might be sore tomorrow.

"Dinnertime for your men?" she asked, following Barson toward a tent that the soldiers were already setting up for him.

"First practice, then dinner," he said, courteously lifting the tent flap for her. "You can rest if you'd like. I should be with you in an hour or so."

"Rest in a tent while your boys play with swords?" Augusta lifted her eyebrows at him. "You're joking, right? I wouldn't miss this for the world."

He grinned at her. "Then come and watch."

They walked together to a small clearing where

most of the other guards were gathered. As they approached, Barson's men respectfully stepped aside, clearing the way for them.

"Why don't you get on your chaise?" Barson suggested, turning toward her. "It will provide you with a good view and keep you safely out of the way."

Augusta smiled, charmed by his concern for her. "Sure, let me get it." Although she'd ridden here on the horse, she'd had the chaise follow them at some distance, just in case it was needed.

Pulling out her Interpreter Stone—a shimmering black rock that resembled a large piece of polished coal with a slot in the middle—Augusta loaded it with a pre-written spell for summoning her chaise and waited. Two minutes later, the chaise arrived, landing softly on the grass. Deep red in color, it was shaped like the piece of furniture it had been named after. However, it was made of a special crystalline material that looked like glass but was warm and soft to the touch, like a plush, padded armchair. Augusta had invented this particular magical object fairly recently, and it had caught on among the sorcerer community immediately. It looked quite incongruous here, among all the trees, and Augusta almost laughed at the looks on the men's faces as they stared at it.

Climbing onto the chaise, Augusta did a quick verbal spell to get it hovering in the air a little to the right above the clearing. Then, comfortably tucking her feet underneath herself, she leaned on one of the sides and prepared to watch the spectacle that was about to unfold.

* * *

Archery practice was first.

Augusta watched in fascination as one man let loose a strange-looking arrow. Large and covered with extra feathers, it appeared to be flying a little slower than usual, making it easier to see mid-flight.

Before she could wonder about its purpose, she saw the feathery arrow get hit by another arrow—an ordinary one this time. Apparently, the large arrow was the target—a target that some soldier had managed to hit with unbelievable accuracy.

Looking down on the ground, she saw that the men were divided into pairs, with one guard sending up those arrows and his partner shooting them down. Every time the target was reached, there would be cheers from the other soldiers. If Augusta hadn't seen this herself, she wouldn't have believed it was possible to perform this feat even once—yet every single one of Barson's men managed to do this. The mathematics involved were staggering, and Augusta marveled at the ability of the human mind to do something so complicated without any conscious calculations.

Finally, it was Barson's turn. Looking up, he gave her a wink, then motioned to his soldiers. To Augusta's shock, not one, but two men sent up the special feathery arrows—and her lover's arrow pierced them both in one shot. The other soldiers cheered, but not any louder than for any of the others. Apparently, it wasn't the first time their Captain had done something so impossible.

After archery, the guards sparred with swords. Augusta watched with bated breath as steel clashed against steel, making her flinch every time someone narrowly avoided an injury. Even though this was only practice, the swords used by the men were quite real—and potentially quite deadly.

All of the soldiers appeared to be highly skilled, however, and nobody was getting hurt, causing Augusta to relax a little. Observing the fighters, she couldn't help but take pleasure in the sight of their strong, fit bodies twisting and turning as they engaged in a kind of macabre dance. There was beauty to war, she thought, watching as they thrust and parried with incredible grace.

Barson was walking around the clearing, giving pointers and instructions to his soldiers. She wondered if he would fight as well—and if so, whether he would be as skilled with the sword as he was with the arrow.

As though in answer to her unspoken question, Barson walked to the middle of the clearing, stopping the fight between the men who were there. "You four," he said, pointing at them, "I need some warm-up."

Warm-up? Augusta grinned, realizing that her lover was probably trying to impress her.

The four big men approached Barson gingerly. Were they actually scared to go four against one?

Augusta knew the Captain of the Sorcerer Guard was good at what he did, but she had never actually seen him in action.

The four soldiers took their positions, surrounding their leader. What happened next was so amazing, Augusta couldn't help but gasp.

Barson started moving slowly, in a strange pattern, somehow keeping all four men in his sight at all times. Then he lashed out with lightning speed, apparently spotting an opening, and Augusta saw a droplet of red welling up from a scratch on one of the soldiers' wrists.

First blood, she thought, mesmerized by what was happening.

The blood seemed to serve as some kind of a signal, and all four guards attacked at once. To Augusta's untrained eye, there was only a flurry of movement. Barson's blade seemed to be everywhere, blocking every move his opponents made with a skill and speed that seemed superhuman. There was something hypnotic in the way Barson moved. Every gesture, every move, was perfectly calibrated. He dodged thrusts, while using the same turn to deliver an attack. His deadly proficiency was breathtaking.

"More," he shouted after a few minutes. "I need more."

Four more fighters joined in. Augusta directed her chaise to fly closer, because all she could see now was a row of bodies surrounding Barson's powerful figure.

Suddenly, there was a scream.

DIMA ZALES

Augusta's heart skipped a beat, but then she saw that one of the other soldiers—not Barson—was on the ground, clutching his thigh. The others stopped fighting, forming a circle around the wounded man.

Landing her chaise, Augusta quickly jumped off and ran toward them. Barson was kneeling beside the man, a look of dismay on his face. The soldiers stepped aside, letting her through, and her breath caught in her throat at the sight of the gushing wound in the man's leg. To her astonishment, Augusta saw that the man was very young—barely more than a boy.

Barson ripped a strip of cloth from his shirt and tied it around the soldier's thigh. "This should help the bleeding. I am sorry, Kiam," he said somberly.

"These things happen in practice," said Kiam, clearly trying to keep the pain out of his voice.

"No, it's my fault," Barson said. "I shouldn't have taken on so many of you. Like a rookie, I couldn't control where I aimed my thrust."

At that point, he seemed to notice Augusta's presence, and she knew what Barson was going to ask before he even said it.

"Can you help him?" he said, looking up at her.

Augusta nodded and walked back to the chaise, where she'd left her bag. Strictly speaking, using sorcery on non-sorcerers was frowned upon. However, these were special circumstances. Now that she wasn't so panicked, Augusta recognized the boy. Kiam was the son of Moriner, a Council member from the north. She remembered the Councilor

42

saying that his youngest son didn't seem to have any aptitude for magic, only for fighting. But even if Kiam had been a nobody, she would've still helped him as a favor to Barson.

Grabbing her Interpreter Stone, Augusta carefully chose the cards she needed. The boy was lucky that she and Blaise had come up with this invention. If she'd had to rely on the old oral spells, Kiam would've likely bled to death while she planned and chanted something of this complexity. Even Moriner, who was considered the foremost expert on verbal spell casting, would've been unable to help his son in time.

Written sorcery was much quicker, especially since Augusta already had some of the components of the spell in her bag. All she had to do now was tailor those components to Kiam's body weight, height, and the specifics of his injury. When she was ready, she walked back and set the Stone next to Kiam, loading the paper cards into it on the way.

The flow of blood from Kiam's thigh slowed to a trickle, then stopped. Within a minute, no trace of the injury remained, and Kiam's face lost its pallor, looking healthy again. The young man got up, as though nothing had happened, and Augusta could see the looks of awe and admiration on the soldiers' faces. She smiled, glowing with pride at her accomplishment.

Without saying a word, Barson squeezed her shoulder with rough affection, and she grinned at him, looking forward to the night to come.

Practice was over for the day.

CHAPTER SIX

❈ BARSON ❈

Barson watched Augusta as she walked away, her hips swaying with the seductive grace that was as much a part of her as her golden brown eyes. She was a beautiful woman, and he was glad she'd chosen him to be her lover. She still pined for that exiled sorcerer, he knew, but not when she was in Barson's bed. He'd made certain of that.

"That was not particularly smooth, I have to say," a voice drawled next to him, interrupting his musings.

Turning his head, Barson saw his right-hand man and soon-to-be brother-in-law. "Shut up, Larn," he said without much heat. "Kiam will be fine, and he'll know better than to jump under my sword the next time."

Larn shook his head. "I don't know, Barson. That kid is a hothead; I've warned you about him before—"

"Yeah, yeah, look who's talking. You think I don't remember all the trouble you got into when you were his age?"

Larn snorted. "Oh please, you're a fine one to talk. How many times did Dara have to plead your case? If it weren't for your sister, you'd still be grounded to this day."

Barson grinned at his friend, remembering all the mishaps they'd gotten into as children.

"He reminds me of you quite a bit actually," Larn said, glancing in the direction of Kiam, who had picked up his sword again, apparently getting ready to practice on his own time. Then, lowering his voice, he said in a more serious tone, "Can *she* hear us?"

"I don't think so," Barson said, though he wasn't entirely sure. One could never be certain with sorcerers; they were sneaky and had spells that could enhance their eavesdropping abilities. However, Augusta would have no reason to do such a spell right now—not when she was getting ready for bed in his tent. "In any case, it's far safer to talk here than anywhere in the vicinity of the Tower."

"That's probably true," Larn agreed, still keeping his voice low. "Why did she come along, anyway?"

Barson shrugged.

"Oh, the legendary Barson strikes again." Larn wiggled his eyebrows lasciviously.

Barson's hand shot out with the speed of a striking cobra, grabbing Larn's throat. "You will show her respect," he ordered, filled with sudden anger.

"Of course, I'm sorry . . ." Larn sounded choked. "I didn't realize—"

"Well, now you do," Barson muttered, releasing his friend. "And you better hope she didn't hear any of this."

Larn paled. "You said she couldn't—"

"And she probably can't," Barson agreed. "The fact that you're still alive is evidence of that." Like all members of the Council, Augusta could be quite dangerous if provoked.

Larn stepped back, rubbing his throat. "Your sorceress aside," he said in a low, raspy voice, "we have some business to discuss."

Barson nodded, feeling a small measure of guilt at his lack of control. "Tell me," he said curtly. Larn was his best friend and his most trusted soldier; soon, he would be family as well. Barson shouldn't have reacted so strongly to his good-natured ribbing. What did it matter what anyone thought of his relationship with Augusta? He must be feeling particularly violent after the practice fight, he decided, not wanting to analyze his actions too much.

"I made a list of the most likely candidates." Larn pulled out a small scroll and handed it to Barson. "Before, I could've sworn that none of these men could do this, but now I'm not so sure."

Barson unrolled the scroll and studied the eleven names written on there, his anger growing again.

Lifting his head, he pinned Larn with an icy stare. "They all fit the behavior pattern?"

"Yes. All of them. Of course, there could always be some other reason for their actions—a mistress or some such thing."

"Yes," Barson agreed. "For ten of them, it's probably something like that." His hands clenched into fists, and he forced himself to relax. Every one of the eleven men on that list was like a brother to him, and the thought that one of them could've betrayed him was like poison in Barson's veins.

Taking a deep breath, he glanced at the list again, mentally running through each of the names. One name in particular jumped out at him. "Siur is on there," he said slowly.

"Yes," Larn said. "I noticed that, too. He didn't come with us this time. Did he tell you why?"

"No. He said he needed to stay in Turingrad. It's Siur, not some rookie, so I didn't press him for explanations."

Larn nodded thoughtfully. "All right. I'll continue working on this list and keeping an eye on the ones already there."

"Good," Barson said, turning away to hide the fury on his face.

No matter what it took, he would get to the bottom of this matter—and when he did, the man who betrayed him would pay.

CHAPTER SEVEN

✳ BLAISE ✳

Wrapping up the Life Capture recording, Blaise came back to the library to check on Gala. To his surprise, he saw her lying on the floor unconscious, in the middle of a huge pile of books.

Worried, he ran to her and crouched down to take a closer look. To his relief, he saw that she looked quite peaceful, her breathing slow and even. She was simply sleeping.

Without thinking too much about it, Blaise picked her up and carried her to one of the guest bedrooms. She was light in his arms, her body soft and feminine, and he found himself enjoying the experience. Reaching the room, he gently placed her on the bed, and as he was covering her with a blanket, she opened her eyes.

For a moment, she seemed confused, then her gaze cleared. "I think I fell asleep," she said in astonishment.

Blaise smiled. "I would've thought you wouldn't know what sleep was like."

"I didn't before, but I learned quite a bit from your books."

He studied her with fascination, wondering if she'd read all those hundreds of books that were lying on the library floor. "How many books did you get through?" he asked.

She sat up in bed, brushing a few strands of long blond hair off her face. "Three hundred and forty nine."

Blaise blinked. "That's very precise. Are you sure it wasn't three hundred and forty eight?"

"Yes, I'm sure," she said seriously, then smiled. "In fact, it was 138,902 pages and 32,453,383 words."

"Are those the exact figures?" He could hardly believe his ears.

Gala nodded, still smiling. In a flash of intuition, Blaise realized that she knew just how much she had impressed him—and that she was enjoying his reaction tremendously.

"All right," Blaise said slowly. "How do you know this?"

She shrugged. "I just know. As soon as I wanted to tell you, the numbers came to me. I guess I must've counted as I was reading, but I don't remember doing it."

"I see," Blaise said, watching her closely. On a hunch, he asked, "What is 2,682 times 5?"

"13,410," Gala said without hesitation.

Blaise concentrated for a few seconds, doing the calculations in his head. She was right. He was one of the few people he knew who could do this kind of multiplication quickly, but Gala had known the answer almost instantaneously.

"How did you do this so quickly?" he asked, curious about the way her mind worked.

"I took 2,682, halved it to get 1,341, and then multiplied it by 10."

Blaise thought about it for a second and realized that her method was indeed the easiest way to solve the problem. He was surprised he hadn't come up with it himself. He would definitely use this shortcut the next time he needed to do some quick calculations for a spell.

Given the purpose of her creation, Gala's analytical and math skills shouldn't have surprised him, but still, Blaise was amazed. He couldn't wait any longer to see what she was capable of. "Gala, can you try to do some magic for me?" he asked, staring at her beautiful face.

She looked surprised by his request. "You mean, like you did earlier, in the gardens?"

"Yes, like that," Blaise confirmed.

"But I don't know how you did what you did." She seemed a little bewildered. "I don't know all those spells you used."

"You don't have to know them," Blaise explained. "You should be able to do magic directly, without having to learn our methods. Magic should come as easily and naturally to you as breathing does to me."

She appeared to consider that for a second. "I also breathe," she said, as though reaching that conclusion after examining herself.

"Of course you do." Amused, Blaise smiled at her. "I didn't mean to imply that you don't."

Her soft lips curved in an answering smile. "All right," she murmured, "let me try doing magic." She closed her eyes, and Blaise could see a look of intense concentration on her face.

He held his breath, waiting, but nothing happened. After a minute, she opened her eyes, looking at Blaise expectantly.

He shook his head regretfully. "I don't think it worked. What did you try to do?"

"I wanted to make my own version of that beautiful flower you created in the garden."

"I see. And how did you go about doing it?"

She lifted her shoulders in a graceful shrug. "I don't know. I replayed the memory of you doing it earlier in my mind and tried to picture myself in your place, but I don't think it works like that."

"No, you're right, that's probably not how it would work for you." Frustrated, Blaise ran his fingers through his hair. "The problem is I don't know exactly how it *would* work for you. I was hoping you would simply be able to do it, just like you did the math problem earlier."

Gala closed her eyes again, and that same look of concentration appeared on her face.

Again nothing happened.

"I failed," she said, opening her eyes. She didn't

seem particularly concerned about that fact.

"What did you try to do?"

"I wanted to raise the temperature in this room by a couple of degrees, but I could feel that it didn't work."

Blaise lifted his eyebrows. Her unusual temperature sensitivity aside, it seemed that Gala did have a good intuition for sorcery. Changing the temperature of an object was a very basic spell, something that Blaise could do just by saying a few sentences in the old magical language.

While he was pondering this, Gala jumped off the bed and came up to one of the windows. "I want to go out there," she said, turning her head to look at him. "I want to see more of this world."

Blaise tried to hide his disappointment. "You don't want to try any more magic?"

"No," Gala said stubbornly. "I don't. I want to go out and explore."

Blaise took a deep breath. "Maybe just one more try?"

Her expression darkened, a crease appearing on her smooth forehead. "Blaise," she said quietly, "you're making me feel bad right now."

"What?" Blaise couldn't keep the shock out of his voice. "Why?"

"Because you're making me feel used, like that object that you intended me to be," she said, sounding upset. "What do you want from me? Am I to be some tool that people use to do magic? Is that my purpose in life?"

"No, of course not!" Blaise protested, pushing away an unwelcome tendril of guilt. In a way, that had been exactly what he had originally intended for Gala, but she wasn't supposed to be a person, with the feelings and emotions of a human being. He had been trying to build an intelligence, yes, but it wasn't supposed to turn out this way. It was to be a means to an end, a way to address the worst of the inequality in their society. All he had thought about was getting the object to understand regular human language, and he hadn't considered the fact that anything with that level of intelligence might have its—or her—own thoughts and opinions.

And now he was a victim of his own success. Gala could certainly understand language—maybe even better than Blaise, given her reading prowess. However, she was no more an object to be used than he was. His original plan of creating enough intelligent magical objects for everyone was sheer folly; if successful, it would just transfer the burden of inequality from one group of thinking beings to another—provided that Gala or others of her kind would even go along with something like that.

Besides, it wasn't like she could even do magic at this point. Or maybe she just didn't want to, Blaise thought wryly. He would certainly be hesitant to display any kind of magical ability in her situation.

She was still looking upset, so he tried to reassure her, "Gala, listen to me, I didn't mean to make you feel like an object. What I told you about my original intentions for you is obviously out of the question now. I know you're not a thing to be used. I'm sorry. It was thoughtless of me not to realize how you felt." He hoped she could see the truth of his words; the last thing he wanted was for Gala to be afraid of him or to resent him.

She looked away for a second, then turned to meet his gaze. "Well, now you know," she said softly. "All I want to do right now is learn more about this world. I want to experience everything about it. I want to see for myself what I just read about in your books, and I want to witness those injustices you're trying to fix. I want to live like a human being, Blaise. Can you understand that?"

CHAPTER EIGHT

※ GALA ※

Gala watched the play of emotions on her creator's expressive face. He was disappointed, she could see that, and it hurt, but she needed him to understand that she was a person with her own needs and desires. She wasn't something to be used to better the lives of people she didn't know and didn't care about.

She could see his internal struggle, and then he seemed to come to a conclusion of some kind. "Gala," he said quietly, looking at her, "I understand what you're saying, but you don't know what you're asking. If anyone found out about you—about what you are—I don't know what they would do. People fear what they don't understand—and even I don't fully understand what you are and what you're capable of. I can't let you go out there, not until we know more about you."

As he spoke, Gala felt the beginnings of

something she had never experienced before. It was a strange churning sensation that started low in her stomach and spread upward, making her chest feel unpleasantly tight. She could feel her blood rushing faster in her veins, heating up her face, and she wanted to scream, to lash out in some way. It was anger, she realized, real anger. She hated not being able to do exactly what she wanted.

"Blaise," she managed to say through tightly clenched teeth, "I. Want. To Go. Out. There." Her voice seemed to rise with every word.

He appeared taken aback by her temper. "Gala, it's just too dangerous, can't you understand that?"

"Too dangerous? Why?" she demanded furiously. "I look human, don't I? How would anybody guess that I'm not?"

She could see him considering her point. "You're right," he said after a moment. "You do appear completely human. But if we go out there together, we'll attract a lot of attention—mostly because of me, not you."

"You? Why?" Gala could feel her anger cooling now that Blaise was no longer being so unreasonable.

"Because I quit the Sorcerer Council two years ago," he explained, "and I've been an outcast ever since."

"An outcast? Why?" Gala had just finished reading about the Sorcerer Council and the power wielded by those who had the aptitude for magic. Blaise seemed to be an unusually good sorcerer—he had to be, in order to create something like herself—

and it didn't make sense to her that he would be an outcast in a world that valued those kinds of skills so much.

"It's a long story," Blaise said, and she could hear the bitterness in his voice. "Suffice it to say, I don't share the views of most on the Council—and neither did my brother."

"Your brother?" She'd also read about siblings, and she was fascinated by the idea of Blaise having one.

He sighed. "Are you sure you want to hear about this?"

"Definitely." Gala wanted to learn everything about Blaise. He interested her more than anything else she'd encountered thus far during her short existence.

"All right," he said slowly, "do you remember what I told you about the Life Captures?"

Gala nodded. Of course she remembered; as far as she could tell, she had a perfect memory. Life Captures were the way she'd initially learned about Blaise's world.

"Well, as I mentioned earlier, Life Captures were invented by a powerful sorcerer named Ganir a couple of years ago. When they first came out, everyone was very excited about them. A single Life Capture droplet could allow a person to get completely immersed in someone else's life, allowing him to feel what they felt, learn what they learned. It was also the first magical object that didn't require knowledge of the sorcery code. All one has to do to record his life is give the Life Capture Sphere a tiny drop of blood. Another drop of blood stops the recording, allowing the Life Capture droplet to form in a special place on top of the Sphere. And then those droplets can be used by anyone, without any special equipment. All one needs to do to experience the Life Capture is put the droplet in his or her mouth."

Gala nodded again, listening attentively. She wanted to try these Life Captures again, to experience them for the first time in the Physical Realm.

"My brother, who was Ganir's assistant at the time," continued Blaise, "was one of the few sorcerers who knew a little bit about how Life Capture magic worked. He saw how it could be used as a learning tool, as a way to teach magic to those who would never be able to gain access to the Academy of Sorcery. He also thought it was a great way for the less fortunate to escape the reality of their everyday life. A regular person could experience what it might be like to be a sorcerer just as easily as the other way around." He paused to take a breath. "My brother was clearly an idealist. He didn't foresee the consequences of his actions—both for himself and for the people he wanted to help."

"What happened?" Gala asked, her heart beating faster as she sensed that this story might not have a happy ending.

"Louie managed to create a large number of Life Capture Spheres in secret and smuggled them out of

Turingrad, distributing them throughout all the territories. He thought it might aid the spread of knowledge, improving our society, but that's not what ended up happening." Blaise's voice grew hard, emotionless. "As soon as the Council learned about Louie's actions, they outlawed the possession and distribution of Life Captures for non-sorcerers, creating a black market and a criminal underclass that specializes in the sale of these objects—thus completely perverting their original purpose."

"So what happened to Louie?"

"He was punished," Blaise said, and she could sense the anger burning underneath. "He was tried and found guilty. For giving Life Capture to the commoners, he paid with his life."

"They killed him?" Gala gasped, horrified at the idea that somebody could lose his life so easily. She was enjoying living so much that she couldn't imagine ceasing to exist. How could people do this? How could they deny each other the amazing experience of living?

"Yes. They executed him. I left the Council shortly after his death. I could no longer stand to be a part of it."

Gala swallowed, feeling a painful sensation in her chest. She ached, as though Blaise's pain was her own. She must be experiencing empathy, she realized, identifying the unfamiliar feeling.

"Could I try more Life Captures, Blaise?" she asked cautiously, hoping she was not causing him additional pain by dwelling on this topic. "I would really like to experience them here, in the Physical Realm."

To her surprise, his face brightened, like she had said something that made him happy. "That's a great idea," he said, giving her a warm smile. "It's an excellent way for you to experience the world."

"Yes," Gala agreed. "I think so."

She also intended to experience the world in person, but for the moment, the Life Captures would suffice.

CHAPTER NINE

※ AUGUSTA ※

Augusta watched her lover getting ready for the upcoming fight. The supple leather tunic hugged his broad frame, and the armor he put on over it looked heavy enough to fell a smaller man. To Barson, however, it was as light as air. Not because of his strength—which was admittedly impressive—but because the armor of the Sorcerer Guard was special. It was spelled to be almost weightless to the wearer and very nearly impenetrable. That was one of the perks of being a soldier in modern-day Koldun: access to sorcery-enhanced weapons and armor.

Seeing that Barson was almost ready, Augusta got up and took her bag, slinging it over her shoulder. Her red chaise was already waiting outside. She planned to fly above the battle, so she could observe everything from a safe vantage point.

"We're going to meet them over on that hill,"

Barson told her as they walked out of the tent. "It's a good spot. Our archers will have a clear shot at anyone approaching, and there's only one road that goes through there, so nobody will be able to sneak up on us."

Augusta smiled at him. "Sounds good." Her lover was as obsessed with military strategy as Augusta was with magic, devouring ancient war books in his spare time.

"I will see you in a few hours." Leaning down, he gave her a brief, hard kiss and walked off, heading toward his soldiers.

Augusta watched his powerful figure for a couple of minutes before climbing onto her chaise. Pulling out her Interpreter Stone, she loaded in a pre-made concealment spell, so that no one on the battlefield would be able to see her or her chaise. Once that was done, she pulled out another spell, a more complicated one this time. It was a way for her to temporarily boost her senses, enabling her to see and hear everything with as much clarity as possible. She'd used it several times before; in the Tower of Sorcery, it paid to hear every whisper.

A quick verbal spell, and she was flying, her chaise far more comfortable than the carpets and dragons of old fairy tales. Rising high above the hill, she saw Barson's men heading over to their chosen battleground and the narrow road stretching into the far distance. With her enhanced sight, Augusta could see much better than usual, and she marveled at the beauty of this northern part of the land, with its tall sturdy trees and rich dark soil. Even the devastation from the drought was not enough to diminish the beauty of the local forests.

Augusta had never visited this area before, generally splitting her time between Turingrad and her own territory in the southern region. The city was the biggest on Koldun, and it was the epicenter of art, culture, and commerce. In contrast to the peasant-occupied surrounding territories, the majority of Turingrad was populated by sorcerers, members of the Guard, and some particularly prosperous merchants.

Directing her chaise to turn north, Augusta peered at the dark mass in the distance. It was so far away that even with her improved vision, she couldn't tell what it was. Curious, she flew toward it.

And when she got close enough to see, she could hardly believe her eyes.

Instead of three hundred men, as Ganir's spies had said, there were at least a couple of thousand.

A couple of thousand peasants ... versus fifty of Barson's soldiers.

* * *

Her heart racing, Augusta stared at the approaching horde. She had never seen such a large gathering of commoners in her life.

They were marching up the dirt road, their lean faces hard with anger and their dirty bodies covered with ragged woolen clothes. In addition to the usual pitchforks, many of them were carrying weapons; she saw maces, clubs, and even a few swords. They were still far from Turingrad, but the very fact that they dared to go toward the capital with such numbers was disturbing on many levels. As someone who had grown up with stories of the Revolution, Augusta knew full well what could happen when peasants thought that they deserved better—that they had the right to take what wasn't given to them.

She had to warn Barson.

Flying back toward the hill, Augusta jumped off the chaise as soon as it landed and ran toward Barson, quickly telling him what she saw. As she spoke, his jaw tightened and his eyes flashed with anger.

"You're turning back, right?" she asked, although it was clearly a rhetorical question.

"No, of course not." He stared at her like she had grown two heads. "This changes nothing. We need to contain this rebellion, and we need to do it here, before they get any closer to Turingrad."

"But they outnumber you by an impossible margin—"

Her lover nodded grimly. "Yes, they do." The expression on his face was storm-black, and she wondered what he was thinking. Was he truly suicidal enough to attempt to go up against all those peasants? She admired his dedication to duty, but this was something else entirely.

Fighting to remain calm, Augusta tried to think of a solution that would contain the rebels and prevent

Barson from getting killed. "Look," she finally said in frustration, "if you're determined to do this, then maybe I can help somehow."

Barson studied her, his gaze dark and inscrutable. "Help us how? Using sorcery?"

"Yes." Sorcerers rarely did this sort of thing, but she couldn't let Barson and his soldiers perish in a battle with some peasants.

To her relief, he looked intrigued. "Well," he said thoughtfully. "Perhaps there is something you can do . . . Do you think you can teleport all of us to them, and then teleport us back at an agreed-upon time?"

Augusta considered his request. Teleportation was not an easy spell. It required very precise calculations, as even the smallest error could be deadly. Teleporting many people at once was an even greater challenge. Still, she should be able to do it, since it was only for a short distance and she would be able to see their destination, thus visually confirming that everything was clear. "Yes, I could do it," she said decisively. "How would that help?"

Barson smiled. "Here is what I have in mind." And he began telling her his insane plan.

CHAPTER TEN

❊ GALA ❊

Back in Blaise's study, Gala examined the Life Capture Sphere. It looked like a large round diamond, and the rest of the room was reflected in it, as though in a mirror. Gala was mesmerized by the elegant mathematics that warped the image of the laboratory, with its arcane bottles and instruments. There was only a single flaw in the spherical shape— an opening with a couple of clear beads inside it.

"Those are the Life Capture droplets," Blaise explained, walking up to it. "They are the physical shape Life Captures take when entering this world."

Taking one of the beads, he put it in her hand. When their hands touched lightly, Gala felt a pleasantly warm sensation in her body—the same strange feeling she experienced every time she was near Blaise. She would have to touch him more when an opportune moment arose, Gala decided, liking the way her body seemed to react to him.

"These appear when the cycle of recording is compete," he said. "To start the cycle, I touched the Sphere with the blood from my finger, and to stop it, I did it again. See that needle there? That's what I used to prick my finger. Droplets show up shortly after."

Gala pricked her finger. The sensation she felt now was most unpleasant. It was pain, she realized. The red substance—blood—started slowly oozing out of the small opening in her finger. She knew that pain was something humans avoided, and she could now understand why.

Reaching out with her bloody finger, she touched the Sphere, waiting for something to happen. When nothing did, she touched it again, wondering what she was doing wrong.

"It's not working for you, is it?" Blaise asked, watching her efforts. "That's not surprising."

"Because I am not human?"

He nodded. "Yes. With time, I suspect you'll be able to create your own droplets or do anything else you wished without the use of the Sphere."

Gala examined herself and saw no evidence to support what he said. If she could create these Life Capture droplets, she did not know how. In the meantime, her pricked finger had already healed.

"Why did Ganir tie pain to this?" she asked.

"I think he wanted a small cost to be associated with this part. Also, it must help functionally with the spell. I suspect something small enters the body through the wound, going to the brain and capturing something important there. When you touch the Sphere again, it leaves your body. Ganir is very secretive about this process, but that's how my brother explained it to me. He was hypothesizing, of course, since only Ganir understands his invention fully."

Gala focused on her body, wanting to try again. She pricked her other finger. The pain was much less unpleasant this time, since she knew what to expect. When she touched the Sphere, now that she knew what to look for, she actually felt something extremely small entering her flesh through her blood. She could also feel how her body immediately attacked the tiny invaders, preventing them from going further in her bloodstream. And her finger healed again, as quickly as before.

"Why don't you try just taking one of the droplets?" Blaise said. "Put it under your tongue and see what happens."

Gala did as he said, and felt like she was being invaded again. It was as though something wanted to take over her brain. This time, she tried to get her body to allow this invasion, but it still didn't work. Sighing, she looked at Blaise and shook her head. "I didn't succeed, but I would like to try again," she said apologetically. "I'm sorry if I'm wasting your precious droplets—"

"It's quite all right. These ones I made myself in order to document the completion of my spell. It doesn't matter if you use them up—I can still recall that time quite clearly and write it all up in my journal, if necessary." He smiled at her reassuringly.

Gala smiled back at him. Knowing that these were Blaise's Life Captures—that they would allow her to view the world through his eyes—was a very powerful incentive. Closing her eyes, she willed her body not to fight the invasion and focused on letting the substance of the droplets travel through her veins. Suddenly, something within her yielded, and she felt the stuff go up to her head and then into her brain. To her annoyance, however, what worked for the human mind didn't seem to work for hers. She felt some hint of foreign emotions, but no visions of any kind.

Frustrated, she opened her eyes. "It failed again, but I think I am close," she told Blaise. "Do you have any less valuable Life Captures?"

"Sure. They're in storage," he said, walking out of his study. Gala followed him, and they went into one of the rooms she remembered seeing on her earlier tour of Blaise's house. Every wall of that room seemed to be covered with wooden furniture—furniture that seemed to consist of dozens of little doors. Cabinets, Gala realized. These were cabinets—miniature closets used for storage purposes.

Bending down, Blaise opened one of the cabinet doors and took out a jar with a few droplets in it. "These are Life Captures of my less important work," he explained, handing her one of the clear beads. "You should feel free to use up as many of these as you want. I document anything particularly important in writing." He waved toward another set of doors, indicating where he kept his written legacy.

Taking one droplet from his hand, Gala put it under her tongue. With all her being, she willed the ability to see what was contained in the Life Capture. She thought of her time back in the Spell Realm and how she was able to get visions. Then she tapped into the part of her mind that was able to do this before. After what felt like hours of concentration, she felt something finally giving and a vision coming on . . .

* * *

Blaise was sitting in his study writing code. At times like these, he didn't mind his self-imposed solitude. Preparing spells required concentration, and distractions could result in significant setbacks. Thankfully, Maya and Esther knew better than to approach his study while he was working. They would simply come, drop off the Life Captures he needed, and quietly leave if he was busy.

He enjoyed coding because it was so exact, so precise. The sorcery code did what you asked it to do. As long as you wrote out the logic of the spell properly, then it was a simple dynamic of 'if variable A is set to such and such value, action B happens.' There was something reassuring about it. A certainty in an uncertain world. His mind liked the predictability of it all. He frequently re-used certain patterns, and they produced the same outcome each time.

The spell he was working on now was different,

much more challenging than usual. It was based on the work of Lenard the Great himself, and Blaise didn't fully understand all of its components—and thus couldn't predict the results. All he knew was that it was his gateway to the Spell Realm—and that it should enable him to send his Life Captures there, shaping the intelligent object he was creating.

Stopping for a second, Blaise wrote down a few things in his journal.

* * *

Gala suddenly became aware that she was Gala and not Blaise. Just a moment ago, she had been him. She had been thinking about sending Life Captures into the Spell Realm to feed the object—the object that was herself. The strangeness of that—of having thoughts about herself prior to her existence—had been jarring. Opening her eyes, Gala looked at Blaise.

"You're out of it already?" He seemed surprised.

"I stopped it," she explained. "I didn't like it. I was not myself. It was the way it had been in the Spell Realm, before I became aware of myself. I felt lost in your mind, and I didn't like that feeling—although I liked your mind quite a bit."

Blaise grinned at her, looking pleased. "Thank you. But just so you know, I've never heard of anybody being able to exit a Life Capture before it ends. I guess there's no point in being surprised with you."

"I *am* different," Gala agreed.

"Life Captures tend to be all-consuming," Blaise said. "That's what most people like about them. Some are even addicted to the experience. When your own life is lacking, being someone else provides a powerful escape. I, like you, don't enjoy the feeling of losing myself, but I embrace the chance to learn more about people by seeing life from their perspective."

"Yes, I could see that. I must admit, I got a chance to learn that you have a beautiful mind," she told him honestly. "So different, yet similar to my own." It had been enlightening to witness his thought processes, and Gala felt like she understood her creator better now.

He gave her a warm smile, his blue eyes crinkling at the corners. "Thank you."

She felt a sudden urge to touch his smiling lips, but she fought the impulse, having gleaned from books that uninvited touches were not socially acceptable. "I would like to see another Life Capture," she said instead. "From someone who is not you." As strange as the experience had been, Blaise was right: it gave her a chance to learn.

Blaise gave her an approving look. "I have some left over from the batch that was meant for your learning while you were in the Spell Realm." Taking out a droplet from a different cabinet, he handed it to Gala.

She put it under her tongue and tried to get her body to use it, like it did the last time. Only this time she focused on not letting it consume her completely, as it did before.

∗ ∗ ∗

She was a village girl, working in a garden near a large field of grass. The day was sunny, and the field was beautiful, with wildflowers that were just beginning to bloom. All of this grass would be gone soon, making way for wheat and other grains.

Looking down, she flexed her arms, noticing the play of muscle underneath her smooth skin. She was strong for a girl, her body toned from laboring on the farm her entire life. She enjoyed that part of her life, the endless cycle of planting and harvesting. Now that the spring was here, her family would soon be hard at work—

∗ ∗ ∗

Gala stopped the vision. It was difficult to stay detached. For a brief moment, she *had been* that girl, and the experience was as disorienting as before.

"This person seems familiar," she told Blaise. "I think I've been inside her mind before, in the Spell Realm."

He smiled at her, no longer startled by her quick exit. "Yes, I'm not surprised you recognize her. I've gotten most of my droplets from Maya and Esther, my friends in the village. They have many talents, including natural healing and midwifery. And in exchange for their services, they've been requesting

Life Captures from women that they help. A payment of sorts, which they've been passing on to me . . ." His voice trailed off, and there was now a thoughtful look on his face.

"What is it?" Gala asked, intrigued.

"It just occurred to me why you might have taken that shape," he said, studying her as though seeing her for the first time.

"What shape?" Gala gave him a questioning look.

"That of a girl."

"You don't like it?" she asked, feeling inexplicably disappointed.

"Oh, no," he reassured her. "I do. Believe me, I like it a little too much." His eyes darkened, color appearing high on his cheekbones, and Gala smiled, delighted that he liked her appearance. Looks were important to people; she knew that also from her readings.

He cleared his throat, still looking a little uncomfortable. "What I meant to say earlier is I think you look like a girl because so many of the Life Captures I sent to you were from the village women—the majority of them, in fact."

Gala nodded. That made sense to her. Her subconscious mind had likely chosen the female form based on the visions she experienced through the Life Captures. And since most of the Life Captures were from women, it was only logical that her mind had decided to take that shape.

"So would you like to see one more Life Capture?" Blaise asked. "I smuggled this one from the Tower of

Sorcery."

"Yes, I would love to," Gala told him.

* * *

The young sorceress was sitting in one of the study rooms in the Tower of Sorcery. For the first time ever, she was writing the sorcery code for her own spell. It was a tremendous milestone in her education, and she wanted to make Master Kelvin proud of her achievements.

This spell was of the more difficult verbal variety, since all students had to learn the old-fashioned way before they could get access to the simpler magical language and the Interpreter Stone. To reduce the possibility of errors, she went over the logic of the spell and verified that everything seemed correct. Of course, she knew that the only way to be certain was to say the spell out loud.

Gathering her courage, she spoke the sentences that she'd prepared, following them up with the arcane words of the Interpreter Spell. Then she watched as a small floating fire sphere appeared in front of her, just as she had coded. She laughed with excitement and exhilaration, feeling like she had just conquered the world.

All of a sudden, there was a flash of bright light in the room and the sphere exploded, shards of glass and burning wood raining everywhere.

The explosion knocked the young woman off her feet, but she managed to remain conscious. The room,

however, was nearly destroyed.
 Her spell had failed.

* * *

Gala stopped the Life Capture and decided not to do any more for the time being. It was just too unsettling for her. This last girl's mind had been filled with such deep negative emotions of disappointment and fear that Gala was still feeling some residual effects of that.

"You're out of it again?" Blaise asked as soon as Gala's eyes opened.

"I don't think I want to learn about the world this way," she told him. "I want to experience everything myself, not through someone else's eyes."

"Gala . . ." Blaise sounded unhappy again, his brow furrowing in a frown. "That's not a good idea. I already explained. If we go out there, everybody is going to be curious about you. The only thing you'll get to experience is their stares. They'll want to know where you come from and who you are—"

"Because of you," Gala said, recalling what he'd told her earlier. "Because you're an outcast."

"Yes, exactly."

"All right," Gala said, coming to a decision. "Then I'll go by myself. I don't want everybody to watch me just because I'm with you. I want to blend in, to live as your regular people." That last part was important to her. She was different, but she didn't want to *feel* different.

"You want to pretend to be one of the peasants?" Blaise gave her an incredulous look.

"Yes," Gala said firmly. "That's what I want."

"That's not a good idea—" Blaise started again, but Gala held up her hand, interrupting him mid-sentence.

"Am I your prisoner?" she asked quietly, feeling herself starting to get upset again.

"Of course not!"

"Am I your property, a magical object that is yours?"

Blaise shook his head, looking frustrated. "No, Gala, of course you're not. You're a thinking being—"

"Yes, I am." Gala was glad he accepted that fact. "And I know what I want, Blaise. I want to go out there and see the world, to live as a normal person."

He sighed and ran his hand through his dark hair. "Gala . . ."

She just stared at him, not saying anything. She had made her wishes clear. She was not an object or a pet to be kept in his house—not when there was so much to see and experience here in the Physical Realm.

"All right," he finally said. "Remember Maya and Esther, the friends I mentioned to you before? They live in the village where I grew up. Esther was my nanny, and I think of her and her friend Maya as my aunts, even though we're not related by blood. I want them to watch over you, if you don't mind, to help guide you until you're more familiar with our world."

"That sounds like a great idea," Gala said, all negative emotions vanishing in an instant. "I would love to meet both of them." In general, she wanted to meet more people, and she liked the idea of getting to know those who were important to Blaise.

"One thing, though," Blaise said, staring at her intently, "you can't tell anybody about your origins. It could get both of us in trouble."

Gala nodded. "I understand." She would do as Blaise asked, especially since she wanted others to see her as a regular human being, not some curiosity of nature.

Her creator looked somewhat reassured. "Good. Then I will take you to the village."

"Is that a village that's part of your holdings?" Gala asked, remembering from her readings that most of the land surrounding Turingrad was divided into territories—and that each territory belonged to some sorcerer.

"Yes." Blaise looked uncomfortable with this topic. "It's part of my territory."

"And the people living there belong to you, right?"

Blaise frowned. "Only by the strictest letter of the law. It's an archaic custom that's an unfortunate leftover from the feudal times. The Sorcery Revolution was supposed to eradicate it, but it failed in that, as it did in so many other things. Despite the Enlightenment, we still live in the Age of Darkness in some ways. This aspect of our society is something

DIMA ZALES

that I would very much like to change."

Gala nodded again. She'd gathered that much from the fact that he was so focused on helping the common people. "I understand," she said. "So when can I go there, to your village?"

"How about tomorrow?" Blaise suggested, still looking less than pleased with the idea.

"Tomorrow would be great." Gala gave him a big smile. And then, unable to contain her excitement, she did something she'd only read about.

She came up to him, wrapped her arms around his neck, and pulled his head down to her for a kiss.

CHAPTER ELEVEN

✳ AUGUSTA ✳

Flying high above the road on her chaise, Augusta observed the shocked looks on peasants' faces as fifty soldiers suddenly materialized out of thin air in front of them. Few laypeople even knew that teleporting spells existed, much less had ever seen the effects of one.

The peasants in the front abruptly stopped, and the people following them stumbled into them, causing a few to tumble to the ground. The fallen immediately got up, holding out their clubs and pitchforks protectively, but it was too late. They'd shown themselves for the clumsy weaklings that they were.

Knowing what was coming, Augusta smiled. They would get a bigger shock in a moment.

"Who is in charge here?" Barson's voice boomed at them, hurting Augusta's enhanced hearing for a moment. She'd used magic to increase the volume of her lover's voice, and she could see that the spell had had its intended effect. Some of the rebels now looked simply terrified.

At that moment, a giant of a man wearing a smith's apron walked out of the crowd. In his hand, he was holding a large, heavy-looking sword. A blacksmith, Augusta guessed. His presence explained some of the weapons the rebels were carrying.

"Nobody is in charge," the giant roared back, trying to match Barson's deep tones. "We're all equals here."

Barson raised his eyebrows. "Well, then, you can tell all your 'equals' that we have an army waiting just up this hill." His voice was at a normal volume now; Augusta's spell only worked for a short period of time.

The peasant openly sneered. "And we have an army about to march up this hill—"

"More like a bunch of hungry peasants," Barson interrupted dismissively.

The man's lip curled in a snarl. "What do you want?"

"It's more about what I don't want," the Captain of the Guard said coolly. "I don't want unnecessary slaughter."

The blacksmith laughed, throwing his head back. "We don't mind killing all of you, and it's quite necessary."

Barson didn't respond, just lifted his eyebrows and continued looking at the man.

"You're afraid of us," the peasant sneered again. "What, you think a little sorcery and threats are enough to make us turn back?"

Augusta's lover gave him an even look. "I would rather not make martyrs out of you. I understand that the drought is making life difficult for everyone, but you are marching on Turingrad. Even if we didn't kill you—and we will, if you force us—a single sorcerer there could destroy you in a moment."

The man scowled. "We'll see about that."

"No," Barson said, "we won't. I will give you a chance to see how futile your rebellion is. Your ten best fighters against one of us—any one of us."

"Oh, right." The man snorted. "And if we win?"

"You won't," Barson said, his confidence so absolute that for the first time, Augusta could see a glimmer of doubt on the blacksmith's face.

A moment later, however, the peasant recovered his composure. "This is pointless," he said, making a move to turn back.

"You're scared of us!" A taunting voice— surprisingly high-pitched and youthful—seemed to come out of nowhere, causing the peasant to stop in his tracks. Turning, the huge commoner stared at the young soldier who was pushing his way to the front.

It was Kiam, the boy Augusta had healed during practice.

Before the peasant could respond, Kiam yelled out, "Ten to one is not enough for you cowards— you're still scared! Why don't you do fifteen to one? Or how about twenty? Think you'd be less scared then?"

The blacksmith visibly swelled with rage, his bearded face turning a dark red color. "Shut your mouth, pup!" he bellowed and, pulling out his sword, charged at Kiam.

Augusta gripped the side of her chaise, tense with anxiety, as the slim youth unsheathed his own sword, preparing to meet the peasant rushing at him like a maddened bull.

The blacksmith lunged at Kiam, and Kiam gracefully dodged to the side, his movements smooth and practiced. Howling, the commoner charged again, and Kiam raised his sword. Before Augusta could even understand what happened, the peasant froze, a red line appearing on his neck. Then he collapsed, his huge bulk hitting the ground with tremendous force. His head, separated from the body, rolled on the ground, coming to a stop a few feet away.

Kiam's sharp sword had sliced through the man's thick neck as easily as a knife moving through butter.

For a moment, there was only stunned silence. Then Barson laughed. "I said ten, the boy said fifteen, but you sent only a single man," he yelled at the shocked peasants.

In response, five other men pushed through the peasant crowd. While none of them were as big as the dead peasant, they all appeared larger and stronger than Kiam. They were also much more cautious than the blacksmith had been, approaching the boy silently, a look of grim determination on their hard faces.

When they reached him, the first man made a lunge for the boy, which Kiam dodged, like before. This time, however, he proceeded to slice at the man's midsection. Another two peasants attacked at the same time, but Kiam, like a dancer, moved his body away from the blows, and swung his sword. Three more men were on the ground in moments. The last man standing hesitated for a moment, but it was too late for him, too. Without giving the man time to make up his mind, the young soldier jumped and sliced.

The last attacker was no more.

Augusta could hear murmuring in the crowd. This was the critical moment, what Barson had been counting on with this demonstration. One fairly small boy against several large men—there could be no clearer statement of the soldiers' fighting abilities. If the peasants had any common sense, they would turn back now.

At least, that's what Barson had been hoping. Augusta had been uncertain about this part of the plan—and she could now see that she'd been right to doubt. The peasants had come too far to be deterred so easily, and instead of retreating, they began to advance, pulling out their weapons. As they got closer to the soldiers, they spread out and started flanking Barson's men.

This was the point at which Augusta needed to teleport the soldiers back. Her hands shaking, she reached for the pre-written spell, and the card slipped from her fingers, falling off the chaise. She gasped, frantically trying to catch it, but it was futile. As the card flew to the ground, Augusta was overcome by a panic unlike anything she had ever experienced.

If her spell failed, she would be responsible for the deaths of Barson and his men.

CHAPTER TWELVE

※ BLAISE ※

Shocked, Blaise took a step back, staring at Gala. Did she realize what she was doing, kissing him like that?

Despite her startling beauty, he had been trying not to think of her this way. She had just come to this world, and in his eyes, she was as innocent as a child. Her actions, however, belied that idea.

This was getting complicated. Very complicated, very quickly.

Swallowing, Blaise thought about what to say. He could still feel her soft lips pressed against his own, her slim arms embracing him, holding him close. He hadn't realized that he would react to her so strongly, that it would take all his strength to step away from that kiss.

She took a step toward him. "Um, Blaise?"

"Gala, do you understand what a kiss means?" he asked carefully, trying to control his instinctive reaction to her nearness.

"Of course." Her blue eyes were large and guileless, looking up at him.

"And what does it mean to you?" Was she just experimenting with him, trying to 'learn' about this aspect of life as she tried to learn about everything else?

"The same thing that it means to everyone, I imagine," she said. "I read about it. There are a lot of stories about men and women kissing if they find each other attractive. And you find me attractive too, right?" There was a questioning look on her delicate face.

Blaise knew he had to tread carefully. Despite his aptitude for sorcery, he was far from an expert when it came to understanding women. The charming creatures had always mystified him, and here was one who was not even human. He might've created her, but her mind was as mysterious to him as the depths of the ocean.

"Gala," he said softly, "I already told you that I find you irresistible—"

She gave him a look that resembled a pout. "But you just resisted me."

"I had to," Blaise said patiently. "You're so new to this world. I'm the first man—the first human—you've ever met in person. How can you possibly know how you feel about me?"

"Well, aren't feelings exactly that? Feelings?" She frowned. "Are you saying that because I haven't seen the world, my feelings are somehow less real?"

"No, of course not." Blaise felt like he was digging himself a deeper hole. "I'm not saying that what you're feeling right now isn't real. It's just that it might change in the very near future, as you go out there and see more of the world . . . meet more men." As he added that last tidbit, he could feel a hot flare of jealousy at the idea, and he squashed it with effort, determined to be noble about this.

Gala's eyes narrowed. "All right. If that's your concern, that's fine. I'll go out there tomorrow, and I'll meet other men. And then I'm going to come back and kiss you as much as I want."

Blaise's pulse leapt. "Why don't I take you to the village right now then?" he said, only half-jokingly.

Her eyes lit up, and she practically jumped with eagerness. "Yes, let's go!"

CHAPTER THIRTEEN

※ AUGUSTA ※

Below, Augusta could see the peasants launching their attack.

Barson and his soldiers were expecting to be teleported, but when it didn't happen, they began fighting with ferocious determination. Soon they were surrounded by corpses. Augusta's lover seemed particularly inhuman in his battle frenzy. Realizing his strategic value, the rebels came at him, one after another, and he dispatched them all with the brutal swings of his sword.

Seeing that the guards were holding their own, Augusta tried to concentrate. She couldn't fly down to retrieve her spell card—not with a bloody battle raging below—so she had to write a new one.

Getting her thoughts together, she took out a blank card and the remaining parts of the spell. All she had to do now was re-create from memory the complicated bit of sorcery code she'd written earlier. Luckily, Augusta's memory was excellent, and it took her only a few minutes to recall what she'd done before.

When the spell was finished, she loaded the cards into the Stone and peered below, holding her breath.

A minute later, Barson and his soldiers disappeared from the battleground, leaving behind dozens of dead bodies and baffled rebels.

* * *

"I am so sorry," she said when she rendezvoused with Barson and his men back on the hill.

Luckily, no one was hurt; if anything, the fighting seemed to have lifted everyone's spirits. The soldiers were laughing and slapping each other on the back, like they had just come back from a tournament instead of a bloody battle.

"We held our ground," Barson told her triumphantly, snatching her up in his strong arms and twirling her around.

Laughing and gasping, Augusta made him put her down. "You're lucky I was able to replace that card so quickly," she told him. "If I'd lost some other card, it would've taken me more effort to replace it, and you'd have been fighting longer."

"Perhaps there is something you can do to make up for that blunder," Barson suggested, looking down at her with a darkly excited smile.

"What?" Augusta asked warily.

"The rebels will be here soon," he said, his eyes gleaming. "Do you think you could thin their numbers a little?"

Augusta swallowed. "You want me to do a direct spell against them?"

"Is that against the Council rules?"

It wasn't, exactly, but it was highly frowned upon. In general, the Council preferred to limit displays of magic around the commoners. It was considered poor taste for sorcerers to show their abilities so openly—and it could be potentially dangerous, if it incentivized the peasants to try to learn magic on their own. Offensive spells were particularly discouraged; using sorcery against someone with no aptitude for magic was the equivalent of butchering a chicken with a sword.

"Well, it's not strictly speaking against the law," Augusta said slowly, "but it shouldn't be obvious that I'm doing this."

Barson appeared to consider the problem for a moment. "What if it looked like natural causes?" he suggested.

"That might work." Augusta thought about a few spells she could quickly pull together. She hadn't expected to do anything like this, but she did have the right components for these spells. She'd brought them for different purposes, but they would help her now too.

Digging in her bag, she pulled out a few cards and rapidly wrote some new lines of code. When she was finished, she told Barson to have his men sit or lie on the ground for a few minutes. "It might get a bit . . . shaky here," she explained.

The peasants were still a distance away when she began feeding the cards into her Interpreter Stone.

For a moment, all was quiet. Augusta held her breath, waiting to see if her spell worked. She'd combined a simple force attack of the kind that might have blown up a house with a clever teleporting idea. Instead of hitting the peasants directly, the spell would be teleported into the ground under the feet of their attacking army. There, beneath the ground, the force would break and shatter rocks, creating the chain reaction she needed—or so Augusta hoped.

For a few nerve-wracking seconds, it seemed like nothing was happening. And then she heard it: a deep, sonorous boom, followed by a powerful vibration under her feet. The earth shook so violently that Augusta had to sit or be knocked to the ground herself. In the distance, she could hear the screams of the peasants as the ground split open under their feet, a deep gash appearing right in the middle of their army. Dozens of men tumbled into the opening, falling to their deaths with frightened yells.

Step one of the plan was complete.

Augusta loaded her next spell. It was one of the deadliest spells she knew—a spell that sought pulsating tissue and applied a powerful electric current to it. It was meant to stop a heart—or multiple hearts, given the width of the radius Augusta had coded.

The spell blasted out, and Augusta could see the peasants who were still on their feet falling, clutching their chests. With her enhanced vision, she could see the looks of shock and pain on their faces, and she swallowed hard, trying to keep down the bile in her stomach. She had never done this before, had never killed so many using sorcery, and she couldn't help her instinctive reaction.

By the time the spell had run its course, the road and the grassy fields nearby were littered with bodies. Less than half of the original peasant army was left alive.

Still feeling sick, Augusta stared at the results of her work. Now they would run, she thought, desperately wanting this battle to be over.

But to her shock, instead of turning back, the survivors rushed toward the hill, clutching their remaining weapons. They were fearless—or, more likely, desperate, she realized. These men had known from the beginning that their mission was dangerous, but they'd chosen to proceed anyway. She couldn't help but admire that kind of determination, even though it scared her to death. She imagined the rebels behind the Sorcery Revolution—the ones who had overthrown the old nobility so brutally—had been just as determined in their own way.

All around her, Barson's soldiers prepared to meet the onslaught, assuming their places and drawing their arrows.

As the peasants got closer to the hill, a hail of arrows rained down, piercing their unshielded bodies. The soldiers hit their targets with the same terrifying precision that Augusta had seen during practice. Every peasant who got within their arrows' range was dead within seconds. Yet the rebels persisted, continuing on, pushing past their fallen comrades. Lacking any kind of structure or organization, they simply kept going, their faces twisted with bitter rage and their eyes shining with hatred. The futility of all the deaths was overwhelming for Augusta. By the time Barson's men ran out of arrows, less than a third of the original aggressors remained.

Tossing aside their useless bows, the guards, as one, unsheathed their swords. And then they waited, their expressions hard and impassive.

When the first wave of attackers reached the hill, they were dispatched within seconds, the soldiers' sorcery-enhanced weapons sharper and deadlier than anything the peasants had ever seen before. Standing off to the side, Augusta watched as waves of attackers came and fell all around the hill.

Her lover was death incarnate, as unstoppable as a force of nature. Half the time, he would singlehandedly tackle the waves of rebels, easily taking on twenty or thirty men. The other soldiers were almost as brutal, and Augusta could see the peasants breaking up into smaller and smaller groups, their ranks diminishing with every minute that passed.

Within an hour, the battle was nearing its morbid conclusion. Staring at the bloody remnants on the field, Augusta knew it was a battle she would never forget.

No, she corrected herself. It was not a battle—it was a slaughter.

CHAPTER FOURTEEN

✳ GALA ✳

"This is spectacular," Gala told Blaise, looking down at the city below. They were sitting on his chaise, a magical object that she found quite impressive. Light blue in color, it reminded Gala of a narrow, elongated sofa—except that it was made of a strange diamond-like material that looked hard, but was actually quite soft and pleasant to the touch. Blaise was navigating it using verbal spells.

Gala especially liked the fact that she could sit so close to Blaise. She enjoyed his nearness; it made her recall the warm sensations she'd experienced when she'd kissed him earlier. Thinking about that kiss, she tore her eyes away from the view below and glanced at Blaise, studying his strong profile.

It bothered her that he doubted her feelings. She obviously lacked real-world experience, but she'd read enough to understand the mechanics of attraction—and what it meant, to feel like that about someone. She was sure that meeting other people wouldn't make a difference in how she regarded Blaise. This trip to the village would serve multiple purposes, she thought, turning her attention back to the city below. It would let her see the world, and it would also reassure Blaise that she knew her own mind. She didn't want to seem ignorant or naive to her creator.

"This is the Town Square," Blaise said, interrupting her musings. He was pointing at a large open area below. "You can see all the merchant stalls surrounding it. And you see that water fountain in the center?"

"Yes," Gala said, her excitement increasing. She liked learning, and it was great to see these things with her own eyes, rather than through a Life Capture or the pages of a book.

"Everybody who visits Turingrad comes to this fountain to throw a coin in the water," Blaise said. "Rich or poor, commoner or sorcerer—they all come here to make a wish."

"Why? Is that a form of sorcery?"

"No." Blaise chuckled. "Just an old custom. It was in place long before Lenard the Great and the discovery of the Spell Realm. A superstition, if you will."

"I see," Gala said, though the concept confused her a little. Why would humans throw their coins into the fountain like that? If the fountain had nothing to do with sorcery, then it obviously couldn't grant wishes.

"And that's the Tower of Sorcery over there," Blaise said, pointing at an imposing structure sitting on top of a large hill. "That's where the most powerful sorcerers live and work. The Council holds meetings there as well, and the first few floors are occupied by the Academy of Sorcery, a learning institution for the young. The Sorcerer Guard is also stationed there."

Gala nodded, studying the Tower with curiosity. It was a large, stately castle, made even more impressive by its location on the mountain. Whoever had built it was clearly making a statement. The building practically screamed 'power.'

Looking at it, Gala realized that something about the mountain bothered her. The shape of it, the steep cliff at one end—it was just too different from the surrounding flat landscape. "Is the mountain real?" she asked Blaise, turning her head to look at him.

"No." He gave her a smile. "It was built by the first sorcerer families over two hundred years ago. They wanted the Tower to be unassailable, so they did a spell to make the earth rise up, creating this hill. The building itself is fortified with all manner of sorcery as well."

"Why did they do this? Was it because they were afraid of the common people?"

"Yes," Blaise said. "And they still are. It's unfortunate, but the memory of the Sorcery Revolution is still fresh in most people's minds."

Gala nodded again, remembering what she'd read

in one of Blaise's books. Two hundred and fifty years ago, the entire fabric of Koldun society had been ripped apart by a bloody revolution. The old nobility had gotten fat and lazy, disconnected from the brewing discontent of their subjects. The king had been among the worst of the offenders, completely oblivious to the changes taking place as a result of the Enlightenment and one man's discovery of something called the Spell Realm.

Lenard—or Lenard the Great, as he would later become known—had been a brilliant inventor who, among his other achievements, managed to tap into a strange place that had the power to alter reality in a way that was uncannily similar to fairy-tale magic. It wasn't a fairy tale, of course, and what was known in the modern era as magic was nothing more than complex and still little-understood interactions between the Spell Realm and the Physical Realm. But his discovery changed everything, resulting in the rise of a new elite: the sorcerers.

It started off as harmless little spells—oral incantations in a complex, arcane language that only the brightest, most mathematically inclined individuals could master. Some of the first sorcerers were from the noble class, but many were not. Anyone, regardless of their lineage, could tap into the Spell Realm, and Lenard encouraged everyone to learn mathematics and the language of magic, to understand the laws of nature. He even went so far as to open a school, a place that later became known as the Academy of Sorcery, where many of the subsequent magical and scientific discoveries took place.

Within a decade, sorcery and knowledge brought about by the Enlightenment began to permeate every aspect of life on Koldun. The sorcerers discovered a way to sustain themselves without food, to move from place to place in a blink of an eye via teleportation, and even to do battle using spells. Before long, the centuries-old feudal system of hereditary nobility began to seem outdated to those who could change the fabric of reality with a few carefully chosen sentences. Notions of fairness and progress, of basic human rights and merit-based societal standing, spread like wildfire, catching the nobles completely off-guard.

By the time the king understood the threat posed by the new sorcerer class, it was too late. The peasants, realizing that their lords were no longer as all-powerful as they once were, grew more demanding, and uprisings erupted all over Koldun as commoners sought to better their quality of life. Most of the sorcerers—though not all—supported the peasants, and those of the lower class who lacked the aptitude for magic banded behind them, seeking the sorcerers' protection against the nobles who still had the king's army on their side.

The end result was a revolution—a bloody civil conflict lasting six years. As it progressed, each side grew more brutal and vengeful, and the atrocities perpetuated by the peasants against their former masters ended up being as horrifying as what the barbarians did in the Age of Darkness. It wasn't until almost every noble family was slaughtered and the king lost his head that the revolution came to an end, leaving the survivors to pick up the pieces of their shattered lives.

It was no wonder that the sorcerers feared the peasants, Gala thought, staring at the Tower. After all, sorcerers were now the new ruling class.

* * *

After several hours of flying, they finally approached their destination. Gala recognized the field below from one of the Life Captures she'd consumed earlier; it was even more beautiful from above. The spring work in her vision must've been completed, and tall stalks of wheat populated the landscape.

Off to the side was a cluster of buildings that Gala guessed to be the village. Unlike the rich, elaborate-looking structures in Turingrad, the houses here were much smaller. Simpler, Gala thought. She remembered reading that many peasant homes were made of clay, and it appeared to be the case here as well.

There was a little clearing between two of the bigger houses, and that was where they landed.

As soon as their chaise touched the ground, the door to one of these houses opened, and two older women came out.

Gala stared at them, intrigued. She'd read about the physical changes that occur in humans throughout their lives, and she wondered about these women's ages. To her, they appeared to be similar to each other, with their grey hair and brown eyes, although Gala found one of them to be more pleasant-looking than the other.

Seeing Blaise, they smiled widely and rushed toward the chaise.

"Blaise, my child, how are you?" the prettier one of the two exclaimed.

"And who is this beautiful girl with you?" the other woman jumped in.

Before Blaise had a chance to answer and Gala could fully register the fact that she had just been called 'beautiful,' the woman who spoke first turned toward Gala and announced, "I am Maya. Who might you be, my child?"

"And I am Esther," said the other one without giving Gala a chance to reply. Her face was creased with a smile that Gala liked very much. In general, despite the woman's more homely appearance, Gala decided that something about her was quite appealing. Both women had a warmth to them that Gala found pleasant.

"Maya, Esther," Blaise said, getting off the chaise, "let me introduce Gala to you."

"Gala? What a pretty name," said Esther, stepping forward and giving Gala a hug. Maya followed her example, and Gala grinned, pleased to find herself the center of attention. Their hugs were nice, but nothing like what she felt when she touched Blaise.

"Blaise, wasn't Gala your grandmother's name as

well?" asked Maya.

Blaise nodded and gave Gala a conspiratorial smile. "Yes. A lovely coincidence, isn't it?"

"Well, come inside, children," Esther said. "I've just made some delicious stew—"

"I'm not so sure about delicious, but it's definitely stew," Maya said with a wicked grin, and Gala realized that she was teasing the other woman.

Blaise shook his head. "I'd love to, but I can't," he told Esther gently. "Unfortunately, I have to go. However, if you don't mind, Gala will be staying with you for a few days."

The women looked taken aback, but Maya recovered quickly. "Of course, we don't mind," she said. "Anything for you and your lovely young friend."

Esther nodded eagerly. "Yes, anything for you, Blaise. How do you two know each other?" she asked, visibly curious.

"It's a long story," Blaise said, his tone brooking no further questions on this topic. "Maya, would you mind giving Gala a tour of the village while Esther and I catch up for a minute?"

Esther frowned. "Are you sure you won't stay? We'd love to have you for a few days. You need some sun, and you should eat something. I bet you lived on magic since our last visit," she said disapprovingly.

"Blaise has important business to attend to," Gala said, coming to Blaise's rescue. She could see that he looked tense, and she sensed that he didn't want to be here, away from the comforting precision of the code he'd come to depend on so much. From the brief glimpse of his mind she'd gotten in that Life Capture—and from what she'd learned about his brother—she knew that her creator was still hurting, that he wasn't ready to face the outside world yet.

"Well, I don't like it one bit," Esther announced, pursing her lips. "Promise us you'll come back soon."

"Oh, don't worry. I will not leave Gala by herself for long, you can be sure of that," Blaise said, and Gala felt the warmth in his gaze as he looked upon her.

Gala smiled and took a step toward Blaise. Standing up on tiptoes, she wrapped her arms around his neck and pulled his head down for another kiss. His lips were warm and soft, and Gala eagerly savored the sensation. To her relief, this time he didn't step away. Instead, he pulled her deeper into his embrace and kissed her back fiercely, sending shivers of heat down her spine.

When he released her, her heart was beating faster, and she could see the pleased looks on Maya and Esther's faces. She'd succeeded in reinforcing the impression the two women must've already had— that she and Blaise were lovers. It was something that Gala hoped would be a reality at some point, and in the meantime, it provided an explanation for her relationship with Blaise. Not that anyone would ever guess that Gala was Blaise's creation, she thought wryly. From what she'd learned thus far, nobody could imagine that a person could've originated the way Gala did.

Now that it was time for her to part from Blaise, Gala experienced doubt for the first time. All of a sudden, seeing the world was not nearly as appealing, since it meant she would have to be apart from Blaise for the next few days. He hadn't even left yet, and she already missed him—and wanted more of those kisses. From everything she'd read, she knew people rarely developed strong feelings for each other so quickly, but there were always exceptions. It was also possible that the usual rules didn't apply to her, since she wasn't human.

"Bye, Gala," Blaise said, giving her a smile, and she smiled back, shaking off the brief moment of weakness. The village was beckoning her. This was her chance to experience life here, among the common people. She had a strong suspicion that if she backed out now, she would not be able to talk Blaise into doing this again.

"Bye, Blaise," she said, determined to be strong about this. Turning, she started walking toward the beautiful field that she could see nearby. Maya followed her, waving a goodbye to Blaise as well.

As Gala approached the field, her pace picked up until she was running as hard as she could. She could feel the wind in her hair and the warmth of the sun on her face, and she turned her face up, laughing from sheer joy.

She was living, and she loved every moment of it.

CHAPTER FIFTEEN

❋ AUGUSTA ❋

"Are you sure you're going to be all right?" Barson asked, looking down at Augusta with concern. He had just walked her to her quarters, and they were standing in front of her office.

"Of course." Augusta smiled up at her lover. "I'll be fine." She couldn't deny that she still felt a little shaky after the battle, but the best cure for that was getting right back to her everyday routine—and that meant resuming work on her ongoing projects.

"In that case, I'll let you get to your spells," Barson said, leaning down to give her a kiss.

Out of the corner of her eye, Augusta spotted a young sorceress approaching them and pausing deferentially a few feet away.

"Um, excuse me, my lady..." The woman appeared uncomfortable, her hands nervously twisting together.

Barson smirked, clearly amused by the girl's reverent manner, and Augusta turned her head toward him, giving him a narrow-eyed look. "What is it?" she asked the girl, annoyed to be interrupted.

"Master Ganir sent me to look for you," the sorceress quickly explained. "He is requesting your presence in his office."

Augusta frowned, unhappy at being summoned like an acolyte. Had Ganir already heard about the battle and her involvement in it? If so, that was fast, even for him.

"Maybe he wants to explain how three hundred peasants became three thousand," Barson murmured, bending his head so that the girl couldn't hear him.

Startled, Augusta looked up at him, meeting his coolly mocking gaze. Was Barson implying that Ganir had misinformed them on purpose?

Tucking that thought away for further analysis, she told her lover, "I will see you later," and walked decisively down the hall, forcing the young woman to jump out of her way.

It was best to get this unpleasantness over with quickly.

CHAPTER SIXTEEN

❋ BARSON ❋

As soon as Augusta was out of sight, Barson left the sorcerers' quarters and headed toward the Guard barracks in the west wing of the Tower. He and Augusta had ridden ahead of his soldiers, and he had less than an hour to do what needed to get done.

Walking in, he saw the familiar hallway with the row of rooms where he and his men lived when they were on duty. His own quarters were nearly as lavish as those of the sorcerers, but even his lowest-ranked soldiers had comfortable accommodations. It was something he'd made sure of when he'd taken over as Captain of the Guard.

Normally, after a hard trip like this one, he would've gone straight to his room to take a long bath, but there was no time to waste. He had to confront the traitor—and he had to do it now, while he could still catch him unaware.

Stopping in front of Siur's room, he paused to

listen to the sounds coming from within. It seemed that his trusted lieutenant was engaged in a bit of bed play.

All the better, Barson thought, a thin smile appearing on his lips. There was nothing better than catching your enemy with his pants down—literally.

Without further ado, he pushed open the door and entered Siur's bedroom.

As he had suspected, there were two naked bodies on the bed. From the moans and the flashes of red hair he could see under Siur's straining bulk, the woman had to be one of the local whores that frequently visited the guards. The two of them were so occupied with each other, they didn't even react to Barson's entry.

Starting to get annoyed, Barson banged his gauntleted fist against the wall. Siur and his bedmate jumped, cursing, and Barson watched with cruel amusement as the woman scrambled out of bed, pulling a sheet around her plump naked body.

"Captain!" Siur gasped, hopping out of bed and swiftly pulling on his britches. "I didn't see you there . . ." The wide-eyed look of shock on his face was almost comical.

"Surprised to see me?" Barson asked in a silky tone, watching as the whore ran out of the room. "Or just surprised to see me alive?"

"What? No, Captain! I mean, yes—" Siur was clearly caught off-guard. His eyes were shifting from side to side, reminding Barson of a trapped animal.

"Why were you unable to join this mission?"

Barson demanded, not giving the man a chance to regain his composure. "Why did you stay behind?"

"Well, I—" Siur clearly wasn't expecting to be questioned, and Barson could see him frantically trying to come up with a plausible answer. His hesitation was damning.

"Tell me everything," Barson ordered, looking at the man he'd once regarded as a brother. "Why did you do this?"

Siur blinked, backing away. "I don't know what you're talking about—"

"Don't lie to me. At least show me that much respect."

"Captain, Barson, I—" The soldier kept moving backward, and Barson saw what he was after the very second the man's hand closed around his sword.

Barson unsheathed his own sword. "Tell me the truth," he said coldly, "and you will die quickly and painlessly." He was glad the traitor was showing his true colors; up until that moment, he hadn't been completely sure of the man's guilt.

With an enraged cry, Siur attacked. His momentum carried him across the room, his sword swinging.

Barson met his fierce attack, parrying every blow and watching carefully for an opening to disarm his opponent. Normally, Siur would've already been dead, but Barson didn't want to kill him yet. He needed information, and the traitor was the only one who could provide it.

Siur fought like a berserker. Faced with the

prospect of interrogation, the man was apparently trying to go for a quick, glorious death—something that Barson had no intention of allowing. They fought for what seemed like forever. If Barson hadn't been so tired from his earlier ordeal, this would've been easier. As it was, he had to restrain himself from killing Siur every couple of minutes, while simultaneously preventing the soldier's deadly blows from reaching his body.

His moment finally came when Siur made a violent thrust at Barson's shoulder. With one flick of his sword, Barson grazed his opponent's left side, drawing the first blood. Siur jumped back with a pained hiss, then attacked Barson with even more desperation. The soldier knew he would now grow weaker with every minute that passed, and Barson found it more difficult to restrain himself from dealing the traitor a killing blow.

"You can't make me talk, no matter what you do," Siur panted, executing a triple feint attack. Barson easily defended himself; he'd personally taught this maneuver to Siur, and the man had never particularly excelled at it. That Siur used it now was a sign that he was no longer thinking straight.

Silently taking advantage of this opening, Barson slashed the man's right shoulder, slicing through his naked flesh with ease. It was fortunate the soldier wasn't wearing armor; otherwise, Barson's task would've been even more difficult. Siur stumbled, letting out a pained cry, but pressed on, his eyes glittering with rage and desperation.

A trickle of sweat ran down Barson's back, intensifying his longing for a bath. Deciding to bring the fight to its inevitable conclusion, he pretended to favor his right side, leaving his left exposed for a brief moment. Siur immediately took the bait, going for a killing blow to the heart.

At the last moment, Barson twisted his body, letting the man's sharp sword scrape the side of his armor, cutting through it and leaving a shallow scratch on his skin. At the same time, Barson's gauntleted fist landed on Siur's right arm with massive force, causing the traitor's sword to fly across the room.

"Now we talk," Barson muttered, punching Siur in the face and knocking him out.

CHAPTER SEVENTEEN

※ AUGUSTA ※

The wizened old man was working behind his desk when Augusta entered his lavish study. His workspace was nearly the size of her entire quarters in the Tower. Being the head of the Council certainly had its privileges.

"Augusta." He raised his head, regarding her with a pale blue gaze. Although Ganir's face was wrinkled and weathered, his white hair was still thick, flowing down to his narrow shoulders in a style that had been popular seven decades ago.

"Master Ganir," she responded, slightly bowing her head. Despite her dislike of him, she couldn't help feeling a certain grudging respect for the Council Leader. Ganir was among the oldest and most powerful sorcerers in existence, as well as the inventor of the Life Capture Sphere.

"You need not be so formal with me, child," he

said, surprising her with his warm tone.

"As you wish, Ganir," Augusta said warily. Why was he being kind to her? This was very much unlike him. She had always gotten the impression that the old sorcerer didn't care for her. Blaise had once let slip that Ganir thought they didn't suit each other—an obvious insult to Augusta, since the old man had treated Blaise and his brother with an almost fatherly regard.

In response to her unspoken question, Ganir leaned back in his chair, regarding her with an inscrutable gaze. "I have a delicate matter to discuss with you," he said, lightly drumming his fingers on his desk.

Augusta raised her eyebrows, waiting for him to continue. She wouldn't have thought her interference with the rebels was a particularly delicate matter, and she didn't know why he didn't just bring up her actions at the next Council meeting. Of course, it was possible he wanted something from her—a possibility that made her uneasy.

"As you know, when you were with Blaise, I did not always act approvingly," Ganir began, shocking her by echoing her earlier thoughts. "I have since come to regret that attitude." Pausing, he let her digest his words.

Caught completely off-guard, all Augusta could do was stare at him. She had no idea why he was bringing up ancient history now, but it didn't seem like a good sign to her.

"I wish I had supported you then, back when you

and Blaise were together," the Council Leader continued, and the sadness in his voice was as unusual as it was surprising. "He was one of our brightest stars . . ."

"Yes, he was," Augusta said, frowning. They both knew what lay behind Blaise's self-exile. It was Ganir's own invention that had led to that disastrous situation with Louie—and to Augusta losing the man she had loved.

Then, with a sudden leap of intuition, she knew. Ganir's summons had nothing to do with the battle she'd just returned from . . . and everything to do with the man she'd been trying to forget for the past two years.

"What happened to Blaise?" she asked sharply, a sickening coldness spreading through her veins. Even now, despite her growing feelings for Barson, the mere thought of Blaise in danger was enough to send her into panic.

Ganir's faded gaze held sorrow. "I'm afraid his depression has led him to a new low," he said quietly. "Augusta, I think Blaise has become a Life Capture addict."

"What?" This was not at all what she had expected to hear. She wasn't sure what she did expect, but this was definitely not it. "A Life Capture addict?" She stared at Ganir in disbelief. "That doesn't sound like Blaise at all. He would consider it a weakness to drown himself in someone else's memories. In his work, yes, but not in other people's minds—"

"I had trouble believing this at first as well. The

only thing I can think of is perhaps the isolation has broken his spirit . . ." He shrugged sadly.

"No, I don't see how this could be true," Augusta said firmly. "If nothing else, he would never abandon his research. What made you decide that he's an addict?"

"I have someone reporting to me from his village," Ganir explained. "According to my source, Blaise has been getting enormous amounts of Life Capture droplets. Enough to stay in a dream world all waking hours."

Augusta's eyes narrowed. "Are you spying on him?" she asked, unable to keep the accusatory note out of her voice. She hated the way the old man seemed to have his tentacles in everything these days.

"I'm not spying on the boy," the Council Leader denied, his white eyebrows coming together. "I just want to make sure he's healthy and well. You know he doesn't talk to me either, right?"

Augusta nodded. She knew that. As much as she disliked Ganir, she could see that he was hurting, too. He had been close to Dasbraw's sons, and Blaise's coldness had to be as upsetting to him as it was to Augusta herself. "All right," she said in a more conciliatory tone, "so your source is telling you that Blaise acquired a lot of Life Captures?"

"A lot is an understatement. What he got is worth a fortune on the black market."

Ganir was right; this didn't sound good. Why would Blaise need so much of that stuff if he was not addicted? Augusta had always considered Life

Captures to be dangerous, and she was extremely cautious in how she used the droplets herself. She had even spoken up about the risks of Ganir's invention in the beginning—a fact that she suspected had something to do with the old sorcerer's dislike of her.

"What makes you so sure he got them for himself?" she wondered out loud.

"It's not definitive, of course," Ganir admitted. "However, no one has seen him for months. He hasn't even shown up in his village."

Augusta did not think this was that unusual, but combined with the large quantity of droplets, it did not paint a pretty picture. "Why are you telling me this?" she asked, even though she was beginning to get an inkling of the Council Leader's intentions.

"I want you to talk to Blaise," Ganir said. "He will hear you out. I wouldn't be surprised if he still loves you. Maybe that's why he's suffering so much—"

"Blaise left *me*, not the other way around," Augusta said sharply. How dare Ganir imply that their parting was to blame for Blaise's current state? Everyone knew it was the loss of his brother that drove Blaise out of the Council—a tragedy for which they all bore varying degrees of responsibility.

Why hadn't she voted differently? Augusta wondered bitterly for a thousandth time. Why hadn't at least one other member of the Council? Every time she thought of that disastrous event, she felt consumed with regret. If she had known that her vote wouldn't matter—that the entire Council, with the exception of Blaise, would vote to punish Louie—she would've gone against her convictions and voted to spare Blaise's brother. But she hadn't. What Louie had done—giving a magical object to the commoners—was one of the worst crimes Augusta could imagine, and she'd voted according to her conscience.

It was that vote that had cost her the man she loved. Somehow, Blaise had found out about the breakdown of the votes and learned that Augusta had been one of the Councilors who'd sentenced Louie to death. There had been only one vote against the punishment: that of Blaise himself.

Or so Blaise had told her when he'd yelled at her to get out of his house and never return. She would never forget that day for as long as she lived—the pain and rage had transformed him into someone she couldn't even recognize. Her normally mild-tempered lover had been truly frightening, and she'd known then that it was over between them, that eight years together had not meant nearly as much to Blaise as they had to her.

Not for the first time, Augusta tried to figure out how Blaise had learned the exact vote count. The voting process was designed to be completely fair and anonymous. Each Councilor possessed a voting stone that he or she would teleport into one of the voting boxes—red box for *Yes*, blue box for *No*. The boxes stood on the Scales of Justice in the middle of the Council Chamber. Nobody was supposed to know how many stones were in each box; the scales would simply tip whichever way the vote was leaning. There should have been no way Blaise had known how many stones were in the red box on that fateful day.

"I'm sorry," Ganir said, interrupting her dark thoughts. "I didn't mean to imply that you're to blame. I just think Blaise is still in pain. I would go speak to him myself, but as you probably know, he said he would kill me on sight if I ever approached him again."

"You don't think he'd do the same thing to me?" Augusta asked, remembering the black fury on Blaise's face as he threw her out of his house.

"No," Ganir said with conviction. "He wouldn't harm you, not with the way he felt about you once. Just talk to him, make him see reason. Maybe he would like to rejoin our ranks again—he's been away from the Tower long enough."

Augusta raised her eyebrows. "You want him back on the Council?"

"Why not?" The Council Leader looked at her. "Like you, he's one of our best and brightest. It's a shame that his talents are going to waste."

"What about Gina? She took his place, so what's going to happen to her if he comes back?"

"We'll have fourteen Councilors," Ganir said. "I wouldn't want to replace Gina. She's an asset."

Augusta stared at him. "It's been thirteen ever since the Council began. You know that."

Ganir didn't look particularly concerned. "Yes. But that doesn't mean things can't change. For now, let's not worry about this. We'll cross that bridge when we get to it."

"Do you really think the others would welcome him back?" Augusta asked dubiously.

"He was never forced out. Blaise left on his own. Besides, if you and I team up, everyone will have to follow."

Augusta gave him an incredulous look. She and Ganir, team up? That was an idea she'd have to get used to.

"All I can promise is to speak with him," she said, and then walked out of the old sorcerer's study.

CHAPTER EIGHTEEN

※ BLAISE ※

"So who is this girl?" Esther asked as soon as she and Blaise were alone. "How did you meet? How long have you two known each other?"

Still reeling from Gala's kiss, Blaise shook his head at the barrage of questions. "This is not why I wanted to speak to you, Esther," he said. "I have a favor to ask."

"Of course, anything," his former nanny said immediately, though Blaise knew she had been hoping to learn more about Gala and was likely disappointed at the lack of gossip coming her way.

"I want you to look after Gala," he said, giving Esther a serious look. "I don't want her to draw any needless attention to herself—and it's best if her connection to me is kept secret."

"Why?" The old woman looked puzzled. "Is she a fugitive?"

Blaise shook his head. "No. She's just . . . different."

Esther frowned at him. "She seems very young and innocent. Did you involve her in something you shouldn't have?"

"In a manner of speaking," Blaise said vaguely. He wasn't certain how Maya and Esther would react if they knew the truth about Gala's origins. Even other sorcerers would be shocked to learn what he had done; how would someone with much more rudimentary understanding of magic feel? Even in this enlightened age, most peasants were superstitious, and many still believed the old tales of undead monsters and ghosts. If they knew Gala was not really human, she would never be able to experience the world as a regular person.

Esther continued looking at him, and he sighed, not wanting to lie to the woman who'd raised him after his mother's death. "Esther," he said carefully, "Gala has a power that the Council might find . . . threatening."

His former nanny stared at him, her expression slowly hardening. She hated the Council even more than he did, blaming them for Louie's death. She'd raised his brother too, nursing him from infancy, and his loss had affected her deeply. "I will watch her," she promised grimly.

"Good," Blaise said, relieved. "Also, keep in mind, she's been somewhat sheltered." He decided to settle for a half-truth here.

Now Esther seemed confused. "A sheltered young

girl who's a threat to the Council? How did you come across her?" Then she held up her hands. "Never mind. I know you're not going to tell me."

Blaise grinned at her. "You're the best, Nana Esther."

"Uh-huh," she responded, giving him a narrow-eyed look. "And don't you forget it."

"I won't," Blaise said, leaning down to give her an affectionate kiss on the cheek. Straightening, he reached into his pocket. Pulling out a drawstring purse filled with coin, he pressed it into Esther's hand. "Here is a little something for Gala's room and board—"

"Blaise, that's a small fortune!" She stared at him in shock. "You could buy a house with that money. It's too much for just feeding one skinny girl."

Blaise was about to tease Esther for always trying to feed everyone, but then he realized something. He'd never asked Gala if she wanted food. In fact, he didn't even know if she needed to eat like a regular person, or if, like him, she could sustain her body's energy levels with sorcery. He mentally kicked himself for being so inconsiderate. Of course, he thought with relief, if she did need to eat, he was certain that she wouldn't starve now—not with Maya and Esther around.

Thinking about food reminded him of the challenging situation the peasants were facing. "How are the crops?" he asked, switching topics. The drought that had begun a couple of years ago was the worst in a generation, affecting the entire land of

Koldun from one end of the ocean to another and decimating crops in most territories.

Esther gave him a smile. "Your work really made a difference, child. We're doing much better here than people elsewhere."

Blaise nodded, satisfied. When the drought first started, he'd had the crazy idea of doing a spell to strengthen the seeds, imbuing them with resistance to certain pests and reduced need for water. The resulting improvements, as he'd planned, were hereditary, enabling his subjects to grow and harvest healthy crops even during these difficult times. "I'm glad," he said. "The others in the village don't know, do they?"

"No." Esther shook her head. "They know we're faring better than other regions, and that you're a good master, but I don't think they realize the full extent of your help."

Blaise sighed. He often felt like he wasn't doing enough to help his people—and certainly not enough for other commoners on Koldun. That was part of the reason he had created Gala, though that hadn't exactly worked out as planned.

"I will check on her soon," he said, getting ready to take his leave. "I'm sure everything will be fine, but please, just keep an eye on her."

The old woman snorted. "If I could keep you and your brother out of trouble when you were boys, I'm sure I'll be able to manage with that young companion of yours."

Blaise chuckled. It was true; if it weren't for

Esther, he was sure one of them would've lost an arm or an eye long before they reached maturity. He and Louie had been quite adventurous as children. "Goodbye, Esther," he told her.

And with one final look at the field where Gala was running, he walked toward his chaise.

CHAPTER NINETEEN

※ GALA ※

The wheat was up to Gala's chest as she ran through the field. She could feel the stalks tickling the skin on the exposed parts of her body, and she loved the sensation. She loved *all* sensations.

She kept running until she could feel the muscles in her legs getting tired, and then she lay down on the ground, shielding her eyes with her palm as she looked up at the clear blue sky. The sun was bright, and the clouds had so many different shapes . . . Gala felt like she could look at them forever.

She truly loved the Physical Realm, she realized, and was genuinely grateful to Blaise for her existence. Existing was obviously far superior to oblivion. Having read all those books, she knew that humans had only a short span of time during which they could be in existence. It seemed wrong to her, and sad, but that was the way things were. She wondered if the same rules applied to her. Somehow she doubted it; without knowing where the conviction came from, she felt like she might have complete control over how long she could exist. And if that feeling was correct, she intended to never stop existing.

After a while, she got tired of lying there and got up, walking back to where she'd left Maya.

The older woman was standing there with a completely horrified expression on her face.

"Is something wrong?" Gala asked, figuring that was the appropriate response. She was determined to blend into the human society as well as she could. The books and the Life Captures had given her some theoretical foundation for normal behavior, but there was no substitute for real-world experience.

"Oh, my lady, you are ruining that beautiful dress," Maya said, wringing her hands.

Gala blinked. This seemed to be actually worrying Maya. Quickly analyzing the situation, she came to the conclusion that Maya's reaction and her form of address made sense. The dress that Blaise had given her had to be unusually nice and expensive. From what she knew, humans divided themselves into social classes—a needlessly complex hierarchy that Gala didn't think had any good rationale. Because of this dress—and because Maya and Esther had seen Gala in Blaise's company—they likely assumed she was a sorceress and thus a member of the upper class.

That was not what Gala wanted. "Will everyone in

the village call me a lady?" she asked Maya, frowning.

The old woman gave her a reproving look. "For now, in that dress, they will. If you roll on the grass a few more times, they might think you are an orphan homeless girl." She sounded disgruntled about that last possibility.

"That's fine," Gala said. "I wish to be seen as one of the village women." Going by what the books said, she didn't think the common people would behave naturally in front of a sorceress. She wanted to fit in, not stand out.

Maya appeared taken aback, but recovered quickly. "In that case," she said, "let's go talk to Esther and see what we can do."

They walked together toward the other woman, who had already finished her conversation with Blaise.

"She wants to play at being a commoner," Maya said to Esther, gesturing toward Gala.

"How do you know she's not one?" asked Esther, eying Gala's dress.

Maya snorted. "Master Blaise would not settle for anything less than a sorceress. You know how smart he is. He would have nothing to talk about with a common girl."

Esther gave her friend a look that puzzled Gala. "What happened to you and his father is not the lot of every sorcerer-commoner love affair," she muttered to Maya under her breath.

"Are you Blaise's mother?" Gala asked Maya, intrigued by this conversation. Although the older woman didn't look like Blaise, there was a pleasing symmetry to her features that Gala's creator also possessed.

"No, child," Esther said, chuckling. "She was his father's floozy after his mother died."

"I was his mistress!" Maya straightened to her full height, her eyes flashing with anger.

"Is floozy the same thing as a prostitute?" Gala asked curiously. "And if so, what is the difference between a floozy and a mistress?" In her readings, she had only come across the word 'prostitute.' Apparently, it was a profession in which a woman sold sexual services to men. It was frowned upon in Koldun society, although Gala didn't really understand why. Based on what she'd learned about sex, it seemed like prostitution might be a pleasant— and fun—way to earn a living.

Physical intimacy, in general, was something that was of deep interest to Gala. She knew that the way her and Blaise's bodies reacted to each other when they kissed was sexual in nature. The feeling was among the more fascinating sensations she had experienced thus far, and she wanted to learn as much as she could about it.

In response to Gala's blunt question, Esther laughed and Maya flushed a deep red before storming off.

"Oh, no . . . what did I say?" Gala asked Esther, embarrassed at her obvious faux pas. "I didn't mean to offend . . ." She really needed to learn how to interact with people properly.

"Don't worry about it, child," Esther said, still chuckling. "Maya is far too sensitive about the subject. I was just teasing her a bit, and you didn't do anything wrong. You were just curious."

"So did Blaise's father enter into sexual relations with Maya?" Gala persisted, wanting to understand. "And did he pay her for it?"

Esther shrugged, smiling. "Well, yes, my child, he did. But I think old Dasbraw really did love Maya later on. At first, he just needed something to distract him from his wife's death. He took care of Maya, sure, but she was not sleeping with him for the money or even for his gifts. Still, they didn't get married, obviously, and the girl is insecure about that. I like to tease her sometimes, get her mad. One of these days she'll probably strangle me in my sleep." The old woman grinned, apparently delighted at the prospect of such a dire fate—a reaction that Gala found confusing.

"Can you tell me more about Blaise's parents?" Gala asked. "You said his mother died?"

"Yes," Esther confirmed. "She was killed in a sorcery accident when Blaise was a little boy. His father passed away much later. His mother is where Blaise gets his handsome looks, but he inherited his smarts from both of his parents. Both Dasbraw and Samantha were on the Sorcerer Council." There was a note of pride in her voice, and Gala realized that Esther felt like Blaise's parents' accomplishments were her own. It likely had something to do with the prevailing social structure and how each sorcerer had 'their people,' Gala decided.

"Louie, his brother, was born right before Samantha died. I took care of the little one all by myself," Esther continued, her eyes filling up with moisture.

Gala stared at her, realizing that the subject had disturbed the woman emotionally. She had somehow managed to upset the only two human women she'd met.

"I am sorry, child," said the old woman, wiping away her tears. "I was much attached to those boys. When Louie died, it was as though part of myself died with him."

Gala nodded, not sure what to say to that. She felt bad that the woman was hurting.

As though sensing her discomfort, Esther gave her a shaky smile and tried to change the topic. "So why hasn't Blaise told you some of this himself?"

"Blaise and I met quite recently," Gala explained, hoping that the woman wouldn't pry further.

Esther didn't. Instead, she just gave Gala a warm look. "I could tell he cares about you," she said kindly, "and I'm sure you'll get to know each other better soon."

Gala smiled. Hearing what Esther said made her feel good. While it was unlikely that Blaise cared for her all that much, it was still a nice fantasy. From what she knew about human emotions, there needed to be some kind of courtship period, during which humans generally participated in sexual relations—something that hadn't occurred between herself and

Blaise yet, to Gala's disappointment. Of course, she was also not human, so she didn't know if Blaise could grow to care about her. She knew he found the form she had assumed appealing, but she was uncertain if his feelings could extend beyond simple physical attraction.

"Why don't we go into the house, so you can change?" Esther suggested, bringing Gala out of her thoughts.

As soon as they entered the house, Maya greeted them with a dress in her hands.

"I am so sorry," said Gala, still worried over her earlier misstep. "I didn't mean any insult—"

"That's all right," Maya said, flashing Esther a mean look. "Unlike this one, you didn't mean to offend me, so you don't need to apologize. You are just entering adulthood, and you probably haven't seen much of the world. How old are you, anyway? Eighteen, nineteen?"

Gala considered that question for a second. "I'm twenty-three," she said, making up a number. She didn't think telling them how long she had really been in existence would be prudent.

"Oh, of course." Maya didn't seem surprised. "Sorcerers always look younger than their true age. Our Blaise doesn't look a day older than twenty-five, although he's already in his thirties."

Gala smiled, glad to learn yet another tidbit about her creator. Then, taking the dress Maya was holding out to her, she studied it critically. "Do you think it will make me look plain?" she asked, hoping that the piece of clothing would enable her to walk around unnoticed.

Esther chuckled. "Making you look plain is something that would require high sorcery, child."

"It won't make you look plain," Maya chimed in, "but it will make you look less like a lady, especially since you'll be in the company of two old crones like ourselves."

"If anyone asks, you're our apprentice," instructed Esther. "We're what you'd call village healers, so we do a bit of midwifery, take care of minor injuries, and occasionally look after young ones."

Gala nodded thoughtfully. She remembered Blaise mentioning that he got his Life Captures from Maya and Esther. Their profession explained how they were able to get so many droplets—and why those had been primarily from women.

Thinking about the Life Captures reminded her of her purpose for coming here. "I would like to go explore the village," she told them, eager to get started on her plan to see the world.

Esther frowned. "Not so fast. When was the last time you ate? You look like a stick," she said disapprovingly.

Gala felt insulted. A stick? That didn't sound good. She had seen sticks; they looked fine to her, but she didn't think it was a compliment to call a human being that. "I am not hungry," she said, trying to keep the hurt note out of her voice.

"Ah, so she is a sorceress," said Maya knowingly. "They can live on the sun, like the trees."

Esther snorted. "Oh, they can still eat. Even Blaise eats sometimes. Maybe real food will put some meat on those bones of hers." And without waiting for Gala to say something, she walked determinedly toward the kitchen.

"Do I really resemble a dead piece of wood?" Gala asked Maya, still thinking about the 'stick' comment.

"What?" Maya looked shocked. "No, of course not, my lady! You're beautiful. Esther wants to feed everyone—hell, she thinks I'm too skinny!"

Gala immediately felt better. Maya was much rounder than Gala herself, although she also didn't have Esther's plush curves.

"Eat something, my lady," Maya urged, smiling. "It'll make that old woman happy."

"Of course, I would love to eat something," Gala said honestly. It was yet another new thing for her to try.

A few minutes later, the three of them sat down at the kitchen table.

Gala quickly discovered that the sensation of eating was highly enjoyable. She hadn't had a single Life Capture experience of it and thus had no idea what to expect. Eating was probably the second most pleasurable thing she'd experienced, Gala decided—the first being those kisses with Blaise.

"Look at her wolfing down that stew," Esther said with satisfaction. "Not hungry, my foot. That magical sustenance is not food, I tell you."

"You should teach our young apprentice how to cook, so she can make this stew for Blaise," Maya told Esther, barely containing her laughter, and winked at Gala.

"I just might do that," Esther said seriously, giving Maya a frown. "And I'll show her how to bake bread. His mother used to make food for Blaise sometimes, and I have seen him eat it."

Gala noticed that the two women paradoxically liked and disliked one another. It was very strange.

"If you are going to teach the lady to cook for Blaise, you should teach her something fancier than this slop," Maya said derisively, apparently continuing their bickering.

"Oh, I don't mind learning how to make this wonderful stew," Gala protested. She loved the rich flavor of the soup on her tongue.

Both women started laughing.

"I think she really means it," Maya said between bouts of laughter.

Gala was utterly confused. "I would like to learn how to make it," she insisted.

Maya grinned at her. "Just take onions, garlic, cabbage, potatoes, and some chicken, and put it all in a pot for a couple hours. Oh, and be sure to forget to put enough salt and be too busy to stir it properly—"

"Hey, at least my cooking is better than yours, you old crone," Esther said, and the two women laughed again, reinforcing Gala's impression of the strangeness of their relationship.

CHAPTER TWENTY

※ BARSON ※

Pouring a pitcher of cold water on Siur's face, Barson watched calmly as the traitor regained consciousness, coughing and sputtering.

"Welcome back," he said, observing with amusement as the man realized that he was in Barson's room, securely tied to the wooden column that supported the tall, domed ceiling.

"Are you going to torture me now?" Siur sounded bitter. "Is that your plan?"

Barson slowly shook his head. "No, I don't have to do anything as barbaric as that," he said, gesturing toward the large, diamond-like sphere sitting in the middle of the chamber.

Siur's eyes went wide. "Where did you get that?"

"I see you know what it is. That's good," Barson said, giving the man a cold smile. Getting up, he took the Life Capture Sphere and rubbed it against Siur's still-bleeding shoulder before placing it back. "Now every thought—every memory that comes to your mind—will be mine to know."

Siur stared at him, his face nearly bloodless.

"People will say anything under torture," Barson explained calmly. "I've found this to be a much better way to get real answers. You might as well talk, you know. If I have to pry the information out of your mind, I will make sure you're known to everyone as the treacherous rat that you are."

"So if I talk—?" There was a tiny ray of hope on Siur's broad face.

"Then I will say you died in battle, as an honorable soldier should."

Siur swallowed, looking mildly relieved. He obviously knew this was the best he could hope for at this point. Dying in battle meant that his family would be taken care of and his name respected. "What do you want to know?" he asked, lifting his eyes to meet Barson's gaze.

Barson suppressed a satisfied smile. There was a reason he'd studied psychological warfare so thoroughly; now this ordeal would be over with quickly. "Who bought the information from you?" he asked, watching the man carefully. He already knew the answer, but he still wanted to hear it said out loud.

"Ganir," Siur replied without hesitation.

"Good." Barson had suspected the old sorcerer was the one behind the disappearances. The irony of using Ganir's own invention against his spy didn't escape Barson. "And how long have you been reporting to him?"

"Not long," Siur answered. "Only for the past few months."

Barson's eyes narrowed. "And who reported to him before you?"

"Jule."

That made sense. Barson remembered the young guard who had been killed in battle less than six months ago. It was far more understandable for Jule to get tempted by Ganir's coin; to a low-ranking soldier, the money must've seemed quite attractive. Siur's betrayal was much worse; he had been in Barson's inner circle and thus could've done some real damage with his spying.

"How much did you tell Ganir?"

Siur shrugged. "I told him what I knew. That you'd met with those two sorcerers."

Two? Barson exhaled, trying to conceal his relief. When two of the five sorcerers he'd spoken with disappeared, he had been deeply alarmed, expecting the worst. He had also realized then that there had to be a spy in their midst—someone close to him who could've seen or known something.

The fact that Siur didn't know about the other visitors was a tremendous stroke of luck, as was the fact that none of these sorcerers knew much of value. They had just held preliminary discussions, and Barson had been careful not to show his hand fully. If Ganir succeeded in questioning them, he wouldn't have come across anything particularly damning. In fact, losing two potential allies was a small price to pay for discovering Siur's treachery.

"Did Ganir kill them?" Barson asked softly.

"I don't know," Siur admitted. "I just know they disappeared."

Barson gave a short laugh. "Yes, I noticed that much. Went to explore the ocean storms, Ganir said. So tell me, Siur, why did you stay behind on this mission?"

"Ganir told me to."

"So you knew about the three thousand men instead of three hundred?"

"What?" Siur appeared genuinely shocked. "No, I didn't. There were three thousand peasants?"

"Yes," Barson said, unsure if he believed the man.

"I didn't know," Siur said. "Captain, I didn't know, I swear it! I would've warned you if I knew."

Barson looked at him. Perhaps he would have; there was a big difference between selling information and sending all your comrades to their deaths.

Siur held his gaze, his face pale and sweating. "Are you going to kill me now? I told you everything I know."

Barson didn't respond. Walking over the Sphere, he brought it back and pressed it against Siur's wound again, concluding the recording. He had to watch it now, to make sure Siur's thoughts matched his words. Picking up the droplet that had formed inside the Sphere's indentation, he gingerly put it under his tongue and let it take over his mind.

When Barson regained his sense of self, he gave Siur a somber look. "You told the truth. Since I'm a man of my word, your good name is safe."

"Thank you." Visibly shaking, Siur squeezed his eyes shut.

A swish of Barson's sword, and the traitor was no more.

＊ ＊ ＊

Wiping the blood off his sword, Barson walked toward Augusta's quarters. He'd found it suspicious that Ganir wanted to talk to her. He doubted the old sorcerer could've learned about Augusta's involvement in the battle so quickly, which left only two possibilities.

Ganir was either using her to spy on Barson as well—or he was suspicious of her, just as he had been of the two sorcerers who'd gone 'exploring the storms.'

Barson considered the first possibility—a thought that had occurred to him in the past. But somehow he couldn't see Augusta being a spy. She was fairly open in her dislike for Ganir, and she had far too much pride to let herself be used in such manner. If it came down to it, she'd be the one plotting something, instead of being someone's pawn.

That left the other option—that of Ganir learning that Augusta was Barson's lover and taking action against her. Even this seemed unlikely. She was a member of the Council and quite powerful in her own right. Making her disappear would be a significant challenge. In fact, if Ganir did try to take on Augusta, there was a chance that she would make the problem of Ganir disappear instead.

So what had Ganir wanted with Augusta? To his frustration, Barson was no closer to figuring that out.

Entering Augusta's room, he was relieved to find her there, changing her clothes. And to his surprise, he realized that a small part of him *had been* worried for her safety. Rationally, he knew she was more than capable of taking care of herself, but the primitive side of him couldn't help thinking of her as a delicate woman who needed his protection.

"Are you going somewhere?" he asked, noticing that she was putting on one of her special-occasion dresses. Made of a deep red silk, it made her golden complexion glow.

"I just need to run an errand," she said— somewhat evasively, he thought.

Barson suppressed a flare of anger. He wasn't stupid; the last time he'd seen her wear a dress like this was at one of the spring celebrations. Was she dressing up for something—or someone? And did this have anything to do with her earlier conversation?

There was only one way to find out.

Coming up to her, Barson wrapped his arms around her narrow waist and bent his head to nuzzle her soft cheek. "What did Ganir want?" he murmured, kissing the outer shell of her ear.

"I don't have time to discuss it now," she said,

slipping out of his embrace in an uncharacteristic gesture of rejection. "I'll see you when I get back."

And in a whirl of silk skirts and jasmine perfume, she walked out of the room, leaving Barson angry and confused.

CHAPTER TWENTY-ONE

❊ AUGUSTA ❊

Exiting the Tower, Augusta got on her chaise and headed toward Blaise's house, mentally steeling herself for the upcoming encounter. She could feel her heart beating faster and her palms sweating at the thought of seeing Blaise again—the man who had rejected her, the man whom she still couldn't forget. Even now that she had found some measure of happiness with Barson, memories of her time with Blaise were like a poorly healed wound—hurting at the least provocation.

Closing her eyes, she let the wind blow through her long dark hair. She loved the sensation of flying, of being high up in the air, above the mundane concerns and small lives of people on the ground. Of all the magic objects, the chaise was her favorite because no commoner could ever operate it. Flying required knowing some basic verbal magic, and non-sorcerers would not be able to do more than slowly float away to their deaths.

Passing by the Town Square, she made an impulsive decision to land in front of one of the merchant shops. Out here among the noise and bustle of the marketplace, on this beautiful day in late spring, it was hard to remain negative. Perhaps there was a good explanation for Blaise's obsession with Life Capture droplets, she thought hopefully. Perhaps he was running an experiment of some kind. After all, she knew he had always been interested in matters of the human mind.

Walking over to one of the open-air stalls, she bought some plump-looking dates. They were Blaise's favorite snack, when he deigned to stimulate his taste buds with some sweets. They would make a good peace offering, assuming that Blaise would agree to see her at all. Happy with her purchase—and fully cognizant of the futility of it all—she got back into the air.

Her former fiancé's house was not far, a walkable distance from the Town Square, in fact. Blaise was one of the few sorcerers who had always maintained a separate residence in Turingrad, as opposed to spending all of his time in the Tower. He had inherited that house from his parents and found it soothing to go there in the evenings instead of remaining in the Tower to socialize with the others. When she and Blaise had been together, she'd spent a lot of time at his house as well—so much, in fact, that she'd even had a room of her own there.

Thinking about his house again brought back those bittersweet memories. They'd taken occasional walks together from his house to this very Town Square, and she remembered how they'd always talked about their latest projects, discussing them with each other in great detail. It was one of the things she missed the most these days—those intellectual conversations, the back-and-forth exchange of ideas. Though Barson was an interesting person in his own right, he would never be able to give her that. Only another sorcerer of Blaise's caliber could do that—and there were none, as far as Augusta was concerned.

Finally, she was there, in front of Blaise's house. Despite its location in the center of Turingrad, it looked like a country house—a stately ivory stone mansion surrounded by beautiful gardens.

Approaching cautiously, Augusta came up the steps and politely knocked on the door. Then she held her breath, waiting for a response.

There was none.

She knocked louder.

Still no effect.

Her anxiety starting to grow, Augusta waited another couple of minutes, hoping that Blaise was simply on the top floor and unable to hear her knock.

Still nothing. It was time for more drastic measures.

Recalling a verbal spell she had handy, Augusta began to recite the words, substituting a few variables to avoid scaring the entire town. This particular spell was designed to produce an extremely loud sound—except, with the changes she introduced, it would only be heard inside Blaise's house. Thankfully, the code for vibrating the air randomly at the right amplitude was relatively easy. Following the simple logic chains with the Interpreter litany, she put her hands against her ears to block out the noise coming from inside the building.

The sound was so powerful, she could practically feel the walls of the house vibrating. There was no way Blaise could ignore this. In fact, if he was anywhere in the house, he would likely be half-deaf from that spell—and quite furious. It was probably not the best way to start their conversation, but it was the only way she could think of to get his attention. She would much rather deal with furious Blaise than the addict she was beginning to be afraid she would find.

The fact that he didn't respond to the noise spoke volumes. Only someone absorbed in a Life Capture would have been immune to the spell she'd just cast. The alternative—that he'd finally left his house after months of being a hermit—was an unlikely possibility, though Augusta couldn't help but cling to that small hope.

The scary thing about Life Captures was that people addicted to them sometimes died. They would get so absorbed in living the lives of others, they would neglect their health, forgetting to eat, sleep, and even drink. Although sorcerers could sustain their bodies with magic, they had to do spells in order to keep up their energy levels. A sorcerer Life Capture addict would be nearly as vulnerable as a regular person if he or she forgot to do the appropriate spell.

Standing there in front of the door, Augusta realized that she had a decision to make. She could either report this lack of response to Ganir or she could risk going in.

If this had been a commoner's house, it would've been easy. However, most sorcerers had magical defenses in place against unauthorized entry. In the Tower, they frequently did spells to prevent their locks from being tampered with. From what she could recall, however, Blaise rarely bothered to do that. Trying to unlock his door using sorcery was likely her best bet.

A quick spell later, she was entering the hallway, seeing the familiar furnishings and paintings on the walls.

Looking for either Blaise himself or the evidence of his addiction, Augusta slowly walked through the empty house, her heart aching at the flood of memories. How could this have happened to them? She should've fought harder for Blaise; she should've tried to explain, to make him understand. Perhaps she should've even swallowed her pride and groveled—an idea that had seemed unthinkable at the time.

Starting with the downstairs, Augusta went into the storage area, where she remembered him keeping important magical supplies. Opening the cabinets, she found several jars with Life Capture droplets, but there was nothing extraordinary about that. Most sorcerers—even Augusta herself, to some degree— used the Life Captures to record important events in their lives or their work.

One cupboard drew her attention. In there, she saw more jars that didn't seem to be sorcery-related. Blaise always labeled everything, so she came closer, trying to see what was written on them.

To her surprise, she saw that all the jars had one word on them: Louie. These were likely Blaise's memories of his brother, she realized. The fact that he still had them—that he hadn't consumed them as a hardened addict would—gave her some small measure of hope. One of those jars looked particularly intriguing; it had a skull-and-bone symbol on it, as healers would sometimes put on deadly poisons. She had no idea what it could be.

In the corner of the room, she saw some broken jars on the floor. Amidst pieces of glass, there were more droplets, lying there as though they were trash. Curious, Augusta approached the corner.

To her shock, on a few of the jars, she saw labels with her name on them. Blaise's memories of her . . . He must've thrown them away in a fit of rage. Closing her eyes, she drew in a deep, shuddering breath, trying to keep the tears that were burning her eyes from escaping. She hadn't expected this visit to be so painful, the memories to be so fresh.

Reaching down, she pocketed one of the droplets,

doing her best to avoid cutting her hand on the shards of glass lying all around it. Then, trying to regain her equilibrium, she exited the room and headed upstairs.

All around her, she could see dust-covered windowsills and musty-looking furnishings. Whatever Blaise's mental state, he clearly wasn't taking care of his house. Not a good sign, as far as she was concerned.

Going from room to room, she determined that Blaise wasn't there after all. Relieved, Augusta realized that he must've left the house after all. That *was* a good sign, as addicts rarely came out unnecessarily. Unless they ran out of Life Captures—which Blaise hadn't, judging by the jars downstairs. Could it be that Ganir was wrong again? After all, his spies had apparently misinformed him about the size of the peasant army Barson's men would be facing. Why not this also? But if they weren't wrong, then what did Blaise want with all those Life Captures he'd been getting?

Consumed with curiosity, she entered Blaise's study again, the familiar surroundings making her chest tighten. They'd spent so much time here together, exploring new spells and coming up with new coding methodologies. This was where they'd invented the Interpreter Stone and the simplified arcane language to go with it—a discovery that had transformed the entire field of sorcery.

Perhaps she should leave now. It was obvious that Blaise wasn't home, and Augusta no longer felt comfortable invading his privacy in this way.

Turning, she started walking out of the room when an open set of scrolls caught her attention. They were ancient and intricate, reminding her of the type of writings she'd seen in the library of Dania, another Council member. As though her feet had a mind of their own, Augusta found herself approaching the scrolls and picking them up.

To her shock, she saw that they had been written by Lenard the Great himself—except she'd never seen these notes before. She and Blaise had studied everything the great sorcerer had done; without the base of knowledge laid by Lenard and his students, they would've never been able to create the Interpreter Stone and the accompanying magical language. She should've come across these scrolls before, and the fact that she was seeing them now for the first time was incredible.

Skimming them in disbelief, Augusta comprehended the extent of the wealth of knowledge Blaise had been concealing from the world. These old scrolls contained the theories on which Lenard the Great had based his oral spells—the theories that provided a glimpse into the nature of the Spell Realm itself.

Why had Blaise not told anyone about them? Now even more curious, she reached for another set of notes lying on the desk.

It was a journal, she saw immediately—Blaise's recording of his work.

Fascinated, Augusta riffled through the papers

and began reading.

And as she read, she felt the fine hair on the back of her neck rising. What was contained in these notes was so horrifying she could hardly believe her eyes.

Putting down the journal, she cast a frantic glance around the study, wanting to convince herself that this couldn't possibly be real—that it was all the ramblings of a madman. Her gaze fell upon the Life Capture Sphere, and she saw a single droplet glittering inside.

Reaching for it with a trembling hand, she put it in her mouth, letting the experience consume her.

* * *

Sitting there in his study, Blaise couldn't stop thinking about Gala—about his wondrous, beautiful creation. Closing his eyes, he pictured her in his mind—the perfect features of her face, the deep intelligence gleaming in her mysterious blue eyes. He wondered what she would become. Right now, she was like a child, new to everything, but he could already see the potential for her intellect and abilities to surpass anything the world had ever seen.

His attraction to her was as startling as it was worrisome. She was his creation. How could he feel this way about her? Even with Augusta, he hadn't experienced this kind of immediate connection.

Trying to suppress those thoughts, he turned his attention to the fascinating matter of her origin. The way she'd described the Spell Realm was intriguing; he would've given anything to witness its wonders himself.

Perhaps there was a way. After all, Gala's mind was quite human-like, and she had survived there . . .

* * *

Gasping, Augusta regained her sense of self. Breathing heavily, she stared around the study, reeling from what she'd just seen. What had Blaise done? What kind of monstrosity had he created?

This was a disaster of epic proportions. If Augusta understood correctly, Blaise had made an inhuman intelligence. An unnatural mind that nobody—not even Blaise himself—could comprehend. What would this creature want? What would it be capable of?

Unbidden, an old myth about a sorcerer who had tried to create life entered Augusta's mind, making her stomach roil. It was the kind of tale that peasants and children believed, and logically, Augusta knew there was no truth to it. But she still couldn't help thinking about it, remembering the first time she'd read the horror story as a child—and how frightened she had been then, waking up screaming from nightmares of a ghoulish creature that killed its creator and his entire village. Later on, Augusta had learned the truth—that the sorcerer in question had actually been experimenting with cross-breeding various animal species and that one of his creations (a wolf-bear hybrid) had escaped and wreaked havoc on the neighboring town. Still, by then it was too late. The story had left an indelible impression on Augusta's young mind, and even as an adult, the idea of unnatural life terrified her.

Blaise's creation, however, was not a myth. She—*it*—was an artificially created monster with potentially unlimited powers. For all they knew, it could destroy the world and every human being in it.

And Blaise was attracted to it. The thought made Augusta so sick she thought she might throw up.

No. She couldn't allow this to happen. She had to do something. Grabbing Lenard's scrolls, Augusta tucked them in her bag. Then, consumed by rage and fear, she channeled her emotions into a cleansing fire spell—and let it loose in the room.

CHAPTER TWENTY-TWO

※ BLAISE ※

Flying back home, Blaise tried to convince himself that he'd done the right thing—that Gala needed to see the world on her own, to experience everything she wanted. The fact that he already missed her was not a good reason to limit her freedom.

His trip back was much faster than his flight to the village. He'd purposefully gone slower before, giving Gala a chance to see Turingrad, but now there was no reason to linger. He knew this town like the back of his hand, and there were far too many unpleasant memories associated with this view—especially that of the gloomy silhouette of the Tower.

Passing by the Town Square, he remembered how Esther would yell at him for swimming in the fountain as a child. As a boy, he had enjoyed diving for the coins, and she had always scolded him, saying that it was inappropriate for a sorcerer's son to be swimming in the dirty fountain water.

Thinking of Esther and watching the people below, he reflected on what he had tried to do for them. He had wanted to give them the power to do magic, to improve their lives. And instead, he'd ended up creating something miraculous—a beautiful, intelligent woman who was as far removed from an inanimate object as anything he could imagine. He might have failed in his original task, but he couldn't regret having Gala here. Knowing her had already brightened his life immeasurably. For the first time since Louie's death, Blaise felt some measure of excitement—happiness, even.

Being without her for the next few days would be a challenge. He needed to find something to do to occupy his mind, Blaise decided.

One thing that occurred to him was the challenge of figuring out why Gala couldn't do magic. By all rights, as an intelligence born in the Spell Realm, she should have the ability to do magic directly, without relying on all the spells and conventions that sorcerers used. It should be as natural to her as breathing—and yet it didn't seem to be, for now at least.

What would happen if a regular human mind ended up in the Spell Realm? The crazy idea startled Blaise with its simplicity. Would that mind die immediately—or would it be able to return to the Physical Realm, perhaps imbued with new powers and abilities?

The more he thought about it, the more exciting

the idea seemed. The way Gala had described the Spell Realm had been wonderful, and it would be amazing if a person—if he himself—could see it (or experience it using whatever sense passed for sight in that place).

Would it be insane for him to try to go there? To enter the Spell Realm himself? Most people would think so, he knew, but most people lacked real vision, rarely taking the kind of risks that led to true greatness.

What would happen if he did succeed in entering the Spell Realm? Would he gain the kind of powers he suspected Gala might have? If so, he would be unstoppable—the most powerful sorcerer who ever lived. He would be Gala's equal, and if she still didn't master magic by then, he could even teach her how to harness her inherent abilities. He would be able to do what he'd only dreamed of so far: implement real change, real improvement in the world.

He would be a legend, like Lenard the Great.

Taking a deep breath, Blaise told himself to calm down. This was all great in theory, but he had no idea if this would be feasible or safe in practice. He would have to be careful and methodical in his approach.

After all, he now had something—or rather, someone—very important to live for.

* * *

Landing next to his house, Blaise stared in shock at

the red chaise sitting in front of his door.

A very familiar chaise—one that had been the prototype for them all.

Augusta's chaise.

And it was in front of his house.

What was his former fiancée doing here? Blaise felt his heartbeat quickening and his chest tightening with a mixture of anger and anxiety. Why did she come here today of all days?

Mentally bracing himself, he opened the door and entered the house.

She was walking down the stairs as he entered the large entrance hall. At the sight of her, Blaise felt the familiar sharp ache. She was as stunning as he remembered, her dark brown hair smooth and piled on top of her head, her amber-colored eyes like ancient coins. He couldn't help comparing her darkly sensual looks to Gala's pale, otherworldly beauty. When Augusta smiled, she often looked mischievous, but the expression on her face now was that of shock and fear.

"What have you done?" she whispered, staring at him. "Blaise, what have you done?"

Blaise felt his blood turning to ice. Of all the people out there, Augusta was one of the few who could've made sense of his notes so quickly. "What are you doing here?" he asked, stalling for time. Perhaps he was wrong; perhaps she didn't know everything.

"I came by to check on you." Her voice shook slightly. "I wanted to see if you were all right. But you're not, are you? You've gone completely insane—"

"What are you talking about?" Blaise interrupted.

"I know about the abomination you created." Her eyes glittered brightly. "I know about this thing you've unleashed on the world."

"Augusta, please, calm down . . ." Blaise tried to inject a soothing note into his voice. "Let's talk about this. What exactly are you accusing me of?"

Her face flamed with sudden color. "I am accusing you of creating a terrible creature of magic that can think for itself," she hissed, her hands clenching into fists. "A horror that, to your own surprise, took on a human shape!"

So she knew everything. This was bad. Really bad. Blaise couldn't let her go to the Council with this information, but how was he supposed to stop her? "Look, Augusta," he said, thinking on his feet, "I think you misunderstood the situation. It's true that I tried to create an intelligent object, but I failed. I didn't succeed—"

"Don't lie to me!" she yelled, and he was struck by her uncharacteristic loss of composure. He had never seen her in this kind of state before; in all the years that he'd known her, she'd raised her voice only a handful of times.

"I know you had Lenard's notes, which you hid from everyone," she said furiously. "You are the ultimate hypocrite. You, who always said knowledge should be shared, even with the common people. Oh, and before you insult me with any more lies, you should know that I used that droplet in your Sphere. I know that you created it and that it took human shape—and I saw your perverted reaction to it." If looks could kill, the expression on her face would have left him in a pile of dust.

"You're wrong," Blaise said heatedly, figuring he had nothing left to lose. "It lived for a while, but it went back to the Spell Realm shortly after I made that recording. Its Physical Realm manifestation was not stable. You saw the notes; you know I left its physical form open-ended."

She stared at him, her eyes bright with emotion. "Liar. I don't believe a single word you're saying. You don't even know what you've done. This thing could lead to the extinction of our entire race—"

"What?" Blaise said incredulously. "How could it lead to the extinction of our race? Even if it was stable, that doesn't make sense—"

"It's not human!" Augusta was clearly beside herself. "It's an unnatural creature with unimaginable powers. You don't know what it's capable of; for all you know, it could wipe us out with one blink of its pretty blue eyes!"

"Augusta, listen to me," Blaise tried to reason with her. "*She* is intelligent—highly intelligent. She would have no reason to do something so cruel. With intelligence comes benevolence. I have always believed that—"

"Just because you believe it, doesn't mean it's true," she said, her voice shaking with anger. "And even if you're right, even if this thing doesn't intend us any harm now, its mere existence puts us all in jeopardy. If it has its own intelligence—an unnatural intelligence that was created, not born—it can spawn more creatures like itself, perhaps even smarter and more powerful. Then those new abominations will create something even more frightening, and this cycle can go on until we are nothing but ants to these beings. They will stomp on us, like we're nothing more than cockroaches. Mark my words, this will be the beginning of the end."

Blaise stared at Augusta in shock, struck by the idea of Gala creating others like herself. He hadn't considered this possibility before, but it made sense in a strange way. Except he didn't see it as a bad thing, the way Augusta did. In fact, he thought with excitement, this could be the development that would finally change their world for the better. He pictured highly intelligent, all-knowing, all-powerful beings that would view humanity as their parent race . . . and the vision was tremendously appealing.

Then another possibility occurred to him. If he succeeded in his goal of getting to the Spell Realm and gaining powers, then the line between the beings he just envisioned and humans would become blurred anyway. Even if Augusta's fears had some basis in reality—which he strongly doubted— humans could end up being equals of these marvelous creatures.

Of course, sharing these thoughts with Augusta would not be the smartest move at this point. "Look, Augusta, even if you're right," he said instead, "these beings would not want to harm us. They would be too much like us. With higher intelligence, they will surely possess a morality that will be above ours. We don't have anything to fear—"

"You're a fool." Augusta's expression was full of scorn. "Does morality stop you from squashing a pesky insect?"

"If I knew the little critter was self-aware, I would not kill it." Blaise was firmly convinced of that fact. "And if I knew it was my creator, I certainly would not."

"You're just blinded by lust," she hissed, her beautiful features twisting into something ugly. "It's not human! This creature of yours is not real. It's not going to love you, like you want it to. Did you design it to be capable of emotions? Of love?" And without giving Blaise a chance to respond, she said snidely, "No, of course you didn't. You didn't even know it would look like a woman."

Blaise felt an answering flare of anger, and he suppressed it with effort. "You have no idea what you're talking about," he said evenly. "You don't know her—"

"Oh, and you do?" Her eyes narrowed into slits.

"Are you jealous?" Blaise asked in disbelief. "Is that what this is? You and I are over. We've been over ever since you voted to murder my brother!"

"Jealous?" She looked livid now. "Why would I be jealous of this, this . . . *thing*? It's nothing more than a few strings of code and life experiences of some dirty peasants. I have a man now—a real man, not some hermit hiding among his books and theories!"

"Good," Blaise snapped, hanging on to his temper by a thread. "Then you won't interfere in my life again—"

"Oh, don't worry, I won't," she said, her voice low and furious. "It's not me you'll be dealing with—it's the Council." And she began walking down the stairs, toward Blaise.

"You will not go to those cowards with this!" Blaise felt his own anger starting to spiral out of control. He would *not* let the Council kill another person he cared about.

"I'm going to do whatever I want," she said sharply. "And you're going to face the consequences of your actions, just like Louie did—"

At the mention of his brother, Blaise felt something snap. "You're not going anywhere," he said fiercely, physically blocking the stairs.

"Get. Out. Of. My. Way." Her eyes were blazing like fire. Her hand flashed toward him, slapping him across the face before he realized what she was about to do.

His face stinging and his mind in turmoil, Blaise caught her wrist before she could strike him again. She screamed with rage, yanking her arm out of his grasp and stumbling back a few steps. And before Blaise could do anything, he heard her starting to recite the words of a familiar deadly spell.

Blaise's blood boiled in his veins. He'd never done battle with another sorcerer like this, but he recognized what she was doing. She was about to hit him with a blast of pure heat energy—a spell that would incinerate him on the spot.

His mind oddly clear despite his heart racing in his chest, he started chanting his own spell. It was what he used to protect himself during particularly dangerous experiments. A few key phrases and an Interpreter litany later, he was surrounded by a magical force structure that embedded nothingness in its walls. And just as he finished and saw the telltale shimmer in the air, Augusta's spell hit.

It was like the sun had descended into his house. Even through his shield, Blaise felt the unbearable heat. Within seconds, he was covered with sweat. All around him, the walls and furniture were on fire, and thick, acrid smoke filled the staircase.

"Augusta!" he yelled, terrified for her. Without a protective spell of her own, she would be burned to a crisp.

A moment later, however, the smoke began to clear, and Blaise saw her standing on the top of the staircase, still very much alive. The wave of relief that washed over him was strong and immediate; no matter what she'd done, he couldn't wish his former lover dead—not even if it meant that Gala would be safe.

Of course, right now he had to save his house. Thinking frantically, Blaise recalled a verbal spell he'd used in his youth—a spell that would wash his hands in a matter of seconds. All he needed to do was enhance its potency.

As he began saying the words, he could hear

Augusta starting her own verbal coding effort. It distracted him for a second, and he realized that she was working on a teleporting spell for herself. If his own spell failed, Blaise would be the only one to burn.

Shutting out her voice, he focused on his code, changing some parameters to have the soapy water multiplied a thousand fold. Foam started streaming from his hands, covering the blazing fire all around him in a matter of seconds. Now he could pay attention to Augusta—only it was too late.

Just as he started up the stairs, she finished her own spell and disappeared into thin air.

She couldn't have gotten far—long-distance teleportation was difficult under the best circumstances and required far more precise calculations than what she would've had time to do—but all she needed was to get out the door and to her chaise. Still, even knowing the futility of his actions, Blaise rushed down the stairs and out of the house.

And in the distance, he saw a red chaise flying rapidly away. Pursuit at this stage would be pointless and dangerous.

Still shaking with anger in the aftermath of the confrontation, Blaise went back into his house, determined to salvage as much of it as he could. When he entered, he saw that the foam had contained the fire in the hallway and on the stairs. It was only when he went upstairs that he learned the full extent of Augusta's wrath.

His entire study—all the notes he'd made, all his journals, everything from the past year—was gone.

Somehow she had managed to burn everything.

CHAPTER TWENTY-THREE

※ GALA ※

After the meal, a change of clothing, and numerous instructions on how to appear more like a commoner, Gala was finally on her way to see the rest of the village.

Walking through the streets, she studied the small, cheerful-looking houses and stared at the peasants passing by—who stared right back at her. "Why are they looking at me?" she whispered to Maya after two men almost fell off a horse trying to get a good look at her. "Is it because I look strange and different?"

"Oh, you look different, all right." Maya chuckled. "Even in that plain dress, you're probably the prettiest woman they have ever seen. If you didn't want to be gawked at, we should've put a potato sack over your head."

"I don't think I would like that," Gala said

absentmindedly, noticing a large gathering up ahead. Stopping, she pointed at the crowd. "What is that?"

"Looks like the court is meeting for judgment," said the old woman, frowning. She was about to turn away and walk in another direction, but Gala headed toward the gathering and the two women had no choice but to tag along.

"Um, Gala, I don't think that's the best place for you," Esther said, huffing and puffing to keep up with Gala's brisk pace.

Gala shot her an apologetic look. "I'm sorry, Esther, but I really want to see this." She had read a little bit about laws and justice, and she had no intention of passing up this opportunity.

Before her escorts had a chance to voice another objection, Gala walked straight into the gathering, which seemed to be taking place in a miniature version of the Town Square she'd seen in Turingrad.

There was a platform in the middle of the square, and a few people were standing on it. Two bigger men were holding a smaller one, who appeared quite young to Gala's inexperienced eye. The youngster looked like he wanted to run away, the expression on his round-cheeked face that of fear and distress. Near the platform, Gala could see a group of similar-looking people—a family, she guessed. They looked angry for some reason.

A white-haired older man, who was standing on the platform, began to speak. "You are accused of horse theft," he said, addressing the lad, and Gala could hear the disapproving murmuring in the crowd. Even Maya and Esther shook their heads, as though chiding the young horse thief. "What have you to say to this charge?" the white-haired man continued, his dark eyes prominent in his weathered face.

"I am sorry," the young man said, his voice shaking. "I will never to do it again, I promise. I didn't mean any harm—I just wanted to have some fun . . ."

The white-haired man sighed. "Do you know what they do to horse thieves in other territories?" he asked.

The lad shook his head.

"They hang them in the north, and they chop their heads off in the east," the old man said, giving the youngster a stern look.

The horse thief visibly paled. "I'm sorry! I truly didn't mean it—"

"Luckily for you, we do things differently here," the old man interrupted, cutting off the lad's pleas. "Master Blaise does not believe in that kind of punishment. Because you admitted your guilt and because the horse was returned to its rightful owners, your punishment is to work on the farm of the people you stole from for the next six months. During that time, you will help them in any way you can. You will clean their stables, repair their house, bring them water from the well, and perform whatever other tasks you are capable of doing."

A middle-aged man from the family Gala had noticed before stepped forward, addressing the white-haired man. "Mayor, with all due respect, our children would have starved without that horse, with the drought and all—"

The mayor held up his hand, stopping the man's diatribe. "Indeed. However, fortunately for you and for the accused, you got your horse back safe and sound, didn't you?"

"Yes, Mayor," the man admitted sheepishly.

"In that case, the thief will make up for his crime by helping out at your farm. Hopefully, this will teach him the value of hard work."

The middle-aged man still looked unhappy, but it was obvious that he had no choice. This was the punishment for the horse thief, and he had to accept it.

"And with that," the mayor announced, "the court is over for today. You can all go forth and enjoy the fair."

"The fair?" Gala asked, curious about the sudden wave of excitement in the crowd.

"Oh yes," a young woman to her right replied. "Didn't you hear? We've got the spring fair starting today. It's right on the other side of the village." And with that, she flounced off, apparently eager to get to this event.

Gala grinned. The girl's enthusiasm was contagious. "Let's go," she told Maya and Esther, starting to walk in the direction where she saw most people heading.

"What? Wait, Gala, let's discuss this . . ." Maya hurried after her, looking anxious.

"What is there to discuss?" Gala continued walking, feeling like she would burst from excitement. "Didn't you hear what that woman said? I'm going to this fair!"

"This is not a good idea," Esther muttered under her breath. "I'm pretty sure this is not what Blaise meant when he said to make sure she doesn't draw any attention to herself. Her at the fair—she's going to get attention galore!"

"Yes, well, how do you intend to stop her?" Maya muttered back, and Gala smiled at their exchange. She liked having the freedom to do what she wanted, and she intended to see and experience as much of this village as she could.

* * *

The fair was as amazing as Gala had thought it might be. There were merchants all over the place, their colorful stalls displaying various goods and interesting-looking food products. Right beside them, there were games and attractions, and Gala could hear laughter, loud voices, and music everywhere. In the center of the fair, there was a big platform where she could see young people dancing.

Gala approached a merchant closest to her. "What are you selling?" she asked him.

"I have the best dried fruit at the fair, for you or your mother and aunt." He smiled widely, offering Gala a handful of raisins.

She took a couple and put them in her mouth,

enjoying the burst of sweet flavor on her tongue. Esther took out a small coin and gave it to the merchant, thanking him, and they continued on their way.

"Ale for the ladies?" a man yelled out from one of the stalls. There were huge barrels stacked on each side of him, and Gala wondered if they contained this ale he was offering.

"I will get some," she said, curious to try the drink she'd read about.

"No, you won't," Esther said immediately, frowning. "I don't want you drunk on your very first day with us."

"Oh, come on, let the lass have some fun," the ale merchant cajoled. "She won't feel more than a little buzz from just one drink."

"All right, fine," Maya grumbled, handing a coin to the man. "Just one drink."

Gala grinned. She would've tried this ale regardless, but she was glad she didn't have to argue with the two women.

Looking satisfied, the merchant took a mug, walked over to the pile of barrels, and started pouring from one of them into the mug. Gala noticed the way the barrels shook with the man's movements, as though swaying in the wind.

"Hurry up," a male voice said behind Gala. Turning around, she saw a young, well-built man standing there. As soon as he saw Gala's face, his eyes widened, and his cheeks turned red. He mumbled an apology, his gaze traveling from the top of her head all the way down to her toes.

Gala gave him a small smile and turned around to look at the merchant again. She was getting used to these stares.

The merchant handed her the mug, and she took a sip, swirling the drink around her mouth to better taste it. It wasn't nearly as delicious as the raisins, but it did send a warm feeling down her body. Liking the sensation, Gala downed the mug in several large gulps and heard chuckles from the men standing in line behind her.

"You should pace yourself," Maya admonished, and Esther gave Gala another frown.

"I've never had ale before," Gala tried to explain, not wanting the two women to worry. "I think I like it even better than your stew." Turning to the merchant, she asked, "Can I have another one?"

At this, Maya grabbed Gala's hand and dragged her away from the confused ale merchant and his customers. Gala let herself be led only as far as the next stall and then stood her ground firmly.

"You are strong for one so small," Maya said, looking impressed when Gala resisted her tugging. "It's as though she grew roots," she told Esther. "I can't make her move another inch."

"This is just a clown stall," Esther told Gala, sounding exasperated. "There is nothing for you to see here."

Gala didn't agree. To her, the stall was fascinating, surrounded as it was by dozens of children. Children—these miniature humans—were an enigma to Gala. She had never been a child herself, unless one counted her brief stage of development in the Spell Realm. Then again, she reasoned, perhaps she was like a child now compared to the person she would become.

Another thing that interested her was the man with the painted face. He was wearing strange-looking clothing and doing what seemed like sorcery for the children—pulling out coins from their ears and then making those coins disappear. He also seemed to be doing it without any kind of verbal or written spells. When she focused on his hands, however, she saw that he was actually hiding the coins in his palm. A fake sorcerer, she thought, watching his antics with amusement.

Suddenly, there was a loud shout. Startled, Gala looked back toward the ale merchant's stall, where she heard the sound coming from.

What she saw made her freeze in place.

One of the older children had pushed a younger girl into the stack of barrels at the ale merchant's stall. The large barrels swayed perilously, and Gala could see the top barrel beginning to fall.

Time seemed to slow to a crawl. In Gala's mind, she saw the chain of events exactly as they would play out. The barrel would fall on top of the girl, crushing her frail human body. Gala could even calculate the precise weight and force of the falling object—and the child's odds of survival.

The young girl would cease to exist before she'd had a chance to enjoy living.

No. Gala couldn't stand to see that. Her entire body tensed, and without conscious thought, she raised her hands in the air, pointing them at the barrel. Her mind ran through the necessary calculations with lightning speed, figuring out the exact amount of reverse force necessary to hold the falling object in place.

The barrel stopped falling, floating in the air a few inches above the girl's head.

The silence was deafening. All around Gala, the fairgoers stood as though frozen in place, staring at the near-accident in morbid fascination. The ale merchant recovered first, jumping toward the shocked child to pull her away from under the barrel.

As soon as the girl was not in danger, Gala felt her focus slipping, and the barrel fell, breaking into little bits of wood and splashing ale all over the place.

The rescued child began to cry, her small frame shaking with sobs, while the spectators seemed to breathe a collective sigh of relief. Many of them were staring at Gala with awed expressions on their faces, and one woman took a step toward her, addressing her in a quivering voice, "Are you a sorceress, my lady?"

"She had nothing to do with that; it was the clown," Maya told the woman, lying unconvincingly.

Esther grabbed Gala's hand. "Let's go," she said urgently, dragging Gala away from the crowd.

Gala did not resist, following the old woman docilely. Her mind was in turmoil. She had done it. She had done direct magic, as Blaise had designed her to do. It hadn't been a spell—certainly she hadn't said or written anything. Instead, it was as though something deep inside her knew exactly what to do, how to let some hidden part of her mind take over. All she'd known was that she didn't want the child hurt, and the rest had seemed to just . . . happen.

When they were sufficiently far away from the crowd, she stopped, refusing to go any further. "Wait," she told Maya and Esther, bending down to pick up a small pebble lying on the ground.

"What are you doing?" Esther hissed. "You just drew a lot of attention to yourself!"

"Just wait, please." This was too important to Gala. Throwing the pebble in the air, she focused on it, trying to replicate her actions from before. *Don't fall, don't fall, don't fall*, she mentally chanted, staring at the pebble.

The little rock didn't react in any way, falling to the ground in a completely normal fashion.

"What are you doing?" Maya was watching her actions with disbelief. "Are you throwing rocks?"

Gala shook her head, disappointed. Why didn't it work for her again? She'd stopped that barrel, so why not this rock?

Esther approached her, putting an arm around her shoulders. "Come, let's go home, child," she said soothingly. "We'll give you some more stew—"

"No, thanks, I don't want any stew right now," Gala said, stepping away. "I'm sorry I drew attention to myself, but I don't regret that the little girl is unharmed."

"Of course." Maya glared at Esther. "You did the right thing. I have no idea how you did it, but it was the right thing to do."

Gala smiled, relieved that she hadn't messed up too much. Looking back toward the stalls, she noticed the music again, a lively melody playing in the distance. It called to her, tempting her with the promise of beauty and new sensations. "I'm not ready to go home yet," she told Esther. "I want to see more of the fair."

Now even Maya looked alarmed. "My lady . . . Gala, I don't think you should go back to that fair now—"

"I want to dance," Gala said, watching the figures in the distance. "I want to dance to that music."

And without waiting for her chaperones' reply, she hurried toward the music.

CHAPTER TWENTY-FOUR

✳ AUGUSTA ✳

"Blaise did what?" The expression on Ganir's face as he sat behind his desk was priceless. If Augusta hadn't been so distressed herself, she would've enjoyed Ganir's reaction more. As it was, she was still shaking from the aftereffects of the magical battle—and from learning about the horror that Blaise had unleashed on Koldun.

"He created an unnatural being—a thing forged in the Spell Realm," Augusta repeated, pacing around the room. "And then he attacked me when I tried to reason with him. He's gone completely insane. It would've been far better if he had been an addict—"

Ganir frowned. "Wait, I'm still not clear on this. You're saying he created an intelligence? How could he have done this?"

"I know exactly how he did it," Augusta said, remembering the notes she'd found. "He simulated the structure of the human mind in the Spell Realm, and then developed it using Life Captures—the same Life Captures that you thought he was getting for himself."

Ganir's eyes widened. "He must've used some of my research on the human brain," he breathed, his voice thick with excitement. "But he had to have gone leaps and bounds beyond what I had discovered in the process of creating the Life Capture Sphere—"

"He also had some help from Lenard's writings," Augusta told him, stopping in front of his desk. "He had a secret stash of them that he had never shared with anyone."

"Lenard's writings?" Ganir's eyes lit up. "The boy has them? I heard a rumor once that Dasbraw had something like that, but that wily bastard always denied it."

"Wasn't he your good friend?" Augusta asked scornfully. "I thought the two of you were thick as thieves in your youth."

"We were." Ganir's wrinkled face creased into something resembling a smile. "But Dasbraw always liked his secrets when it came to sorcery. I think he resented the fact that he started off as my apprentice . . ." For a moment, there was a faraway look in his eyes, but then he shook his head, bringing himself back to the present. "So you're saying that Blaise has them? Those writings?"

"He doesn't have them anymore," Augusta said with poorly concealed satisfaction. "I had to use a fire spell when he tried to detain me." She didn't mention that, at this very moment, the precious writings were sitting inside her bag, safe and sound. In the Tower, it always paid to have some leverage.

"You burned Blaise's house?" Ganir gaped at her, his mouth falling open in shock.

"I had no choice," Augusta said sharply, annoyed at the Council Leader's reaction. "You weren't there. He refused to listen to reason. You don't know what he's become, how obsessed he is with that creature. He's completely under its control now." The expression on Blaise's face as he blocked her way flashed through her mind. He had been determined to keep her from going to the Council, she was sure of that. Would he have killed her to protect that abomination? Once, Augusta would've thought such a thing impossible, but not anymore—not after she took that droplet and experienced the depth of his feelings for his horrifying creation.

Ganir looked taken aback. "That doesn't sound like Blaise," he said dubiously. "You said he tried to attack you?"

"He wanted to stop me from telling the Council," Augusta said, a little less certain now. Blaise hadn't attacked her, exactly, but she had felt threatened nonetheless. "He even tried to lie to me that the creature's form was unstable, and it was no longer in existence—"

"So, *are* you going to tell the Council?" Ganir interrupted, staring at her.

"I should, shouldn't I?" Augusta met the old

sorcerer's gaze. "They need to know about this thing. It's dangerous, and it needs to be eliminated."

"What do you think would happen to Blaise if they found out what he had done? They won't just get rid of his creation and let him be."

Augusta swallowed. Now that she was thinking more clearly, she realized that Ganir was right—that telling the Council would doom Blaise as well as the abomination he'd created. And she couldn't let that happen, no matter how upset she was with him. The thought of Blaise dead, gone, was as unbearable as the idea of him being attracted to that monstrosity. "What would be the alternative?" she asked. The old man cared about Blaise, and she doubted he wanted to see him brutally punished any more than she did.

Ganir leaned back in his chair, his face assuming a thoughtful expression. "Well," he said slowly, "first of all, there is a small chance he didn't lie to you. If he was surprised that this being took the shape that it did, then he probably doesn't understand it fully. It's very possible that she—*it*—is indeed unstable and gone by now."

Augusta snorted dismissively. "I wouldn't hold my breath for that possibility—he was just desperate to save the creature. You think I don't know after all those years together whether he's lying or telling the truth?"

"All right," Ganir conceded, "let's suppose you're right. I'm still not convinced, though, that this intelligence is as big of a threat as you think—"

Augusta gripped the edge of his desk. "You're not

convinced?" She could hear her voice rising as the old childhood nightmare reared its ugly head. "I took that droplet—I was in Blaise's head—and he himself doesn't know what this creature is capable of! It could have powers that are beyond anything we can imagine. What if it turns against us? What if it decides to wipe us all out?"

Ganir blinked. "What kind of powers does it have? What can it do?"

"I don't know," Augusta admitted, taking a step back and drawing in a shaky breath. "And neither does Blaise. That's the problem. Just because it hasn't done anything yet, doesn't mean we're safe. It's only been in existence for a short time."

The old man looked at her. "In that case, why don't we just let it be? We have never seen anything like it before—an intelligence that was created, not born, a being from the Spell Realm—"

"No." Augusta shook her head, everything inside her rejecting that idea. "We can't take that kind of risk. The thing needs to be destroyed *now*, before it has a chance to destroy us. For all we know, it might be growing more powerful with every moment it's in existence. This is our chance to contain this situation. If we don't stop it now, we might never be able to do so in the future. Think about it, Ganir. What if it ends up creating more abominations like itself?"

The old sorcerer looked stunned. He obviously hadn't considered that angle. Augusta could see him wavering, and she pressed her advantage. "Can you imagine how powerful an entire army of creatures from the Spell Realm might be?"

Ganir's eyes widened, as though some new thought occurred to him. "You said it took a female shape, right?" he said slowly. "And you said Blaise is attracted to it?"

Augusta nodded, staring at him in horror. Was he implying what she thought he was implying? "Ganir, are you suggesting—?"

"That she and Blaise could reproduce?" He raised his eyebrows. "I have no idea, but I would be curious to find out . . ."

Augusta felt like throwing up. "Curious? About whether the monster could spawn?" Was the old man sick in the head?

The Council Leader appeared inexplicably amused. "If Blaise is attracted to it, it can't be all that monstrous."

Augusta squelched the urge to lash out at him with another fire spell. "You're missing the point," she said coldly instead. "This is not some sorcery experiment we're talking about. Blaise created this thing in order to give magic to the commoners. His actions—and his intentions—are dangerous and treasonous. He needs to be stopped. If you're not going to help me with this, I will have no choice but to go to the Council—and we both know how that would likely end for Blaise." Augusta was mostly bluffing, but the old man didn't need to know that.

Ganir's eyes narrowed. "All right," he said, staring at her. "We'll contain the situation ourselves, as you suggested. Where is this creature now?"

"I don't know. I didn't find any traces of it in Blaise's house."

"In that case, I will send some of my men to look for her. They will be given instructions to report anything strange. If the creature is as powerful as you think, we are bound to learn about it eventually." He paused for a moment. "And if we don't hear about any unusual sorcery activity, then Blaise was either telling the truth or the being is not a threat, as far as I'm concerned."

Augusta didn't agree with that last bit, but now was not the time to argue. "And when it's found?"

"Then I will have it captured and brought here, to the Tower, where we can interrogate it and determine if it truly represents a danger to us."

This time she couldn't contain herself. "Ganir, it needs to be destroyed—"

The Council Leader leaned forward. "And it will be, if it's as dangerous as you say," he said, his tone dangerously soft. "But before we do anything rash, we need to find out more about it. I will study it, and then, if need be, I will destroy it myself."

We'll see, Augusta thought, but held her tongue. Right now, they needed Ganir's spies to locate the thing.

CHAPTER TWENTY-FIVE

※ GALA ※

The dance floor was filled with people of all ages, laughing, chatting, and twirling to the music. Pausing on the edge of the floor, Gala took in the sight, her head spinning a little. Her foot tapped to the rhythmic notes, and she wanted to laugh too—at least until she felt mildly disoriented.

The sensation was just different enough that Gala realized she was experiencing something strange. Suddenly it hit her: the ale. This was what people referred to as being drunk.

Frowning, Gala considered the situation. According to what she'd read, drunk people did stupid things and did not act like themselves. She didn't like the idea of that happening to her.

Closing her eyes, she focused on her body, consciously examining the effects of the drink. Instantly, she felt a reaction similar to the one that had been interfering with her Life Capture immersion earlier; it was as if some part of her body was working to dispose of all traces of alcohol. A few seconds later, she was completely clear-headed.

"May I ask you to dance?" a familiar male voice said, and Gala opened her eyes, surprised to find a man standing no more than two feet away from her.

It was the young man she'd seen at the ale merchant's stall.

He beamed a bright smile at her, and Gala realized that he probably hadn't seen the incident with the child. Otherwise, he might act cautiously around her, as some people now appeared to be doing.

Happy to be treated like a regular person, Gala gave him a smile in return. "Sure," she said. "But you'll have to teach me how to do it."

"It will be my honor," he said, offering her his hand. She took it cautiously. His palm was warm and a little damp, and Gala quickly decided that she didn't enjoy his touch. Nonetheless, she saw no harm in dancing with him at a distance, as she saw other couples doing.

Walking onto the dance floor, Gala listened closer to the patterns in the music that was playing. She loved the structured aspect of the fast beat, the clever mathematical precision of the sounds. They pleased her ears tremendously.

Watching the other women out of the corner of her eye, Gala did her best to mimic their movements, trying to follow the rhythm of the tune.

"You're a natural," the young man said, and there was a note of admiration in his voice. "I don't think you need any instruction from me." He was moving his body to the music, but it didn't seem like he was hearing the same melody as Gala because his version of dancing was much clumsier, almost awkward.

The melody changed, became quicker, and Gala could feel the corresponding increase in her heart rate. "Who wrote this beautiful music?" she asked, marveling that she could be so moved by simple sound.

The young man grinned at her. "It was Master Blaise, of course," he said. "He's a prolific composer. You haven't heard his music before?"

Gala shook her head, her heart beating even faster at the mention of Blaise. She wanted him here with her, instead of this man whom she didn't like very much. The fact that Blaise could make her feel things without even being there was amazing. Now that she knew he'd composed this melody, she was surprised she hadn't realized it herself. Writing music likely required the same mathematically inclined mind that would be good at sorcery. Of course, there had to be more to such genius than that, and she doubted that every sorcerer was capable of creating such beauty. In a way, she and this music were alike, both being Blaise's creations.

While she was pondering this matter, the man she was dancing with stepped closer to her. "What is your name?" he asked, leaning toward her. She could smell ale on his breath and a hint of something that reminded her of Esther's stew.

"I am Gala," she told him, moving away just a little.

He gave her a wide smile. "Very nice to meet you, Gala. I am Colin."

Gala kept following the dancers' movements, getting better and better with every step. In the meantime, her dancing partner kept fumbling and missing steps. It didn't matter to her, though; she still found dancing to be a lot of fun. "You're amazing at this," Colin exclaimed when she executed a particularly complex move without missing a beat, and she grinned, pleased at the praise.

The song ended.

"Can I have the next dance?" Colin asked.

Gala nodded her head in agreement. The song that was starting next was even nicer than the first, slower and more melodious. However, before she could start moving to the music, her dancing partner stepped closer to her. Out of the corner of her eye, she could see the other dancers doing the same, the men coming up to the women and putting their hands on the women's sides and shoulders.

Gala frowned, taking a small step back. She didn't want Colin that close to her. Something about this felt extremely wrong. There was only one person whose hands she wanted on her body, and he was back in Turingrad. "I changed my mind," she told Colin politely, backing away further.

"Oh, come on, it's just a dance," he said, smiling and reaching for her. His fingers wrapped around her wrist, and she could feel the moist heat emanating from his skin. It made her stomach turn.

"Get your hand off me," Gala ordered, tugging futilely at her wrist. He was physically stronger than her, and she was starting to feel anxious at the dark excitement visible in his eyes.

"Oh, come on, don't be like that . . ." He was still smiling, but the expression didn't seem the least bit friendly anymore.

"Let go," she said a bit louder, and saw some people look their way. Her heart was pounding like it was about to jump out of her chest, and she felt like her skin was crawling from his touch.

"Don't be such a grouch," he muttered, pulling her closer. "It's just a dance—"

At his refusal to let go, the volatile brew of emotions inside Gala seemed to explode, her vision blurring for a second. It was as though something inside her lashed out at Colin, and she could see him stumbling back with a look of shock on his face. A vile smell began to permeate the room, and Colin's face twisted with something resembling shame and fear.

Her wrist finally free, Gala felt an overwhelming urge to not be there. And as Colin took a confused step toward her, she found herself standing just outside the dance floor, behind Maya and Esther.

"We should go," she said, still feeling sick from the encounter—and shaking from the knowledge that she'd inadvertently done sorcery again, teleporting herself in full sight of all the dancers.

Esther turned toward her, looking startled. "Where did you come from? You were just there, dancing with that lad—"

"I want to leave," Gala told her, rubbing her wrist where she could still feel the disgusting sensation of Colin's touch. "I didn't want to get close to him, but he grabbed me—"

"He grabbed you?" Maya gasped. "Why, that bastard . . . You should've kicked him in the nuts!"

"It looks like she did *something* to him," Esther said, staring at the dance floor with a worried frown.

Casting a quick glance in that direction, Gala saw Colin walking off with a strange gait. "Let's go," she said, tugging at Esther's sleeve. "I want to leave. He might be coming this way." She felt unsettled and disturbed, and she wanted to get away from this place as quickly as possible.

"Of course," Maya said, throwing a glare at the young man. "Let's go home, so you can get some rest."

Gala nodded, wanting nothing more than to experience the sleeping activity again. From what she'd felt before, it was not unlike some of the experiences she'd gone through in the Spell Realm.

CHAPTER TWENTY-SIX

※ BARSON ※

Hearing a knock, Barson got up from the chair where he was reading and went to open the door. It was one of the rare times when he got to relax in his quarters, and he was not happy about the interruption.

His mood didn't improve when he saw Larn standing outside. The expression on his future brother-in-law's face was rather peculiar.

"Come inside," Barson said curtly. He could already tell that something was amiss.

Larn stepped into Barson's room and closed the door behind him.

"Well?" Barson prodded when Larn didn't seem inclined to speak. "What did you learn?"

"So far, Ganir has not left the Tower," Larn said. "He's been mostly in his office, and there have been a number of people going in and out."

"That's not really news." Barson frowned at his best friend. "It's always that way with the old man."

"Well, yes," Larn said, his tone uncharacteristically hesitant. "But one of his visitors this afternoon was, um, Augusta."

Again? Barson could feel his frown deepening. Why would she see Ganir twice in one day? He knew there was no love lost between them.

"There's one more thing." Larn looked increasingly uncomfortable.

"What is it?"

"You won't like this one . . ."

"Just spit it out," Barson said, his eyes narrowing. "What is it?"

Larn swallowed. "Remember, I'm just the messenger—"

Barson took a step toward him. "Just say it," he gritted out between clenched teeth. It had to be something bad if his friend was so afraid to tell him.

"As you requested, I asked a few of our men to keep an eye on Augusta today, after her first meeting with Ganir," Larn said slowly, "and as it so happened, a couple of them were at the market when her chaise landed there."

"And?"

"And they were able to follow her when she took off again. She only flew a few blocks and then landed in front of a house."

"What house?" As far as Barson knew, there were very few houses located so close to the center of Turingrad. It was a highly desirable location, and every house in that area was more like a mansion, owned by the most powerful sorcerer families. One sorcerer in particular came to mind—

"It belongs to Blaise, the man she was supposed to marry," Larn said, confirming Barson's hunch. "She landed in front of it and went inside."

"I see," Barson said calmly. His insides were boiling, but he didn't let anything show on his face. "Anything else?"

"No." Larn looked relieved at Barson's lack of reaction. "The men couldn't stay there for long; they had guard duty at the Tower and were only at the Market to pick up a few things. However, I asked one of our new friends to keep an eye on Blaise, just in case."

Barson nodded, still keeping his expression impassive. "You did well," he said evenly. "Thank you for that."

"Of course." Larn turned to walk out, then looked back at Barson. "Should they continue to follow her as well?"

"Yes," Barson said quietly. "They should."

His control lasted long enough for Larn to exit the room. As soon as the door closed behind him, Barson headed to the corner where a sand-filled potato sack was hanging from the ceiling. His hands clenched into massive fists, red-hot jealousy filling every inch of his body. Unable to contain himself any longer, he lashed out, punching the bag over and over again, until his knuckles were sore and sweat ran down his back. Pausing, he ripped off his tunic, and then continued, venting his rage with furious blows.

* * *

A light jasmine scent reached Barson's nostrils, bringing him out of his mindless state. The bag in front of him was slowly deflating, the sand trickling out through a tear made by one particularly hard strike.

Turning, he saw Augusta sitting on his bed and watching him. She must've just entered his room.

"Augusta, what a pleasant surprise." He forced himself to smile despite the anger still flowing through his veins.

She smiled back, but the expression on her face was strangely distracted. Was she thinking of *him*, that sorcerer bastard she had been engaged to? Barson drew in a calming breath, reminding himself to tread lightly. Augusta was fiercely independent, and she wouldn't take kindly to being spied upon or questioned like an errant child.

Oblivious to his dark mood, she was looking around the room now, studying it like she was seeing it for the first time. "Some light reading before exercise?" she asked, gesturing toward the book he'd left lying on the chair.

"Yes," Barson managed to answer evenly. "I found a new gem in the library archives. It's about the military exploits of King Rolun, the ancient conqueror who united Koldun." He was glad for the small talk, as it was enabling him to push aside his jealous fury and think. The fact that Augusta was in his room chatting about books was a good sign. If she had gotten back with Blaise, he doubted she would come here so casually. She didn't look uncomfortable or guilty, either. Barson considered himself a good judge of people, and he couldn't feel any duplicitous vibes coming from her. She was distracted, yes, but it was more like she had a lot on her mind.

As though to confirm his thoughts, she turned toward him with a warm smile. "You like those old stories, don't you? I never pegged you for a scholar before."

"I like learning about old military tactics," Barson said, watching her closely. He still couldn't see any sign of guilt or regret on her face. She was either an amazing actress or her visit to her former lover had been purely platonic.

Augusta's smile broadened. "Did you know that King Rolun's blood flows through my veins?" she asked. "Most of the old nobility is descended from him."

"No," Barson lied. "I didn't know that." Rolun's blood flowed through his veins, too—not that anyone cared about it these days. Barson had known about Augusta's lineage from the very beginning; she was one of the few sorcerers whose family was of noble origin, and he could see traces of her heritage in her high cheekbones and regal posture. It was one of the reasons he had been so attracted to her in the first place.

"You're descended from him, too, aren't you?" Augusta said, surprising him. "Wasn't your mother from the Solitin family?"

Barson stared at Augusta, wondering how she had known that. It wasn't a big secret, but he hadn't realized she was sufficiently interested in him to study his background. "Yes," he said, watching her reaction. "That's right. Back in the day, we would have been a perfect match."

Her eyes gleamed brighter. "Indeed, oh my noble lord," she murmured, "we would have been an excellent match . . ." And holding his gaze, she gave him a slow, bewitching smile.

Barson's blood heated up again, but this time for a different reason. He didn't know what took place during her visit to Blaise, but it didn't seem like the sorcerer had satisfied her needs.

It would be Barson's pleasure to fix that promptly.

Before he had a chance to do anything, however, Augusta rose gracefully to her feet. "I had a horrible day," she said softly, untying her shiny brown hair and letting it fall to her waist. "I think I may require your unique skills, warrior."

He didn't have to be asked twice. Taking a few steps toward her, Barson closed his fist around the bodice of her red dress, pulling her toward him. The fragile silk ripped in his grasp, but neither one of them noticed as Barson channeled the remnants of his fury into a deep, hungry kiss.

CHAPTER TWENTY-SEVEN

※ BLAISE ※

Blaise stared at the devastation in his study in shock and disbelief, his heart still pounding from his encounter with Augusta. She had found out about Gala—she, who had always been against anything she couldn't easily comprehend, against anything that could upset her way of life. In hindsight, he shouldn't have been surprised that Augusta had voted for Louie's punishment. Like the rest of the Council, she had felt threatened by his brother's actions—and there was no doubt that today she had been terrified by the very idea of Gala.

The floor and walls were black with soot, and Blaise's desk was nothing more than a pile of ashes, testifying to Augusta's wrath. But the worst thing about this was not what she had done to his study— it was what he feared she would do to Gala. If the Council believed Augusta's story, they would be looking for Gala in a matter of hours.

Blaise felt a strong urge to hit something—preferably himself, for letting Gala go off on her own. He should've never left her alone at the village, no matter how much she wanted to see the world as an ordinary person. Now she was there unprotected, with only two old women for company.

He needed to be there with her.

Casting a glance around the study, Blaise saw that his Interpreter Stone had survived Augusta's fire. Picking up the still-warm rock, he rushed downstairs to his archive room, where he kept most of his pre-written spell cards. It was lucky that Augusta had only destroyed his most recent work and the bulk of what he needed was still available.

Taking as many potentially useful spell components as he could, Blaise left the house and got on his chaise. His mind was filled with one thought: getting to Gala before it was too late. Even now Augusta could be talking to the Council, convincing them of the ridiculous idea that Gala was dangerous, and there was no time to waste.

He was flying for a half hour when he noticed something strange behind him. In the far distance, there was a small dot on the horizon—almost like a bird, except it was too large to be one. Blaise cursed under his breath. Was he being followed?

There was only one way to tell. Taking out a few spell cards, he prepared an eyesight-enhancing spell and fed the cards into the Interpreter Stone. When his vision cleared, everything was sharper; it was as though he was an eagle, able to spot even a tiny insect crawling on the ground far away. Turning his head, Blaise peered into the distance.

What he saw made his blood run cold.

There was another chaise flying behind him—a sure sign that he was being pursued by another sorcerer, since no one else could fly these things. However, it wasn't Augusta, as he'd initially suspected. This particular chaise was grey, and the man sitting in it was someone Blaise didn't recognize, which meant he couldn't have been a sorcerer of note. Not that the man's aptitude for sorcery mattered in this case; if he could fly, then he could also likely handle a Contact spell—and the Council might even now be aware of where Blaise was heading.

Looking away, Blaise stared straight ahead, his mind furiously searching for a solution. He wanted to protect Gala, not lead the Council straight to her. He couldn't let them follow him to the village— which meant he had to make them think this trip was about something else.

Subtly adjusting his flight path, Blaise directed his chaise toward a famous carpentry shop located on the outskirts of Turingrad. Since a lot of his furniture got destroyed, a new desk and some other items might actually be useful. And if Augusta had told the Council about her fire spell, then ordering new furnishings should hopefully seem like a normal thing for Blaise to do.

* * *

Getting home after the carpentry store, Blaise began to pace, trying to think of what to do next. In a way, it was good that Gala was away from here; the first place the Council would look for her would be his house. Unfortunately, the second place would be the villages in his territory—exactly where she was right now.

The crazy idea of teleporting himself to the village came to mind, but he immediately dismissed it. Writing a spell as complex as that would take a long time, and would be extremely dangerous. If he miscalculated even a tiny bit, he could easily end up materializing in the ground or inside a tree—and then Gala would be left without anyone to protect her.

No, there had to be something else he could do.

To start off, Blaise decided, he needed to warn her and her guardians of the potential danger. They had to leave the village and go some place where the Council would not think to look for them, while he figured out a way to join them there.

Going to the archive room, he pulled out his cards and began working on a Contact spell—a way to send a mental message to someone far away. It was a fairly complicated spell, one that would have been a pain to do verbally. Now, however, with written spell-casting, it should only take him a few minutes to pen a message and the details of the person he wanted to contact.

Sitting down at an old desk, he composed a message to Esther:

"Esther, do not be alarmed. This is Blaise and I am using the Contact spell I told you about once. To prove my identity, as we agreed on that occasion, I am mentioning the time you caught me spying on my father. Now listen to me carefully. I have reason to fear for Gala's safety. She is in danger from the Council, and I need your help. Please take her to Kelvin's territory. I know about his reputation, but that's precisely why Neumanngrad might be the last place they would expect her to be. Please use whatever money you need—I will pay for everything. Stay at the inn on the southwest side of Neumanngrad when you get there, and try to be as inconspicuous as possible. I will hopefully join you soon."

The next thing he did was compose a message to Gala. He wasn't sure if the Contact spell would work with her, but he still intended to try. His message to her was shorter:

"Gala, this is Blaise. I am thinking of you. Please listen to Esther when she asks you to go to a different area and try to be discreet.

Yours, Blaise."

Thus happy with both notes, Blaise fed the cards into the Interpreter Stone. Combining spells like this was efficient, since some of the code for both messages would be shared.

Getting up, he was about to leave the room when he felt something unusual—something he hadn't experienced in two years.

It was the mildly invasive sensation of another sorcerer sending him a Contact spell.

Surprised, Blaise nonetheless relaxed and let the message come to him, curious to learn who could be reaching out to him.

To his shock, it was Gala.

"Blaise, it's great to hear from you." Like all Contact spells, her words came in the form of a voice in his head—a voice that was really his inner voice, but that somehow took on a different tone. *"I can't believe you are speaking in my mind. I miss you, and I hope to see you soon. I have so much I want to talk to you about.*

Yours, Gala."

Blaise listened to her message with awe. How had she managed to do this? When he saw her last, her magical abilities had been virtually nonexistent, and now she was able to do a complex bit of sorcery in less time than it would take to write a basic spell. It could only mean one thing: she was starting to do magic directly, as he'd hoped she would be able to do.

Excited, he sat down to compose a response to Gala. It took him several minutes to prepare the spell. He wrote:

"Gala, I'm so excited you've mastered this form of communication. I miss you. How is your time in the village so far? Did Esther explain to you about the trip to Neumanngrad?"

There was no response back. Disappointed, Blaise waited several minutes before admitting to himself that none was coming.

Getting up, he decided to occupy himself by putting his house to rights while he figured out what to do next.

He would not let Augusta and the Council wreck his life again, not if he could help it.

CHAPTER TWENTY-EIGHT

✳ GALA ✳

Gala was almost back at Esther and Maya's house when she heard a strange voice in her head. It was as though she was speaking to herself in some strange way. As she listened, however, she realized it was a message from Blaise.

After she heard everything, she grinned in excitement. Blaise wanted her to travel and see more of the world. And the best part was that he was thinking of her! Filled with delight, Gala felt an overwhelming urge to talk to him, to reach out to him in the same way he had just contacted her. And suddenly, she felt herself responding, even though she didn't understand how she was doing it.

"Blaise, it is great to hear from you," she began, her excitement spilling out into the mental message.

To her disappointment, he didn't respond right away. But she noticed Esther staring at her intently.

"Did he get in touch with you too?" the older woman asked.

"If you mean Blaise, then yes," Gala said, smiling.

"Good," Esther said. "Then I hopefully don't need to convince you that we must go."

"Oh, you don't have to convince me," Gala told her earnestly. "I would love to see more of the world."

And by the time Esther explained to them where they were going, Blaise came back to Gala with his response.

Smiling, she began to think of the answers to his questions, but whatever it was that helped her do this before was no longer there. She couldn't seem to tap into the part of her mind that made mental communication so easy and effortless before. After several fruitless attempts, Gala gave up in frustration.

"Come, help us pack, child," Esther said, leading Gala into the house. "We need to get going right away."

* * *

The trip to Kelvin's territory took a couple of days, with Gala enjoying every moment of their travels—unlike Esther and Maya, who grumbled about how uncomfortable it was to be stuck on a buggy for such a long time. The two women complained about roadside food (which Gala loved), the scenery (which Gala found most fascinating), the chill at night (which Gala found refreshing), and the heat of the sun during the day (which Gala found pleasant on her skin). Most of all, however, they complained about Gala's boundless energy and enthusiasm for the simplest things—something they could not even begin to understand, much less relate to.

Unlike her first eventful day at the village, the trip passed without any further incidents. Maya and Esther did their best to keep Gala out of sight of the passersby, and Gala did her best to occupy herself with observing the world around her—and with surreptitious attempts to do magic.

To her great disappointment, she couldn't replicate anything she'd done before. She couldn't even get in touch with Blaise. He had contacted her a couple more times, saying how much he missed her, but she had been unable to respond—a form of muteness she found extremely unpleasant. The lack of control over her magical abilities drove her crazy, but there was nothing she could do about it now. She was hoping, however, that her creator would ultimately be able to teach her how to tap into that hidden part of herself. When she saw Blaise again, she was not about to let him out of her sight until she learned to do sorcery at will.

As they left Blaise's territory and entered Kelvin's, Gala began to notice a number of differences between the villages and towns belonging to the two sorcerers. The houses they passed now were smaller and shabbier, with signs of neglect everywhere, and the people were leaner and less friendly. Even the plants and animals seemed weaker and more weathered somehow.

When they rode by a large open field with sad-looking remnants of wheat, Gala asked Esther about the differences in their surroundings.

"Master Blaise has enhanced our crops," Esther explained, "so that we wouldn't suffer as much in this drought. He's a great sorcerer, and he cares about helping his people—unlike Kelvin, who doesn't give a rat's ass." That last bit was added in a tone of obvious disgust.

Gala frowned in confusion. "Why don't all sorcerers do this for their people? Enhance their crops, I mean?"

Esther snorted."Why not, indeed."

"They just don't care enough," Maya said bitterly. "They're so out of touch with their people, they might not even understand the concept of hunger. They probably think we can just subsist on spells and air, the way they do."

"Also," Esther said, "I don't know much about sorcery, but I think Master Blaise came up with some very complicated spells to do this for us. I don't know if every sorcerer could replicate them, even if they were inclined to try."

"Couldn't Blaise teach them?" Gala asked.

"He probably could, if those fools would listen to him." Esther's nostrils flared with anger. "But they've tarred him with the same brush as his brother, and he's already on thin ice in the Tower. Enhancing crops could be potentially interpreted as giving magic to the people, and that's the last thing the

Council wants."

"But that's so unfair." Gala looked at Esther and Maya in dismay. "People are hungry. They can die from that, right?"

Maya gave her a strange look. "Yes, people can definitely die from hunger—which is something all sorcerers need to realize."

Gala blinked, taken aback. Was Maya lumping her in with the other sorcerers? It didn't sound like she meant the word as a compliment, either.

Esther glared at Maya. "Stop it. You know the girl cares—she's just been sheltered, that's all."

"More like born yesterday," Maya muttered, and Esther purposefully stepped on her foot, eliciting an annoyed grunt from the other woman.

"In any case, child," Esther said, addressing Gala this time, "Blaise has a plan when it comes to getting his crops to the other territories. He's letting us trade the seeds in exchange for other necessities. He knows these seeds will take and will provide others with good crops just like our own, since the improvements he made are hereditary."

Leaving the dying wheat field behind them, they finally reached the inn where Blaise told them to stay. Before they went in, Maya made Gala cover her head with a thick woolen shawl. "So we don't get attacked by some amorous ruffians at night," she explained. "The fewer people who know a pretty girl is staying here, the safer it'll be for us."

The brown inn building was small and rundown, just like the houses they'd passed on the way. It was difficult to believe it could house more than a dozen travelers. Their room upstairs was dirty, cramped, hot, and disgusting—at least according to Maya. According to Esther, they were also being robbed blind.

Gala didn't care; she was just excited to be some place new. When they went downstairs for dinner, she asked the innkeeper about the local attractions, being careful to keep the shawl wrapped around her head.

"Oh, you're lucky," the burly man told her. "Later this week, we have games at the Coliseum. You've heard of our Coliseum, right?"

Gala nodded, not wanting to seem ignorant. In the last couple of days, she'd learned it was best not to ask strangers any questions that could be posed to Maya and Esther instead.

He gave a satisfied grunt. "That's what I thought. If you want to do something today, the market should still be open." His eyes went to Maya's large bosom, and he added, "Be sure to keep your money in hard-to-reach places. Lots of thieves around these days."

"Thanks," Maya said caustically, turning away from the innkeeper's roving gaze. Esther huffed in disdain, shooting him a deadly glare before grabbing Gala's arm and towing her away.

As soon as they were out of the innkeeper's earshot, Esther turned to her and said firmly, "No."

"No way," Maya added, crossing her arms in front of her chest.

Gala stared at them in confusion. "But I didn't ask the question yet—"

"Can we go to the Coliseum?" Esther said in a higher-pitched voice, mimicking Gala's typically enthusiastic tones.

"Yes, can we, please?" Maya mocked, her imitation attempt even better than Esther's.

Gala burst out laughing. She knew she should probably take offense, but she found the whole thing funny instead. The older women were watching her with stoic expressions on their faces, and she finally managed to stop laughing long enough to say, "Why don't we talk about it tomorrow?"

"The answer is going to be the same tomorrow," Esther said, giving Gala a narrow-eyed look.

Gala grinned at her, barely able to contain her excitement at the thought of the upcoming event. "Don't worry about it, Esther—we'll just wait and see. For now, let's go to the market."

And without waiting for their response, she walked out of the inn, going up the road to where she saw a cluster of buildings that typically signified a town center.

CHAPTER TWENTY-NINE

※ BLAISE ※

Once his house was restored, Blaise found himself at loose ends, alternating between being furious with Augusta and worrying about Gala. By now, the Council undoubtedly knew about Gala, and they were probably taking measures to find her. Hopefully, Kelvin's territory would be the last place they would look—assuming Gala did as he asked and kept a low profile.

Still, this was not a sustainable situation. Blaise had to do something to protect her in a more permanent way, and he had to do it soon, before those scared fools mobilized fully. The fact that Gala was not answering his Contact messages worried him a bit, although he guessed that she was not fully in control of her magical abilities yet—something he found mildly reassuring, since it minimized her chances of exposing herself to the world.

Nonetheless, he missed her with an intensity he found deeply unsettling. It was as if a bright light had left his life when he dropped her off at the village.

A persistent idea kept nagging at the back of his mind—that of mastering the route to the Spell Realm. It was possible he was obsessing about it as a way to keep his thoughts occupied, he admitted to himself. In a way, that's what he had done after Louie's death: he'd focused on his work—on creating the intelligent object that turned out to be Gala—in order to keep himself busy. At the same time, however, he suspected that understanding the Spell Realm better could lead to unimaginable advances in sorcery, potentially enabling him to become powerful enough to protect Gala from the entire Council.

Tired of thinking about it, he began planning. Although Augusta had burned many of his notes, Blaise didn't feel particularly discouraged. He had frequently used Life Captures over the past year to record many of his particularly useful experiments, and he still had a lot of those droplets. More importantly, however, it seemed as if his mind had been working on the problem of getting to the Spell Realm ever since Gala had first described it to him, and he had some ideas he wanted to try out.

It was time for action.

He decided to start with a small, inanimate object. If he succeeded in sending that to the Spell Realm and having it come back, it would be an important step toward sending an actual person there.

Thus motivated, Blaise headed to his study, eager to take on a new challenge.

* * *

The spells were finally ready.

Blaise had chosen a needle as the object he would send to the Spell Realm. The spell would examine the needle at its deepest level and break it into its most elemental parts. That would destroy the physical needle, causing it to disappear, but those parts would become information, a message that would go to the Spell Realm and come back to change something in the Physical Realm, like all spells did. In this particular case, however, if Blaise succeeded, the manifestation in the Physical Realm should be identical to the original object.

Cognizant of the danger of new, untested spells and not wishing to suffer his mother's fate, Blaise took precautions. He used the same spell that had protected him during Augusta's attack—the spell that wrapped him in a shimmering bubble. The protection it granted would not last long, but it should be long enough to shield him from whatever havoc the experiment might cause.

Taking a slow, calming breath, he loaded the cards into his Interpreter Stone and watched the needle disappear, as it was supposed to.

Then he waited.

At first nothing happened. He could see the familiar shimmer of the protection spell, but there was no sign of the needle coming back. Frustrated, Blaise tried to figure out if he had made a mistake. The coming-back part of the spell was the trickiest. He assumed the needle would come back to its original location, but the spot remained empty.

All of a sudden, he heard a loud noise downstairs. It seemed to be coming from the storage room.

Blaise ran there, nearly tripping on the stairs in excitement.

And when he entered the room, he froze, staring at the sight in front of him in disbelief.

The needle had come back... in a way. It had returned not to the spot where it lay in his lab, but to the box where he had kept it originally. This return location actually made some sense, unlike the object he was staring at.

Among the shattered pieces of the box and scattered needles on the floor, he saw what he assumed was the original needle—except that now it was more like a sword. A strange, thick sword made of some kind of crystalline material that emitted a faint green glow. Instead of a hilt, this particular sword had a hole at the top.

Blaise carefully picked up the thing that used to be the needle, putting his hand through the hole at the top. It was actually comfortable to hold that way. Despite its size, the sword-like object was impossibly light, no heavier than the original needle. Lifting it, Blaise tried swinging it around the room and discovered that it was both sharp and strong. He was able to cut through his old sofa with ridiculous ease, and the sword-needle didn't break when he banged it on the stone floor.

Both amused and discouraged, Blaise decided to place the needle as a decoration in his hall downstairs. It would work well with the new furniture he had gotten after the fire, as well as some other trinkets he had on display there.

Heading back to his study, Blaise wondered what he had actually learned from this. On the one hand, he'd been able to do something to the needle—something that had obviously involved the Spell Realm. However, the needle had not come back as the same object. It had changed quite drastically. Would the same thing happen if a person went there? Would the person come back as some kind of a monstrosity, assuming he even survived the spell?

It seemed obvious Blaise had made an error in the spell. He had more work to do.

CHAPTER THIRTY

※ AUGUSTA ※

"Augusta, this is Colin. He is a blacksmith's apprentice from Blaise's territory," Ganir told her, gesturing toward the young man standing in the middle of the room. The man was a peasant; it was obvious both from his appearance and from the deferential way he held himself.

Augusta raised her eyebrows in surprise. What was this commoner doing in Ganir's chambers? When the Council Leader summoned her this morning, she had gone eagerly, knowing he likely had news about Blaise's creation.

"Tell her what you told me," said Ganir to the young man. As usual, the Council Leader was sitting behind his desk, observing everything with his sharp gaze.

"I was dancing with her, as I told his lordship," the man said obediently, staring at Augusta with awe and admiration. "Then she just disappeared."

"The 'she' in question sounds like the one we're looking for," Ganir told Augusta. "Physically, she's just as you described—blond, blue-eyed, and quite beautiful. Isn't that right, Colin?"

The peasant nodded. "Oh yes, quite beautiful." There was something about how he said the last word that rubbed Augusta the wrong way—aside from the fact that he apparently lusted after the creature.

Augusta's eyes narrowed. As she had suspected, Blaise had lied about the creature being unstable in the Physical Realm. "Explain what you meant by 'disappeared'," she ordered, looking at the commoner.

"One moment she was backing away," the man said uncertainly, as though embarrassed about something, "then she made me feel awful, and then she was not standing where she was." His face flushed unbecomingly.

"Tell Augusta exactly what happened," Ganir commanded, a slightly cruel smile appearing on his face.

"She didn't want to dance with me, and I was trying to get close to her," Colin admitted, his face reddening further.

"And what happened next?" Ganir prompted. "If I am forced to repeat this question one more time, you might visit the dungeon of this Tower."

The peasant paled at the threat. "I soiled myself, my lady," he admitted, looking like he wanted to disappear through the floor. "She made me feel scared and confused at the same time, and all my muscles involuntarily relaxed. And she just vanished, like she wasn't even there."

Augusta wrinkled her nose in disgust. *Peasants.*

"You are free to go, Colin," Ganir said, finally taking pity on the man. "When you come out, send in the clown."

Still visibly embarrassed, the peasant hurried out of the room.

"So it is definitely a *she*," Ganir said thoughtfully once they were alone again.

"It is an *it*." Augusta didn't like where Ganir was going with this. "We already knew that it had assumed a feminine shape."

"It's one thing to have a feminine shape," the old sorcerer said, a curious expression appearing on his face, "but it's quite different when that shape is one that young men want to dance with. And it's yet another thing altogether when the shape starts acting like a girl and refusing some idiot's attentions."

Augusta gave him a sharp look. What he was talking about was the very thing that made her so uneasy. Blaise's horrible creation was acting human, like it was one of them. "That's partially what makes this thing so dangerous," she told Ganir. "It manipulates people with its appearance, and they don't see it for the horror that it is." The whole situation was sickening, as far as Augusta was concerned.

The Council Leader shrugged. "Perhaps. The fact

that she's so beautiful does make her more noticeable—and easier to track. All my men had to do was ask about a pretty blond who may or may not have done some strange things."

"That is a plus," Augusta agreed, though her stomach clenched with disgust and something resembling jealousy. She hated the idea of this creature out there, seducing other men like she had already seduced Blaise.

"Indeed." Ganir smiled, looking inexplicably amused.

Augusta thought back to what the young man just told them, her eyebrows coming together in a slight frown. "So it sounds like the thing spontaneously teleported itself after making that peasant sick," she said, puzzled. "He didn't say anything about it using an Interperter Stone or doing any verbal spells."

"Yes." Ganir looked impressed. "It seems like she doesn't need any of our tools to connect to the Spell Realm. It makes sense, given her origins."

At that moment, there was a knock on the door, and another man came in. This one was a bit older, with tired-looking features and thin, greying hair.

"My lord, you summoned me?" His voice shook slightly. It was clear the commoner was terrified to be at the Tower.

"Tell her what happened, clown," said Ganir, gesturing toward Augusta.

Augusta gave the visitor a small, encouraging smile. The man looked far too frightened; the last thing they needed was for another peasant to soil himself.

Her ploy worked; the man visibly relaxed. "I was at the fair, entertaining children and doing tricks for them," he began, and Augusta realized that the man was quite literally a clown. "A little girl got pushed into a stack of barrels at the ale merchant's stall next to mine. A barrel started falling on her, and a beautiful sorceress saved the girl by stopping the barrel. She made it float in mid-air, my lady . . ." His tone was almost reverent.

Augusta got chills down her back. The thing could levitate objects, as well as teleport on a whim. Granted, most sorcerers could do a relatively simple verbal spell and make a barrel float, but no one would've been able to do it fast enough to save the child from the falling object.

"Did she utter any words?" she asked, staring at the clown. "Was there anything in her hands?"

"No." The man shook his head. "I don't think she uttered a single word, and I didn't see her holding anything. It all happened so fast."

"Was she alone?" Augusta asked.

"There were two older women with her."

"Please describe them for me," Augusta requested, although she was beginning to guess at their identities.

"It is Maya and Esther, as you would suspect," Ganir interrupted. Looking at the man, he waved toward the door. "You can go now, clown."

"Are you sure it's those old crones?" Augusta asked when the man left the room. She remembered them well. The two old women had constantly meddled in her former fiancé's life, showing up at his house unannounced and generally fussing over him. Blaise tolerated their attentions with good humor, but Augusta had found them annoying.

"Quite sure," Ganir confirmed. "I had both witnesses use a Life Capture and recall the event."

"So what's next?" Augusta asked, taking a few steps toward his desk. "We now know where the creature is, right?"

"No, actually, we don't." Ganir leaned forward, looking at her intently. "Apparently, Esther and Maya's house is abandoned. No one close to them was able to say where the women went. It seems like we'll have to wait longer to locate the creature—or we could try reasoning with Blaise again."

Augusta frowned. Talking to Blaise again sounded like a terrible idea to her. She certainly wasn't about to confront him by herself. "Do you think he would talk to *you*?" she asked doubtfully.

Ganir considered that for a moment. "I don't know," he admitted. "If I thought he'd talk to me, I would not have gotten you involved in this. But it might be worth a try at this point."

"Didn't he vow to kill you on sight?" Augusta asked, recalling Blaise's fury with the man he'd once regarded as a second father.

"He did indeed." Ganir's face darkened with something resembling sorrow. "But we have to get through to him somehow, to contain the situation before the rest of the Council hears about it."

"Yes." Augusta could see Ganir's point. "Something must be done and swiftly, before this creature has a chance to wreak further havoc."

The Council Leader nodded, but there was a thoughtful expression on his face. "Have you noticed that she saved a child?" he said slowly, cocking his head to the side. "This creation of Blaise's might not be as monstrous as you imagine."

"What?" Augusta stared at him in disbelief. "No. That doesn't mean anything. One act of compassion—if that's what it was—does not eliminate the threat that this thing poses. You know that as well as I do."

"Actually, I'm not sure I agree," Ganir said quietly. "I think we need to study her before we make any rash decisions."

"Are you saying you no longer wish to destroy it?"

"I never said we would destroy it. I need to know more about her before I do something so irrevocable."

"You just want to use it," Augusta said incredulously, the truth beginning to dawn on her. "That's what this is all about, isn't it? You just want to use the creature to gain more power—"

Ganir's expression hardened, his eyes flashing with anger. "You're accusing *me* of grabbing for power? I'm already the head of the Council. Why don't you take a closer look at your own affairs instead?"

Confused, Augusta took a step back. She had no idea what the old man was talking about.

"Leave me now," he said, gesturing dismissively toward the door. "I will send word when I hear more."

CHAPTER THIRTY-ONE

※ GALA ※

The market was disappointing. Gala had been expecting something along the lines of the fair she'd seen the other day, but this was nothing like that. There were fewer products on display, and even the trinkets and jewelry seemed drab and of worse quality than what she'd seen in Blaise's village. There were also fewer people actually buying the goods; the majority seemed to be simply browsing, often looking at the products with desperate longing on their emaciated faces. Still, Gala was glad to be out of the inn. Yanking off the shawl, she tied it around her waist, enjoying the cooling breeze on her hair.

As they ventured deeper into the market, Gala saw a number of stalls with foodstuffs, including a variety of breads, cheeses, and dried fruit. It was a more popular area of the market; most villagers seemed to be gathered in this section. Esther bought each of them a pastry filled with something rich and sweet, and Gala was greedily consuming the delicious treat when she heard some yelling behind her.

The noise came from the direction of one of the bread stalls. Curious, Gala turned to see what was going on and saw a figure running through the stalls. There were shouts from the merchant, and a tall man dressed in black started chasing after the runner.

Remembering the trial she'd seen at Blaise's village, Gala wondered if the running person was a thief. She could hear the merchant screaming that he'd been robbed, and she took a few steps in the direction where the figure had been heading. The other market visitors seemed to have the same idea, and Gala quickly found herself swept up by the crowd, everyone pushing and shoving to get to whatever spectacle seemed to be ahead. Casting a glance behind her, Gala saw Esther and Maya hurrying after the crowd with anxious looks on their faces.

Desperate to figure out what was going on, Gala focused on her sense of hearing, and suddenly she could filter out extraneous noise. Now she could hear the sounds of the person running in the distance, as well as the heavier footsteps chasing after it.

"No! Please, let me go!" The high-pitched scream was undoubtedly feminine, and Gala realized that the runner was a young woman—a young woman who had just gotten caught, judging by her hysterical pleas.

As the crowd carried her forward, Gala could hear a harsh male voice speaking of justice, and she managed to break free, now running toward the middle of the market where the screams were coming from.

There were already spectators gathered there, surrounding a small figure huddling on the ground. The black-garbed man was standing over her, holding her arm in an inescapable grip. Looking around, Gala could see fear and pity reflected on many of the faces, as well as gleeful anticipation on a few. She didn't know what was about to happen, but some kind of intuition gave her a sinking feeling in the pit of her stomach. She wished Esther and Maya were here, so she could ask them about this, but they were far behind her at this point.

Staring at the girl, she noticed that she was thin—far thinner than Gala herself—and that her clothing was in rags. Her long brown hair was tangled, and the expression on her pale face was that of sheer terror.

Another man, this one dressed in richer, more elaborate clothing, pushed his way through the crowd, joining the young woman and her captor. There was a sword in a leather scabbard hanging on his left hip and a cruel smile playing on his lips. "You are going to be honored, thief," he said, addressing the frightened girl. "I am Davish, the overseer of these lands."

The thief visibly flinched, the expression on her face changing to that of utter despair. It was as if she had given up all hope, Gala thought, transfixed by the scene in front of her.

"You are being accused of stealing," the overseer continued. "Do you know the punishment for thievery?"

The young woman nodded, tears running down her face. "My lord, please spare my life . . . I took a loaf of bread to feed my two remaining children. My youngest already passed away from starvation. Please, my lord, don't do this—"

The overseer looked amused. "You are in luck," he said. "In honor of the upcoming games at the Coliseum, I am in a good mood and inclined to be merciful."

Gala exhaled, letting out a breath she hadn't realized she'd been holding. She was glad the woman would be spared. Had they been seriously considering killing her for stealing a loaf of bread? The girl had only done it to save the lives of her children, and it seemed incredibly cruel to punish her for that.

The thief sobbed with relief. "I am forever in your debt, my lord—"

"Guard, take her to the execution stone." The overseer issued the order to the black-clothed man. Looking up at the crowd, he announced, "Because I am merciful, her life will be spared. As punishment, she will simply lose her right hand, so she remembers never to steal again."

And before Gala could register the full meaning of the man's words, the guard took action. Holding the girl by her arm, he dragged her, kicking and screaming, toward a slab in the center of the square. Ignoring her struggles, he pressed her forearm against the stone surface, causing her to release the small loaf of bread that she had been clutching in her fist. The evidence of her crime fell to the ground, rolling in the dirt.

Gala instinctively started forward, trying to get through the crowd, but the people around her were packed so tightly that she could hardly move. Her anxiety spiking, Gala squeezed her eyes shut and tried to recall how she had teleported that one time. Nothing came to mind; she simply couldn't make it work.

Opening her eyes, she stared in helpless horror at the scene unfolding in front of her.

The girl was still screaming, her voice hoarse with terror, and Gala could see Davish unsheathing his sword and approaching the girl.

No, Gala thought in desperation, *this could not be happening.*

Making one last heroic attempt, she started shoving her way through the crowd, elbowing and kicking to make her way to the front. People were pushing back at her, yelling, but she didn't care. She needed to get to this girl before it was too late. Up ahead, Davish lifted the sword into the air.

Gala doubled her efforts, heedless of any injury to herself.

The sword swung down with deadly force, and the thief's agonized scream pierced the air. Bright red blood sprayed everywhere, covering the stone platform and splattering on the overseer's elaborate clothing. The guard released his hold on the girl's arm, taking a step back.

Stunned, Gala saw the girl's severed hand fall to the ground next to the bread—and felt something inside her snap again.

"No!" Every bit of her outrage poured out of Gala in an ear-splitting shout. All around her, the crowd seemed to stumble, most spectators falling to their knees and clutching their heads. All of a sudden, Gala found herself free to move, and she ran toward the bloody slab of rock where the girl was huddled, moaning and crying.

It seemed like there was blood everywhere, the metallic scent permeating the air. *How could there be so much blood?* Then Gala saw that the girl was not the only one bleeding. Everyone around them was holding their ears, trying to contain the red liquid trickling out.

And Gala realized with sick horror it was her fault—that her shout had somehow caused this awful occurrence.

Dazed, she approached the thief, who was practically bathing in blood at this point and clutching desperately at her stump of a wrist. Driven by some unknown instinct, Gala put her arms around the girl, hugging her gently. And in that moment, it was as though their bodies became one.

With every fiber of her being, Gala reached out with love and kindness to the victim of this unspeakable injustice. She could feel warm energy slowly flowing from her body into the girl's. Everything inside Gala was focused on one goal and one goal only—to undo the damage that the executioner had caused. She could feel the girl's pain, and she took it into herself, freeing the young woman of that burden. The feeling was agonizing and illuminating at the same time; until then, Gala had had only a rudimentary, book-learned understanding of pain and suffering. Now, however, it was real to her, and she vowed silently to make it so that there would be less of it in the world.

What was happening now was being done by the part of Gala's mind that she had no control over; she was vaguely aware of that. But it didn't matter, because Gala could sense that it was working, that the girl's pain was slowly dissolving and ebbing away. When there was no more pain left, Gala let go of the girl and stepped back.

The young woman stood there, her dirt-streaked face serene and joyful, showing no trace of pain or fear. The bloody stump of her arm was no longer gushing; instead, as Gala watched, the hand slowly re-grew itself, each bone, muscle, and tendon gradually lengthening and thickening. Soon, the fingers appeared, and the hand was as it had been before, slim and feminine—and very much alive.

When Gala looked back at the crowd, she saw that everybody was kneeling, the expressions on their faces strangely blissful. There was blood on their clothing, but nobody seemed to be bleeding or in pain anymore. She had done this too, Gala realized with relief. She had not only taken away the girl's pain, but also that of others in the vicinity, undoing the harm she herself had inadvertently caused.

In the distance, she could see Esther and Maya approaching the edge of the crowd, but Gala knew she was not done yet. The guard and the overseer were next to the girl, kneeling in the same position as the rest of the crowd and rapturously staring at Gala. She came up to them, knowing what she had to do.

She started with the overseer, putting her hands on his temples. She needed to understand why he had done something so horrible. "How could you?" she thought, letting the question reverberate in her head, over and over, as she lost herself in what felt like a series of Life Captures.

He was a small child of rich parents—a child who looked nothing like his father, a child who wished daily that he had been born to a different family. The child relived the many cruelties he had suffered, the endless beatings and demeaning words. Time sped forward, and the child was a young man who acted more like his father with every passing day—a young man who needed to lash out at others to cope with the pain left inside. As the young man matured, he found himself becoming someone who craved power, someone who needed to control others so nobody could hurt him again.

Now Gala understood. The cruel man was as damaged in his own way as the unfortunate girl he'd tried to hurt. The warm, sharing feeling from before came over Gala again, and she reached out to the man's broken mind, trying to mend it as she had healed the girl's hand. The mind resisted, and Gala understood that by doing this, she would be changing the man fundamentally, making him become someone else. Deep inside, she knew she might not have the right to do this, but the instinct to heal was too strong. She needed to do this so he would not hurt anyone else in the future. Gathering her strength, she pushed harder into the overseer's mind and felt it finally letting her in.

"Gala! Gala, are you listening to me?" Maya's voice penetrated the haze surrounding her, bringing Gala out of her mindless state.

Blinking, she stared at Maya and Esther, becoming aware for the first time of the deep exhaustion overtaking her body.

"Come," Esther said, reaching for Gala. She looked anxious, and Gala let her guide her away, too weary to resist as the two women led her out of the square. All around them, she could see the spectators slowly coming out of their strange bliss-like state and starting to look around with confusion. Maya quickly wrapped the shawl around Gala's head again, covering her with the thick scratchy material.

When they got back to the inn, Gala collapsed on her bed and was asleep as soon as her head hit the pillow.

CHAPTER THIRTY-TWO

✳ BLAISE ✳

Blaise was analyzing his last spell when he heard knocking at the door. His heart jumped, and a tendril of fury snaked down his spine. Was this the Council making their move?

Rushing down to the storage room, he swiftly grabbed a bunch of cards he had written for just such a confrontation after his brother's death. It was a mixture of offensive and defensive spells, each optimized for the particular strengths and weaknesses of the Council members.

In the meantime, the knocking continued.

Thinking furiously, Blaise took a generic defense spell and fed it into the Interpreter Stone. It would afford him some protection against both mental and physical attacks, hopefully buying him some time. Approaching the entryway, he called out, "Who is it?"

"Blaise, it's me, Ganir."

Blaise's anger doubled. How dare the old man show his face here after what he'd done to Louie? Ganir's betrayal was in some way worse than Augusta's; the old sorcerer had always treated Louie as a son, and nobody had been more shocked than Blaise to learn of Ganir's vote in favor of his brother's punishment.

Filled with fury, Blaise began to speak, instinctively resorting to a spell designed to paralyze his opponent. He didn't think; he just acted. If the spell succeeded, he had no idea what he would do with the unmoving body of the Council Leader, but he didn't care at the moment, too consumed with anger to be fully rational.

After he was done, Blaise took a deep breath, trying to regain control of his emotions. He didn't know if the spell had been successful, but there was a chance that he had surprised Ganir. When it came to battle, unanticipated moves were the best, and it was unlikely the old sorcerer would've expected him to use such a simple spell.

He felt himself getting calm and clear-headed. Very calm.

Too calm, Blaise realized. Ganir was using a pacifying spell against him—a spell that had partially penetrated Blaise's mental defenses.

The thought of being manipulated infuriated Blaise again, and he felt the unnatural calm dissipate, bringing back some of the volatile emotions he'd experienced earlier. However, Ganir's spell must've been at least somewhat effective, since he was no longer feeling quite so murderous toward the Council Leader—something that Blaise bitterly, but calmly, resented.

At that moment, he heard Ganir's sorcery-enhanced voice. It was loud and clear, as if the old man was standing right next to him and shouting. "Blaise, I am extremely disappointed," the voice said. "I know you hold a grudge, but I thought you were better than this. Attacking me without even looking me in the eye? That's not the Blaise I remember."

Blaise felt his fury returning. The old man was a master of mental games, and Blaise hated being manipulated.

"I will give you a second to walk away," Blaise shouted back, speaking to Ganir for the first time. Tauntingly, he added, "And you're right—I'm not the Blaise you remember. That Blaise died along with Louie. You remember Louie, don't you?"

As he was speaking, Blaise scribbled the rough coordinates of where Ganir was standing on a card and added some code before loading the card into the Interpreter Stone. Then he jumped back a few feet, making sure that he wouldn't be in the radius of the spell.

The spell he unleashed was designed to paralyze his victim mentally—to blast the mind with indecision, fear, shock, and various effects of sleep deprivation. It was far worse than the physical paralysis spell Blaise had used earlier, since this one was an amalgamation of multiple attacks on the mind all rolled into one.

Then he waited.

All seemed quiet. To check if the mental attack worked, Blaise prepared another spell and directed it at the entryway wall, making it as transparent as glass.

Now Blaise could see outside, and he saw Ganir standing there, looking directly at Blaise through the now-see-through wall. It was obvious the old man was unaffected by the spell, but he appeared to be alone. His dark brown chaise stood next to him.

Despite his disappointment, Blaise felt a wave of relief. It didn't seem like this was a Council ambush; they wouldn't have sent the Council Leader just by himself.

"You insult me if you think your spells had any chance of success," Ganir said calmly, his voice still penetrating the walls of the house with ease. In his hands was an Interpreter Stone. He could've struck at Blaise with a deadly spell of his own at any time, but he had apparently chosen not to.

Some of his anger fading, Blaise opened the door. "What do you want, Ganir?" he asked wearily, beginning to tire of this confrontation.

"I spoke to Augusta," Ganir said, looking at him. "The Council does not know of your creation."

"Why not?" Blaise was genuinely surprised.

"Because I convinced her not to tell them for now. There is still a window of opportunity to untangle this mess. Augusta will go to them eventually. I made sure she did not do so yet, but she is scared of what you have done, scared beyond reason."

Blaise felt like he could breathe again. The Council didn't know about Gala. It was only Ganir and Augusta—which was bad enough, but not nearly the disaster it would've been if the entire Council got involved. Still, that didn't mean he had any intention of being civil to Ganir.

"How exactly are you planning to untangle this mess?" he asked, not bothering to keep the bitterness out of his voice. "The same way you did with Louie?"

He could see that his words stung. Ganir flinched, his hand instinctively reaching for the pouch hanging at his waist before dropping to his side. Blaise made a mental note of that pouch—it was likely where the old sorcerer kept his spell cards. Letting the door frame block Ganir's line of sight, he surreptitiously scribbled a quick spell on one of his own cards and prepared to use it at an opportune moment.

In the meantime, Ganir took a step forward. "Blaise," he said softly, "your brother was quite open about his crime. Even I could not hide what he had done from the Council. I tried my best to guide the Council toward a lenient resolution, but they would not listen—and your brother's stubbornness and refusal to even pretend at remorse did not help matters."

Blaise stared at Ganir, remembering the passionate speech Louie had made in front of the Council about the injustices in their society—a speech that had probably sealed his fate. Blaise had agreed with every word his brother had spoken, but even he had thought it unwise to antagonize the other sorcerers so openly. Ultimately, though, the vote was what mattered—and Ganir had voted in favor of Louie's execution.

"Don't lie to me," Blaise said harshly. "You know as well as I do that you're no different from them, that you all voted the same way. And you expect me to believe that you tried to speak on Louie's behalf?"

Ganir looked stunned. "What? I voted against Louie's death. How could you think otherwise?"

Blaise let out a short, hard laugh. "Oh, is that right? You think you can hide behind the fact that all votes are anonymous and nobody knows the exact count? Well, I learned the truth—I know the breakdown of the voting results. There was only one vote against Louie's death, and it was my own. All of you—you, Augusta, every single person on that Council—voted for my brother's execution."

"That's not true." Ganir still appeared shocked. "I don't know where you're getting your information from, but your methods must be flawed. I voted *against* Louie's death, I swear to you. He was like a son to me, just like you were. And Dania voted the same way—against the punishment."

He sounded so earnest that Blaise doubted himself for a moment. Could his source have lied? If so, why? Blaise couldn't think of a reason—which meant that Ganir had to be lying to him now. "Why don't you just admit it, like she did?" he asked scornfully, remembering how Augusta had been unable to conceal the truth of her betrayal from him. Just thinking about it made him want to kill Ganir on the spot.

"Are you talking about Augusta?" Ganir asked in confusion. "Are you saying she voted for Louie's execution?"

"Of course she did." Blaise's upper lip curled. "And so did you."

"No, I didn't," the Council Leader insisted, frowning. "And I didn't know about her vote. I had always assumed she supported you and Louie. Is that why the two of you parted, because you found out about the way she voted?"

Blaise felt the old memories bubbling to the surface, poisoning his mind with bitter hatred again. "Don't," he said quietly. "Don't go there, Ganir, or I swear, I will kill you on the spot."

The old sorcerer ignored Blaise's threat. "I have to say, that's low, even for her," Ganir mused, "though now that I think about it, it makes sense. You know Augusta's family is from the old nobility. She was raised on stories of the Revolution, and any possibility of societal change terrifies her. She acted out of fear, not reason, when she cast her vote, and I wouldn't be surprised if she regrets her actions." Pausing for a second, he added, "You were not the only one suffering after your brother's death, my son."

Blaise looked at Ganir, wondering if there could possibly be any truth to what the old man was saying. If so, then his hatred for the Council Leader had been misplaced this whole time.

"Is that why you vowed to kill me?" Ganir asked, echoing his thoughts. "Because you thought I voted in favor of Louie's execution? I was sure you hated me because I failed to protect your brother—because, even though I was the head of the Council, I couldn't save him."

Blaise was almost tempted to believe him. Almost. "You're an expert when it comes to getting people to do what you want them to do, Ganir," he said wearily. "If you had truly wanted to save Louie, he would still be alive. If nothing else, you and I could've joined forces and fought the others. But you didn't even try—so don't lie to me now."

Ganir looked pained. "Blaise, I'm so sorry. I couldn't go against the rest of the Council at that point—not when it was my invention that was at the heart of the issue. I tried to convince them to be lenient, I truly did, and I got the impression that most of them would vote as I did—against the punishment. I was as shocked as you when the verdict came through—"

"Stop," Blaise snapped, losing his patience. "Just stop. Why are you here?"

"I have an offer," Ganir said, finally getting to the point. "Bring your creation to me, and I will do my best to make sure she is unharmed. I can almost guarantee you will be cleared of any wrongdoing; after all, your spell did not go as planned. Although you intended to do something they disapprove of, you have not succeeded, and that will convince the

Council that no crime occurred." His eyes gleamed with unusual excitement. "In fact, I can even help you regain your rightful place on the Council."

Blaise laughed sardonically. "Oh, I see," he said, chuckling at the old man's transparent intent. "You want Gala for your own purposes. And as for me, does the almighty Ganir need another ally on the Council?"

"I am trying to help you." Ganir was beginning to look frustrated. "Yes, I do find your creation fascinating and would like to learn more about her, but that's not what this is all about. The Council needs you right now—far more than any of those stubborn fools realize. *I* need you. Blaise, please, give up Gala and come back."

Blaise couldn't believe his ears. Give up Gala? It was unthinkable. "The answer is no," he said coldly, reaching for the spell card he had prepared when he'd noticed Ganir's pouch. It was already next to the Stone he was holding in his other hand, and he swiftly joined the two objects, activating the spell.

A second later, Ganir's pouch went up in flames, leaving the old sorcerer without ready-made spells and nearly defenseless.

"Leave, old man," Blaise told Ganir, watching with satisfaction as his opponent threw remnants of the burning pouch on the ground. "I can kill you now, and I will. You have two minutes to get out of my sight."

The sorcerer's pale eyes filled with sadness. "If you change your mind, let me know," he said with quiet dignity. Shuffling over to his chaise, he rose into the air and flew away, leaving Blaise puzzled and disturbed.

CHAPTER THIRTY-THREE

❋ BARSON ❋

Walking into his sister's house, Barson inhaled the familiar aroma of baking bread and scented candles. It smelled like home, reminding him of when their mother would bake delicious rolls for the entire household. Unlike most other sorcerers, their mother enjoyed working with her hands—something that Dara had inherited from her, along with her aptitude for sorcery.

"Barson! I'm so glad you came by." Standing at the top of the staircase, his sister gave him a radiant smile before hurrying down toward him.

Barson smiled back, genuinely happy to see her. He missed Dara, though he couldn't fault her for preferring this comfortable townhouse over cramped quarters back at the Tower. Low-ranking sorcerers received terrible accommodations there, and many of them chose to live outside of the Tower most of the time.

"It's good to see you, Dara," he said, leaning down to kiss her cheek. "Is Larn here also?"

"He should be here soon. He's passing by the well right now," she said, grinning up at him mischievously. Her dark eyes were sparkling, making her look extraordinarily pretty.

Barson sighed, knowing what she was up to. "Did you put a Locator spell on him again?"

Dara's grin widened. "I did indeed. But don't tell him; it'll be our secret."

Amused, Barson shook his head. His sister and his right-hand man had been together for the past two years, and she drove Larn insane with her insistence on using spells in everyday life. For Dara, it was a way to practice sorcery and sharpen her skills, while Larn viewed it as showing off. "All right," Barson promised, "I won't."

"Come," Dara said, tugging at his arm. "Let me feed you. I bet you're starved. That sorceress of yours doesn't cook, I presume?"

"Augusta? No, of course not." The very idea struck Barson as ridiculous. Augusta was . . . well, Augusta. She was many things, but homemaker was not one of them.

"That's what I assumed," Dara huffed. "She does know you need to eat, right?"

"I'm not sure," Barson admitted, taking a seat at the table. "Most sorcerers—unlike you—rarely think about food or consider that others might need it."

"Well, I hope she's good in bed then," Dara

muttered, putting a bread basket and sliced cheese in front of him. "That and some spells is all she seems to be good for."

Barson burst out laughing. His sister was jealous of Augusta's position on the Council and was doing a terrible job of hiding it. "I'm not about to discuss my love life with you, sis," he said after a few seconds, still chuckling.

She sniffed disdainfully, but kept quiet until Barson had a chance to eat some bread with cheese. "So guess what?" she said after Barson ate his second slice. "I was offered a chance to work with Jandison today."

"Jandison?" Barson frowned. The oldest member of the Council was known for his teleportation skills and not much else. It was not exactly the most promising opportunity for Dara, given her ambitions.

"I know," she said, understanding his unspoken concern. "But it's still better than what I do now."

"Do you think Ganir put him up to it?"

Dara shook her head. "I doubt it. I get the sense Jandison doesn't like Ganir very much."

"Oh?" Barson was surprised. He was well-versed in Council politics, but he hadn't heard of any enmity between the two sorcerers. "What makes you think that?"

"A woman's intuition, I guess," Dara said. "It's just a vibe I got from him when he mentioned Ganir's name to me once. When I thought about it later, it actually made a lot of sense. Jandison is the oldest sorcerer on the Council, and I wouldn't be surprised if he thinks he should be the Council Leader instead of Ganir."

Barson gave his sister a thoughtful look. "You know, you may be right. Are you going to accept Jandison's offer?"

"I think so." She smiled. "And yes, I will definitely keep my eyes and ears open."

At that moment, Larn walked into the kitchen, and Barson got up to greet him.

When Barson had first learned of his best friend's involvement with Dara, he had been less than pleased. For one thing, being with a non-sorcerer was looked down upon in the Tower, and Barson had been concerned that her relationship with Larn might be detrimental to Dara's desire to be recognized for her sorcery talent. However, he could see that Larn genuinely loved her, and that ultimately proved to be the most important thing of all. That, and the fact that Larn was one of the few men Barson was not tempted to kill immediately for laying a finger on his older sister.

"So tell me," Barson said to Larn when the three of them sat down at the table, "do you have any news for me?"

Larn nodded, chewing on a piece of bread. "There has been a lot of activity with Ganir recently. Augusta visited his chambers again, and so did a number of commoners."

"Commoners? Why?" Barson looked at his friend in surprise.

"We don't know. Ganir's spies spirited them out of the Tower before we could learn their identities. They were literally brought in to see Ganir and then were taken away immediately. My man only got a quick look at them."

"Anything else?"

"We got a report from our source who's watching Blaise's house."

Barson's hands curled into fists underneath the table. "Did Augusta visit him again?"

Dara shot him a curious look and opened her mouth, but Larn reached over and squeezed her hand in gentle warning. "No," he said. "It was even stranger than that. It was Ganir."

"Ganir visited Blaise?" Barson's temper cooled immeasurably. "I thought they weren't on speaking terms."

"Blaise is not on speaking terms with anyone these days," Dara said. "Once he left the Council, it's like he disappeared. Why would anyone visit him now?"

"Was our ally able to figure out what Ganir wanted?" Barson asked.

"No," Larn replied. "He's petrified of Ganir. They all are. As soon as he saw the old sorcerer arrive, he got out of there as quickly as his chaise could carry him."

Barson's lip curled. "Those sorcerers are such cowards. No offense, Dara."

"None taken." She grinned. "I fully agree with you, in fact. I would've definitely stuck around to learn as much as I could. By the way, speaking of sorcery, I finished working on your armor. It should now be resistant to most of the common spells."

"Thank you, sis." Barson smiled at her. "You're the best."

"I know," she said without false modesty. "And soon they will know it, too."

"Yes, they will," Barson promised her, and for the next few minutes, they ate in companionable silence, enjoying the meal Dara had prepared for them.

When his stomach was comfortably full, Barson looked up at his friend again. "Any news from outside Turingrad? Any more uprisings anywhere?"

"No," Larn said, "everything seems quiet for now. There's just one thing, which is probably nothing."

"What is it?" Barson asked.

"There have been some curious rumors about a powerful sorceress." Larn paused to pour himself some ale. "Apparently, she's beautiful, young, and wise beyond her years . . . They say she heals the sick, brings dead children back to life, and can even make the crops prosper wherever she is."

Dara laughed. "That's ridiculous. Bringing back the dead is impossible, even in theory."

"The common people always make up stories that cast sorcerers in this kind of light," Barson told her. "They want to believe the elite cares about them, that their overlords simply don't know they're suffering."

Larn snorted. "And I'm sure many of them don't—because they just don't care."

Barson shook his head, thinking about the

gullibility of the common people. The peasants had been conditioned to think that the old nobility had been bad, while their new sorcerer masters were an improvement. Of course, with this drought, many of them were starting to see the truth—hence the increasing uprisings throughout Koldun.

Remembering the last rebellion he'd been forced to quell made Barson's thoughts turn back to Ganir. Why had he met with Blaise? Could it somehow be connected with Augusta's visit to her former lover? And what about all those commoners coming to the Tower?

Ganir was obviously playing a deep game, and Barson intended to get to the bottom of it.

CHAPTER THIRTY-FOUR

※ AUGUSTA ※

Approaching Ganir's chambers, Augusta knocked decisively on his door. The old man had been avoiding her for the past couple of days, even going so far as to ignore her Contact messages, and she wasn't about to allow this.

By the time the door swung open, Augusta's temper was reaching a boiling point. Taking a few deep breaths to calm herself, she entered Ganir's chambers.

"How are you, my child?" Ganir greeted her calmly. He was sitting behind his desk, apparently looking over some scrolls prior to her arrival.

"You said you would notify me when your men had some information," she said bluntly. "It has now been several days, and I haven't heard anything from you. Where do we stand as far as locating this creature? If your spies have been unable to find it, then I'm going to have no choice but to speak about this at the upcoming Council meeting—the one that's happening on Thursday."

Ganir sighed. "Augusta, you need to have patience. We can't act in haste—"

"No, we *need* to act in haste," she interrupted. "We need to contain this situation before it gets completely out of control. Did you, or did you not, learn anything thus far?"

He hesitated for a moment, then inclined his head. "Yes," he said. "There is something that I want to show you."

"Show me?"

The old man gestured toward a Life Capture droplet sitting in a jar. "It's from one of my observers in Kelvin's territory," he said softly. "Blaise's creation has been spotted there, at the market in Neumanngrad."

Augusta's pulse jumped in excitement. "Did your observer capture it?"

"No," Ganir said. "That was not his task."

"All right," Augusta said, "so what happened? How was he able to find the thing?"

"You better see for yourself." Ganir picked up the droplet and handed it to her. "Keep in mind, this is from a man who is a sorcerer himself."

Augusta took the droplet and was about to bring it to her mouth when Ganir held up his hand.

"Wait," he said. "Before you do that, I want you to start a new recording." He pointed toward the Sphere sitting on his desk.

"What? Why?" Augusta gave him a confused look.

"I want to keep that Life Capture for more study," he explained. "By you recording yourself using the Life Capture droplet, I will not lose the information that this droplet contains. Instead, I will get a new droplet that will include a few moments before you took the original droplet and a few moments after, as well as a recording of the original."

Augusta stared at him in shock and amazement. Why hadn't she thought of this before? The idea was genius in its simplicity. It was widely believed that the droplets were consumable—gone forever once used. But now it seemed like there was a way to use them over and over again. Why had the old man kept this to himself?

The implications were staggering. If nothing else, it could change the way sorcery was taught. All one needed to do was teach a group of students once and have them record the class via Life Captures. Then the next class could be given those droplets, and their experiences would also be recorded—and so on. This would significantly cut the time each experienced sorcerer had to spend tutoring apprentices—a duty that Augusta particularly disliked.

Of course, now that she thought about it, it was not that surprising Ganir had hoarded this knowledge. Augusta had always suspected the old sorcerer of keeping secrets when it came to some of his discoveries; he took joy in possessing knowledge that no one else had.

Realizing that she was standing there in silence, Augusta approached the Sphere and pricked her finger on a needle lying on the desk. Then she pressed that finger to the magical object and put the droplet she was holding into her mouth.

* * *

Ganir reached for the droplet Vik had brought to him. Carrying it to his mouth, he closed his eyes, letting the droplet consume him.

* * *

Vik was sitting on the roof of a building overlooking the market. The weather was nice, and he was quite content. His only gripe was a large wooden splinter that had gotten stuck in his finger when he was climbing up there.

He could see the whole market from this vantage point, and he made himself comfortable, knowing he was likely in for another boring shift. His job in this territory was to observe public gatherings, which usually meant sitting for several hours and watching people shop. As usual, he was Life-Capturing the experience as Ganir ordered him to do, although Vik honestly didn't see the point in doing that. Nothing of interest ever happened in this region.

He had an Interpreter Stone and cards with spells written on them, ready to be cast. One particularly useful spell enabled him to enhance his vision, making his job a little bit more bearable. There was nothing quite like watching a woman changing in her bedroom, secure in the knowledge that nobody could see her from the street.

Ganir had supplied Vik with many cards that had the intricate code for the spell. Vik was a lousy coder, and he had to take Ganir's word for it when the old man assured him that the vision enhancement spell was actually an easy one.

His hearing was also sharpened, and the sound of a young woman's scream was what first alerted him to the chase happening in the market below. Another thief, he thought lazily. Still, Vik watched the running woman and her pursuer, since he had nothing better to do.

His interest was piqued further when he saw an attractive young woman in the crowd following the usual chase. That she looked like the description of the target barely registered at this point. All they knew of the target was that it was a young maiden with blue eyes and long, wavy blond hair. She was also supposedly very pretty. The woman below definitely fit the description, but so did hundreds of others that Vik had seen in passing—and even a few that he had watched surreptitiously through the windows.

Once the thief was captured, Vik continued to observe the scene. It was certainly more entertaining than watching some old women haggling with the merchants.

He heard Davish speak and was amused at the overseer's mercy. A poor, starving woman with her right hand chopped off would die just as surely as if she were beheaded—except her death would now be slower and more painful.

Like the rest of the crowd, he watched the girl's mutilation with a mix of pity and gruesome curiosity.

And then he suddenly heard the Shriek. His ears felt like they exploded.

His head ringing, Vik realized that someone had used a powerful spell designed to deafen and psychologically control a rioting mob—a spell he had learned about but had never seen used in real life. This version in particular seemed more potent than anything Vik had read about. If it weren't for the defensive shield spell Ganir insisted they all use while on duty, the Shriek would've been the last thing Vik heard. As it was, he was in agony. The unprotected people in the square below were falling to their knees, bleeding from their ears.

Only one person remained standing—the young woman Vik had noticed earlier. Dazed, he watched as the beautiful girl walked toward the execution platform and put her arms around the thief huddling in a bloody ball on the ground.

And then Vik felt it—a sense of peace and warmth unlike anything he had ever experienced before. It was beauty, it was love, it was bliss . . . it was indescribable. The wave seemed to emanate from the center of the square, where the two women stood hugging.

A spell, he realized dazedly. He was feeling the effects of some spell—a spell strong enough to penetrate his magical defenses.

His finger tingled, and he looked down, watching as the splinter slowly came out of his flesh and the wound healed itself, all traces of the injury disappearing without a trace. Even his head, which had been pounding just moments earlier from the Shriek, felt completely normal.

On the ground, he could see the crowd still on their knees, staring at the young sorceress with rapture on their faces. Had they felt it too, the euphoria he'd just experienced?

And then he knew that they had—because when the beautiful girl stepped away from the thief, the peasant woman's hand was whole again. Whatever spell the young sorceress had used, it had been so potent that it had spilled over to the spectators, healing even Vik's minor wound. "What kind of sorcery is this?" he wondered in terrified awe.

Vik now knew why Ganir had dispatched so many of his men to find this girl. As the sorceress touched Davish, Vik pricked his finger and touched the Life Capture Sphere he was carrying with him.

* * *

His heart racing, Ganir regained his senses. For a brief moment, he wondered if he would ever get used to the disorienting effects of his invention, and then his mind turned to what he had just witnessed.

"What had the boy done?" he thought darkly, pricking his finger and touching the Life Capture

Sphere.

* * *

Augusta came back to herself with a gasp. Quickly pricking her finger, she touched the Life Capture Sphere on the table in front of her. The last thing she wanted was to expose her private thoughts to the person who would use this droplet next, as Ganir had just done. It was bad enough that there would still be a moment of her feelings captured for anyone to see—a moment of overwhelming horror and disgust.

Her fears had come true: the thing had unnatural powers.

"What of Davish?" she asked Ganir, trying to remain calm. "In the droplet, the creature was reaching for him."

The Council Leader hesitated for a moment. "He's not . . . exactly himself after meeting her, according to Vik."

"What do you mean?" Augusta gave him a questioning look.

"How much do you know about Davish?"

She frowned. "Not much. I know he's Kelvin's overseer and supposedly not much better than our esteemed colleague."

Kelvin was her least favorite member of the Sorcerer Council. His mistreatment of his people was legendary. Several years ago, Blaise had even petitioned for Kelvin to get kicked off the Council and have his holdings confiscated, but, of course, no one had dared to implement such a precedent against a fellow sorcerer. Instead, Kelvin ended up giving control of his lands to Davish—who turned out to be a mirror image of his master when it came to the treatment of peasants.

Ganir nodded, an expression of disgust appearing on his face. "That's an understatement. Davish's reputation has traveled far and wide. That atrocity they call the Coliseum was originally Davish's idea—"

"What happened to him?" Augusta interrupted.

"Well, apparently after the encounter you just saw, Davish has already begun to change many policies in the territory. He has initiated an aid effort for the families most affected by the drought, and there are rumors that he may close or change the Coliseum games after the upcoming events." Ganir's eyes gleamed. "In short, Davish is a changed man. Literally."

Augusta's stomach twisted unpleasantly. "The creature changed him? Just like that? How do you even change someone?"

"Well, theoretically, there are ways—"

Augusta stared at him. "You can do this, too?"

"No." Ganir shook his head. "I wish I could, but I can't. At most, I could control a commoner's mind for a short period of time. The mathematics and the complexity of deep fundamental change are beyond human capabilities."

Beyond human capabilities? "Doesn't this terrify

you?" Augusta asked, sickened by the thought of this thing having such power.

"Probably not as much as it terrifies you," Ganir said, watching her with his pale gaze, "but yes, the power to make someone lose their essence, their personhood, is a dangerous power indeed. Especially if it is abused."

"So what are we going to do?"

"I am going to dispatch the Sorcerer Guard," Ganir said. "They will bring her here. You saw how the defenses protected my observer from the full power of her spells. I will equip the Guard with even better defenses."

"You are asking them to bring it here alive? You would risk their lives and ours just so that you could study this creature?" Augusta could hear her voice rising in angry disbelief. "Are you insane? It needs to be destroyed!"

"No," Ganir said implacably. "Not yet. If nothing else, Blaise would never forgive us if we destroy her without just cause."

"What does it matter? He hates us anyway," Augusta said bitterly. And turning, she left Ganir's chambers before she said something she would later regret.

CHAPTER THIRTY-FIVE

❋ GALA ❋

"Did you hear? They said she was shooting fire out of her eyes, and her hair was as white as snow, streaming behind her for a solid five yards." The pot-bellied man sitting at the corner table burped, then wiped his mouth with his sleeve.

"Really?" The man's skinny friend leaned forward. "I heard men were blinded when they looked at her, and then she healed them by waving her hand."

"Blinded? I didn't hear that. But they say she brought back the dead. The thief got her head chopped off and then the whole thing regrew."

The skinny man picked up a tankard of ale. "She wasn't one of the Council either. Nobody knew where she came from. They say she wore rags, but her beauty was such that her skin glowed."

Sweeping the floor around the table, Gala listened to the men's conversation with amusement and disbelief. How had they made up all these stories about her? Nobody at the inn had even been at the market—a fact that helped protect her identity nearly as much as the rough shawl Esther insisted she wear when doing her chores at the inn.

Cleaning the inn turned out to be less fun than Gala had expected. She'd volunteered to help around the inn as a way to get out of the room and experience more of life. Although she had enjoyed knitting and sewing—two activities that Maya and Esther had occupied her with after the market fiasco—she had wanted to do something more active. Of course, Maya and Esther had been less than receptive to the idea of her leaving the room. Their biggest fear was that Gala would be recognized.

Gala had doubted that anyone would recognize her, particularly in the disguise she wore around the inn, and she was right. All day long, she had been cleaning, scrubbing pots in the kitchen, and washing windows, and nobody had paid the least bit of attention to a poorly dressed peasant girl with a thick woolen shawl wrapped around her head. To be extra safe, Maya had even smeared some soot on Gala's face—a look that Gala didn't particularly like, but accepted as a necessity in light of what had occurred at the market.

Now, after a full day of physical labor, her back was aching and her hands were beginning to blister from gripping the rough broom handle. Although her injuries healed quickly, she still disliked the feeling of pain. Cleaning was really not fun at all,

Gala decided, determined to finish this particular task and then rest. She couldn't imagine how most common women worked like this day in and day out.

A few times she had tried to do magic again, emboldened by her tremendous success at the market. However, to her unending frustration, it seemed like she still had no control over her abilities. She couldn't even cast a simple spell to get a pot clean; instead, she'd nearly rubbed her palms raw scrubbing it with all her strength.

"Gala, are you still cleaning?" Esther's voice interrupted Gala's thoughts. The old woman had managed to approach Gala without her noticing.

"Almost done," Gala said wearily. She was exhausted and all she wanted to do was collapse into her bed upstairs.

"Oh, good." Esther gave her a wide smile. "Are you ready to help prepare dinner?"

Gala felt a trickle of excitement that battled with her exhaustion. She had never cooked before, and was dying to try it. "Of course," she said, ignoring the way her muscles protested every movement.

"Then come, child, let me introduce you to the cook."

* * *

By the time Gala got back to the room, she could barely walk. Pausing to wash some of the sweat and grime off her hands and face, she collapsed on her bed.

"So did you enjoy cooking dinner?" Maya was sitting on the cot in the corner, calmly knitting another shawl. "Did you find it as fun and educational as you hoped?"

Staring at the ceiling, Gala considered her question for a minute. "To be honest with you, no," she admitted. "I was cutting up an onion, and my eyes began tearing up. Then they brought in the dead birds, and I couldn't look at them. They were plucking out their feathers, and the whole thing was utterly horrible. And then carrying around all those heavy pots and pans . . . I really don't know how those women in the kitchen do it every day. I don't think I would be happy doing that my entire life."

"Most peasants don't have a choice," Maya said. "If a woman is pretty, like you, then she has more options. She can find a wealthy man to take care of her. But if she doesn't have the looks—or the aptitude for sorcery—then life is hard. Maybe not always as hard as cooking dinner at a public inn, but it's not fun and pleasant. Childbirth alone is brutal. I'm glad I never had to go through that."

"Do men have it easier?"

"In some ways," Maya said as Esther entered the room. "In other ways, it's more difficult. Most commoners have to work very hard to grow their crops, plow their fields, and take care of their livestock. If a job is too difficult for a woman to do, then she can ask her husband to help her. A man, however, can only rely on himself."

Gala nodded, feeling her eyelids getting heavy.

Maya's words began to blend together, and she felt a familiar lassitude sweeping over her body. She knew it meant she was falling asleep, and she welcomed the relaxing darkness.

* * *

Gala's mind awakened. Or, more precisely, she became self-aware for the first time.

'I can think' was her first fully coherent thought. 'Where is this?' was the second one.

She somehow knew that places were supposed to be different from where she found herself. She vaguely recalled visions of a place with colors, shapes, tastes, smells, and other fleeting sensations—sensations that were absent in here. There were other things here, however—things she didn't have names for. The world around her didn't seem to match her mind's expectations. The closest she could describe it was as darkness permeated by bright flashes of light and color. Except it wasn't light and color; it was something else, something she had no equivalent name for.

There were also thoughts out there. Some belonging to her, some to other things—things that were nothing like her. Only one stream of thought was vaguely similar to her own.

She wasn't sure, but it seemed like that stream of thought was seeking her, trying to reach out to her.

Waking up with a gasp, Gala sat up in bed, looking around the dark room.

"What happened, child?" Esther asked, putting down the book she had been reading by candle light. "Did you have a bad dream?"

"I don't think so," Gala said slowly. "I think I was dreaming of a time right before my birth."

Esther gave her a strange look and returned to her book.

Gala lay back down and tried to calm her racing heartbeat. This was the first time she had dreamed at all—and she wished Blaise was there, so she could talk to him about it. He would find this dream fascinating, since it had been about the Spell Realm.

Closing her eyes, she drifted off again, hoping her next dream would be about Blaise.

CHAPTER THIRTY-SIX

❋ BLAISE ❋

The confrontation with Ganir left Blaise feeling strangely unsettled. Had the old man been genuine in offering his help? He'd seemed so shocked when Blaise had told him about the vote that Blaise had almost believed his lies.

The Council didn't know about Gala—unless Ganir had lied about that too. But if he hadn't, and if the Council was not involved, then who had been following Blaise that day? Thinking about it, Blaise decided that it could just as easily have been one of Ganir's spies; the old sorcerer was famous for having his tentacles everywhere.

Ganir clearly had some plans for Gala—that much was obvious to Blaise. The Council Leader was far from a fool; he, more than most, would see the potential in an intelligent magical object that had assumed human shape. Of course, Blaise had no intention of letting Gala become Ganir's tool. No matter what Blaise himself had intended for her originally, she was a person, and he needed to make sure she was treated as such.

Walking back to his study, he sat down at his desk, trying to figure out what to do next. If the Council didn't know about Gala, then there was still some time. Somehow Blaise had to get to her without leading Ganir there. His experiments with the Spell Realm were clearly not the answer; it would take too long to perfect something so complicated.

Blaise needed some way to evade whoever was watching his house.

Pondering the problem, he wondered if it would be possible to increase the speed of his chaise. If he could go significantly faster than his pursuer, then he could outrun the spy and collect Gala before anyone caught up to them.

Suddenly, a crazy idea occurred to him. What if, instead of flying, he teleported himself part of the way? If the teleportation was over a sufficiently short distance, it would be significantly safer, reducing the odds of materializing someplace unexpected. In fact, he could always teleport to a spot that he could see with enhanced vision—and from there, he could do it again and again. This would make the trip significantly shorter in length, and make him impossible to track.

The only problem would be the complexity of the code he would need to write—but Blaise was up for the challenge.

CHAPTER THIRTY-SEVEN

❊ BARSON ❊

Walking into Ganir's chambers, Barson forced himself to keep his face expressionless.

"You summoned me?" He purposefully omitted any honorific due to the head of the Council—a subtle insult that he was sure Ganir would not miss.

"Barson." Ganir inclined his head, foregoing Barson's military title as well.

"How may I be of assistance?" Barson asked in an overly polite tone. "Should I put down another small rebellion for you?"

Ganir's mouth tightened. "About that. I regret that I was misinformed about the situation in the north. The person responsible for this grievous error has been dealt with."

"Of course. I would've expected no less from you." Barson would've done the same thing in Ganir's place. The old sorcerer clearly didn't want any witnesses to his treachery.

"I have a small task for you," the Council Leader said. "There is a sorceress who is causing some disturbances in Kelvin's territory. I'd like you to take a few of your best men and bring her to me, so we could have a discussion."

Barson did his best to conceal his surprise. "You wish me to bring in a sorceress?"

"Yes," Ganir said calmly. "She's young and shouldn't present much of a challenge. You can just talk to her and convince her to come to Turingrad. That might be the best way. Of course, if she's reluctant, then you have my leave to use whatever methods of persuasion you deem necessary."

Barson inclined his head in agreement. "It shall be done as you wish."

* * *

Leaving Ganir, Barson walked through the Tower halls, trying to make sense of the Council Leader's request. The sorceress in Kelvin's territory had to be the same one Larn had informed him about—the mystery woman who could supposedly perform miracles. Why did Ganir want her detained? And why would he send the Guard to do it? Sorcerers usually dealt with their own affairs, not wanting to seem vulnerable to outsiders—not even to the Guard. The precedent of non-sorcerers subduing one of the elite would be something most in the Tower would find frightening.

There were only two reasons Barson could think of for Ganir's request: the old sorcerer was either trying to keep this matter hidden from others on the Council, or it was another ploy to send the Sorcerer Guard into a potentially deadly situation. Barson did not for a second believe Ganir's claim of a 'grievous error.' It was obvious the old man had somehow caught wind of Barson's plans and was doing his best to sabotage him.

Of course, it was also possible that Ganir had staged this whole thing in the hopes that Barson would refuse to follow his orders, thus giving him cause to take up action against Barson at the Council level. No doubt the Council Leader thought that if he eliminated the immediate threat of Barson and his closest lieutenants, the rest of the Guard would return to being the sorcerers' loyal tool.

Approaching his chambers, Barson was surprised to find Augusta standing by his door, about to knock. She looked beautiful, but surprisingly anxious.

"I need to speak with you," she said as he got closer.

"Of course." Barson smiled, his heart beating faster at her nearness. "Come inside. We'll talk."

Opening the door, he led her into his room. However, before he could so much as kiss her, she started to pace back and forth in the middle of the room.

Barson leaned against the wall, waiting to see what was on her mind.

She stopped in front of him. "Ganir will summon you," she said, sounding worried. "He'll want to send you on a mission to Kelvin's territory."

"Oh?" Barson did his best to look mildly interested. Augusta was clearly unaware that he had just seen Ganir, and he was curious to hear what she was about to say.

"It's a different kind of a mission. He will tell you that you are to apprehend a dangerous sorceress."

"A sorceress?" Barson continued pretending ignorance. This was a serious stroke of luck. Perhaps Augusta would give him the information he needed.

"Yes," she said, looking up at him. "A powerful sorceress that Ganir wants to use for his own purposes."

"And what purposes would those be?"

"He wants to replace me with her on the Council," Augusta said, giving him a steady look. "As you probably know, Ganir and I don't get along very well."

That wasn't what Barson had been expecting to hear. "Is that right?" he asked softly, lifting his hand to brush a stray lock of hair off her face. Was she lying to him right now? For someone who didn't get along, she and Ganir had certainly been seeing a lot of each other.

Augusta nodded, reaching up to capture his hand with her own, squeezing it lightly. "It's the truth. And that's why I want to ask you for a favor." She paused, holding his gaze. "I don't want her brought in alive."

Barson couldn't conceal his shock. "You want me to go against the Council Leader and kill a sorceress?"

"She's not what she seems," Augusta said, her hand tightening around his palm. "You would be doing the entire world a favor by getting rid of her." Her voice held a note of fear that startled Barson.

He stared at her, trying to figure out what it all meant. "You are asking me to go against the Council Leader and to commit the greatest crime of all—murdering a sorcerer," he said slowly. "You do realize the consequences of this?"

She nodded, her eyes burning with some strange emotion. "I know what I am asking you to do. If you do this for me, Barson, I will be forever in your debt." Her hand still held his own, her tight grip betraying her desperation.

Barson did his best to conceal his reaction to her words. "We will be in this together then, right?" he asked quietly, curving his other palm around her cheek. "If Ganir becomes my enemy as a result, you will be on my side?"

"Always." Augusta held his gaze without flinching.

"Then consider it done," Barson said. He could hardly believe this turn of events. He had been wondering how to get Augusta to join his cause, and she just jumped into bed with him herself—figuratively this time.

Her face lightened, and her grip on his hand eased. Standing up on tiptoes, she kissed him softly on the lips. "Be careful," she murmured, reaching up to stroke the side of his face. "Make it look like she resisted so violently that you and your men had no choice but to kill her. It might even turn out to be true."

"Just how powerful is this sorceress?" Barson asked, his mind turning to the upcoming quest despite the distraction of Augusta's touch. He didn't like the idea of killing a woman, but he suppressed the feeling. A sorceress could be just as powerful as her male counterparts—and potentially deadlier than a hundred of his men. He remembered how useful Augusta had been during the peasant rebellion, and he knew that it would require more than a few swords and arrows to win this fight.

"She's powerful," Augusta admitted quietly, looking up at him. "I don't know just how powerful she is, but I want you to be ready for the worst. I will also prepare some spells to make sure you and your soldiers are well-protected, both physically and mentally, against whatever attacks she might launch against you."

"That would be helpful," Barson said. Although Dara had already given him some protective spells, Augusta was a stronger sorceress, and he would welcome the additional protection for his men.

"I also have a gift for you." Taking a step back, she reached into a pocket in her skirt and took out what looked like a pendant. "This will enable me to see everything that happens in a special mirror," she said, handing it to him.

Barson took the pendant and put it on his commode. "I will wear it when we depart," he promised. It would be somewhat limiting to have his lover watching him, but it would also strengthen their alliance.

For now, though, he wanted to reinforce their bond in a different way. Reaching for Augusta, he drew her toward him.

* * *

"You must let me come." Dara gave him an imploring look. "Barson, let me go with you."

"For the hundredth time, you're not going." Barson knew his tone was sharp, and he softened it a bit before continuing. "It's too dangerous, sis. If anything were to happen to you . . ." He couldn't even complete that horrifying thought. "Besides, you know you're far too important to our cause. If you got hurt, who would continue recruiting for us? You know what happened when Ganir found out I was meeting with those five sorcerers."

His sister stared at him in frustration. "I would be fine—"

"No, there's no guarantee of that." Barson shook his head. "I will not put you in danger like that. Besides, you know that if we are to overtake the Council, we have to be able to fight them. We need to start testing the waters now, to see how my army would fare against one of them. This is a perfect opportunity because we just have one sorceress to deal with, not the entire lot of them."

She still looked unhappy, but she knew better than to argue further. Once Barson made up his mind, there was very little anyone could do to change it.

"So did you have a chance to look at the defensive spells Augusta put in place?" Barson asked, changing the subject.

Dara nodded. "She did a superb job. She must really care about you. The spell that she put on your armor—and on your men in general—will protect you against most elemental attacks, as well as against many that could tamper with your mind. Her anti-Shriek defense, in particular, is a masterpiece."

Barson smiled. He liked the idea of Augusta caring about him.

"Why doesn't she come with you?" Dara asked, looking at him curiously. "If this mission is so important to her, why doesn't she come along?"

"And openly go against Ganir?" Barson's smile widened. "No, Augusta is too smart to do that. There is a Council meeting coming up, and if she's not there, Ganir will know immediately something is going on. My men have explicit orders from the Council Leader to go and capture this sorceress, and if she happens to resist arrest . . ." He shrugged his broad shoulders. "Well, these things happen. It would be much tougher to explain a dead sorceress if Augusta were there—or you, for that matter."

"But you're bringing almost your entire army," Dara protested, "not the few men that Ganir suggested. Won't he be suspicious of that fact?"

Barson chuckled. "How many men I take on a military mission is entirely my prerogative. Ganir doesn't have any say in that."

"Do you think he did it on purpose again?" Dara asked. "Telling you to take just a few of your best men while sending you against a powerful sorceress?"

"I'm not sure," Barson admitted. "It sounds like Ganir genuinely needs this sorceress, but at the same time, I know he'd love to have me and my closest men perish in battle. Maybe it's a win-win proposition for him. If we bring her, he gets what he wants. And if we die during this mission, he will get rid of what he perceives to be a threat—and there will be other opportunities for him to capture her."

"I still wonder why he hasn't killed us all outright," Dara mused, "or gone to the Council with his suspicions."

"Because I don't think he realizes the full extent of our plans," Barson said. "He probably thinks I'm just an overambitious soldier with fantasies of grandeur—"

"That is what you are," Dara interrupted, smiling.

"No." Barson shook his head. "I don't do fantasies. I make plans. Ganir, like all the rest of them, underestimates us. But even if he does have his suspicions, he's too smart to act on them openly. He doesn't know how many supporters we have, or how deep the conspiracy runs. If he openly accuses us of treason, my men will not stand idly by—nor will those we convinced to join our cause. There will be war—a real civil war—and I don't think Ganir is ready for that."

Dara frowned, an anxious look appearing on her face.

"What is it, sis? Are you doubting our plans again?"

"I can't help it," Dara admitted. "Even with all our allies, going up against the Council sounds like an impossible mission."

"You're right." Barson smiled at her. "We're not ready yet. However, if we can get Augusta to join us, that would significantly increase our odds of success."

"Do you really think she would join us? She's part of the Council."

"She has already joined us; she just doesn't realize it yet. Her request goes against my orders—orders that come directly from the Council Leader—which means that we are now both involved in a treasonous conspiracy."

Dara considered that for a moment. "Yes, I could see that. And with her on our side, things would be different."

Barson nodded. He could already see it—the aftermath of the eventual power shift. He would be king and Augusta his queen. Both of them of noble blood, as rulers should be.

"Be careful on this mission, Barson." Dara looked unusually worried. "I don't have a good feeling about this."

Barson gave his sister a reassuring smile. "Don't worry, sis. All will be well. It's just one sorceress. How bad could it get?"

And walking out of Dara's house, he headed back to the Tower, where his men were already preparing to depart.

CHAPTER THIRTY-EIGHT

※ GALA ※

On the day of the Coliseum games, Gala made the decision to venture out of the inn again. Over the past three days, she had done every chore imaginable, from emptying chamber pots (at which point she truly understood the concept of disgust) to making cheese out of the milk that farmers delivered to the inn every morning. While most of the tasks were interesting in their own way—and Gala turned out to be surprisingly good at them—she was beginning to feel caged, a prisoner in the inn where Maya and Esther insisted they stay while waiting for Blaise.

"I am going to attend the games today," she told Esther, ignoring the anxious expression that immediately appeared on the old woman's face. "They say the Coliseum is closing after this, and I would like to see the games at least once."

"I don't think you'd like those games, child," Esther said, frowning. "Besides, what if someone recognizes you?"

Gala took a deep breath. "I understand and respect your concern," she said, determined to allay her guardians' fears. "I considered it thoroughly, and I think it's safe. It has been several days since the market, and nobody has recognized me thus far. The disguise you've given me is such that nobody even looks at me twice. I'm just a peasant girl working at the inn, and nobody will think anything different if I attend the games today. I'll wear the shawl to the Coliseum as well."

Esther sighed. "Child, you are obviously a very talented sorceress and you seem to be getting wiser with every hour that goes by, but Blaise wants us to stay hidden. Here at the inn, we're just a couple of old women with a young niece who's trying to earn a little coin by helping out. I worry about you in a public venue, child. Things seem to happen around you that I don't understand. I don't know how you do what you do, but we can't draw any more attention to ourselves."

"I understand," Gala said soothingly. "But trust me, I have considered all the positives and negatives, and I strongly feel that it will be worth it for me to go there. This kind of event is a rare opportunity, and I must see it for myself since it's the last time the games are taking place."

Esther shook her head in resignation. "Arguing with you is like arguing with Blaise," she muttered, putting on her own shawl. "You two are impossible with all your smooth talk and reason. I don't know what all those positives and negatives are, but I do know it's a bad idea to go. Obviously, I can't stop you any more than I can stop a force of nature."

Gala just smiled in response, knowing she'd gotten her way.

As the three of them were walking out of the inn, she wondered how one would literally stop a force of nature. She'd read about the horrible ocean storms that surrounded Koldun, and now she was curious if those could be stopped. The mainland was protected from these storms by a ridge of mountains all around, but on rare occasions, the storms still crossed the mountains and caused many deaths. Of course, if the mountains could stop the storms, a proper—if complex—spell could likely do the same.

"So far, so good," Maya said as they passed by a crowd of young people and no one paid them any attention. "Maybe you were right, Gala. Just keep your shawl on at all times."

Gala nodded, pulling the shawl tighter around her head. She didn't like the feel of the scratchy material, but she accepted the necessity of wearing it. After all, if it hadn't been for her own actions at the market, she wouldn't have needed the disguise outside the inn at all.

* * *

The Coliseum was the most majestic structure Gala

had ever seen. Maya had managed to get them seats toward the bottom of the huge amphitheater, closer to the stage, and Gala could barely contain her excitement as the start of the games approached.

A drumbeat began at first, followed by some strange, wonderfully energetic music. Gala was mesmerized. A gate slowly opened at the bottom of the amphitheater, and a dozen barrels rolled out, with people balancing on top of them, gripping the barrels with their bare feet. The crowd cheered, and Gala watched in fascination as the acrobats began to perform incredible feats on top of those barrels, coordinating their actions with stunning precision.

More performers came out of the gate, carrying large baskets of fruit that Gala recognized as melons. They threw the melons at the acrobats, and the performers caught the fruit and started juggling it, all the while moving in precise circles all around the arena.

Staring at the intricate flight path of the juggled fruit, Gala felt her mind going into an unusual half-absent, half-euphoric state. She was seeing the exact mathematical patterns that governed the trajectories of the flying melons, along with ones required to keep the barrels balanced, all the while the musical beat and melody had its own harmonious set of vibrations that the jugglers were in sync with. It was so amazing she almost felt like she was one with the acrobats—like she could walk out there, ride a barrel, and juggle a dozen fruits herself to the music.

Grinning, she watched the acrobats performing

their tricks, happy that she hadn't listened to Maya and Esther about attending the event. If she hadn't seen this, she was sure she would've regretted it for life.

By the time the next act came out, Gala was laughing and thoroughly enjoying herself like the rest of the crowd. To her surprise, instead of people, the next performers were bears—wild animals she'd read about in one of Blaise's books.

Two large beasts rolled out on barrels. It was amusing, and at first, Gala continued laughing—until she saw a man with a thick mustache standing in the middle of the stage. He was cracking a long whip all around the bears, and every time he did so, the animals seemed to flinch, reacting to the sharp sound.

Frowning, Gala realized that the bears didn't enjoy being there—that, unlike the acrobats, they didn't thrive on the attention of the crowd. In fact, from what she could tell, all they wanted was to get off those silly barrels and rest, but every time one of them faltered, the ugly crack of the whip sounded, and the animals continued rolling around on stage.

"Why do they make those bears do that?" she whispered to Esther.

"Because it is fun to watch?" Esther whispered back.

"I don't like it," Gala muttered under her breath, unhappy that the animals were forced to do something that clearly went against their nature.

"Should we leave then?" Maya asked hopefully.

"No." Gala shook her head. "I want to see what happens next."

After the bears left the arena, the next act was that of a man swallowing fire, followed by a group of young women dancing in skimpy, colorful costumes. Gala greatly enjoyed all of it, relieved that no more animals were involved.

And just as she was about to decide that the Coliseum games were the best entertainment she could imagine, a voice echoed throughout the arena, cutting through the excited chatter of the crowd. "Ladies and Gentlemen, now is the moment you have all been waiting for." There was a drumroll. "I give you . . . the lions!"

The crowd went silent, all their attention focused on the stage. Gala waited to see what would emerge as well, some intuition making her stomach tighten unpleasantly.

The gate opened again, and a dozen men dressed in heavy armor came out, dragging heavy chains behind them. At the other end of those chains were the lions—the most beautiful creatures Gala had ever seen.

The chains were hooked to choking collars with spikes that were digging deeply into the animals' necks. In obvious pain, roaring and screaming, the lions were forced to walk toward the middle of the arena. Once more than a dozen lions were there, the armored men attached the chains to the hooks in the ground and hurried away, poking the lions with long spears to keep the animals from attacking them. This seemed to infuriate the beasts even more, and their roars grew in volume, causing some women in the crowd to squeal in excitement.

Her horror and disgust growing with every moment, Gala watched as the gates opened yet again, letting in a group of men into the arena. Unlike the guards before, these men were armed with nothing more than a few short, rusty-looking swords. They stumbled out into the arena, several of them tripping over their own feet, and Gala realized that they had been pushed out—that they didn't want to be there any more than the poor lions. The expressions on the men's faces were those of fear and panic.

Gala's heart jumped into her throat as two lions began to stalk one of the men in the arena. He was backing away, waving his sword at them, his motions desperate and clumsy—and Gala realized that *this* was the entertainment.

The lions and the people were about to fight to the death.

A rage more powerful than anything Gala had ever felt before started building inside her. It filled her until all she could see, all she could focus on, was the terrifying scene about to unfold.

"Stop," she whispered, barely knowing what she was saying. With the corner of her eye, she could see Maya and Esther looking at her worriedly, feel them tugging at her sleeve, trying to lead her away, but it was as though her feet grew roots. She was frozen in place, unable to do anything but watch the hideous spectacle below.

A loud roar, then a blur of yellow... A lion pounced, tackling a man to the ground, and Gala felt the now-familiar sensation of losing control, of letting that other, unknown part of herself take over. She was vaguely aware that something inside her was calculating the distance from her seat to the middle of the arena—and then she was out of her seat, floating toward her destination.

Everything seemed to grow silent. Even the lions stopped roaring, turning their heads to watch the amazing sight of a human girl flying through the air. It was so quiet, Gala could hear the clinking of chains as the lions moved toward the center of the arena where she was about to land, leaving their prey without a second glance.

And then Gala was among them, surrounded by the beautiful, fierce creatures. She knew they could be dangerous, but she didn't feel any fear. Instead, all she felt was wonder. Without conscious thought, she reached out and touched the gorgeous animal closest to her. His fur felt rough, almost bristly, but underneath, the lion was warm—as warm as Gala herself. In that moment, she knew that they were one and the same—both flesh and bone, a manifestation of thought and matter in the Physical Realm.

Reaching out to the lion with her mind, she tried to reassure him, to tell him she was a friend, here to help them. And the lion seemed to understand. Purring, the beast lay down in front of her, his long whiskers pleasantly tickling her ankle.

Bending down, Gala touched the chocker around

the lion's neck. The animal whimpered, and she willed the chains and the chocker removed, desperate to free the majestic creature. With a loud clang, all the instruments of feline torture came off, not just on the lion next to her but on all of them.

The lions roared as one, and then the biggest one came up to her. Still dazed and feeling no fear, Gala extended her hand to him, smiling as he licked her palm with his rough tongue.

Slowly beginning to calm down, she became aware of murmuring in the crowd. Looking up, she saw everyone watching her—and realized what she had done. She had lost control again, and she had done it in the most public venue possible.

Her hand instinctively rose to touch her shawl, but she felt her hair blowing in the breeze instead. Her disguise was gone, the shawl lying in a heap on the floor of the arena. It must've fallen off at some point without her noticing.

Gala's breathing quickened. Thousands of eyes were staring at her right now. Blaise had asked her to be discreet, and she'd failed him again and again, in the most spectacular fashion. Her discomfort growing with every moment, Gala cast a frantic glance around her. The lions were calmly standing there, like a wall of animal flesh, and at the far side of the arena were the men who were supposed to fight them, all huddling together and watching her with shock and disbelief.

And Gala knew what she had to do. Her mind went to that place inside herself that she was now beginning to recognize—the place that had enabled her to do sorcery before. It was a far cry from being able to control her abilities, but at least now she recognized when she was about to use them.

As though from a distance, she felt she was about to do exactly what she'd done the other day at the dance. Focusing with all her might on Esther, Maya, and the lions, Gala let the desire to be away overwhelm her. Closing her eyes, she willed them all back to the place that had served as home for the past several days.

She willed them back to the inn.

And when she opened her eyes, that was exactly where they were all standing—she, the lions, and the two elderly women.

Unfortunately, in front of them, on the dead field of wheat, were hundreds of heavily armed soldiers.

They were headed for the inn, and seeing Gala materializing with her strange entourage gave them only the briefest of pauses. Their faces were hard, expressionless, and Gala suddenly knew that they were there for her—that what Blaise had feared had come to pass.

Her heart jumped, and in her desperate panic, her mind succeeded in doing something she had been futilely trying to do for the past several days: it reached out to Gala's creator.

"Blaise, I think we have been found."

CHAPTER THIRTY-NINE

※ BLAISE ※

Rubbing his eyes, Blaise fought his exhaustion in order to write yet another line of code. His brain was barely functioning, but he was only a few hours away from completing the spell that would take him to Gala in a series of teleporting leaps. His task was complicated by the fact that he'd only had a couple of pre-written spell cards with teleportation code, and that the code would have only applied to one person—not a person and his chaise flying in the air, as Blaise was planning to do. That meant that he was essentially doing the spell from scratch, which always took much longer.

Deep in thought, he got that sensation again, the one that preceded Contact.

"Blaise, I think we have been found."

As though a glass of cold water had been thrown into his face. Blaise jumped up from his chair, his heart hammering. The voice had been Gala's, and it had spoken clearly in his head. He was so shocked he didn't even have a chance to ponder the fact that Gala had somehow altered the Contact spell enough that her actual voice had sounded in his mind.

There was no more time to sit and finish the teleportation spell. He had to get to Gala, and he had to do it now.

Grabbing his Interpreter Stone and the spell cards he had been painstakingly working on, Blaise ran out of the house. He had enough of the spell done by now that he would be able to tele-jump a good portion of the way to Neumanngrad. The rest of the way he would fly. It would be faster than finishing the spell right now.

Jumping onto his chaise, Blaise rose up into the air and quickly fed one of the cards into the Stone. He didn't even bother to look behind him to see if he was being followed. Now that Gala had been found, it didn't matter anymore. All he cared about was getting to her as quickly as possible.

When he materialized a few miles away, he looked ahead with his enhanced vision, making sure his path was clear, and quickly scribbled the next set of coordinates onto a pre-written card. Then he fed that into the Stone too.

By the time he ran out of cards, he was still a distance away. Cursing, he tried to get his chaise to go faster, his blood running cold at the thought of Gala being there with only two old women to protect her. He had been a fool to let her go see the world on her own, and he would never make that mistake again. Whatever happened next, they would be together, he mentally vowed to himself.

As he was getting closer to his destination, he heard thunder and saw large clouds forming. The first raindrops hit his skin soon thereafter, quickly turning into a torrential downpour. Below, Blaise could see the parched ground greedily absorbing the water—the first such rain since the drought had begun.

Squinting, he peered through the wall of water, trying to see what lay ahead. And in the distance, he spotted the inn.

What he saw there shook him to the very core of his being.

CHAPTER FORTY

✳ GALA ✳

Cornered. They were cornered.

The word hammered inside Gala's skull as she stared at the soldiers moving swiftly toward her. Out of the corner of her eye, she could see Esther and Maya frozen in place, shock and fear reflected on their pale faces. Even the lions seemed dazed, disoriented by being teleported so suddenly from place to place.

She had gotten them out of the Coliseum and brought them into a situation that seemed a thousand times worse.

Closing her eyes, Gala tried to will herself and her companions away, but when she opened them, she was still standing there. Her magical abilities, never reliable, had apparently deserted her again. Though she felt that part of her mind churning, she couldn't control it enough to teleport them this time.

A surge of panic sharpened her vision. Gala could suddenly see everything, right down to each mole and scar on the soldiers' faces. Instead of one big formation, they were organized into small groups, each one with archers in the middle and men with large two-handed shields standing in a semi-circle at the front. They looked grim and determined, the archers already drawing their arrows and the swordsmen holding the hilts of their weapons tightly, their muscular forearms tense in anticipation.

They were ready for battle.

No, Gala thought in desperation. She couldn't let this happen. If the soldiers were there for her, then she needed to face them herself. She couldn't allow Maya, Esther, or the lions to get pulled into this.

Gathering her courage, she began walking toward the army.

"Gala, wait!"

She could hear Esther yelling behind her, and she picked up the pace, wanting to leave the old women far behind. "Stay there," she yelled back, turning her head to see the lions following her and Maya and Esther trailing in their wake. Gala willed them to stop, to turn back, but her magic was no more in her control than the dual emotions of fear and desperation that made her whole body shake.

Not knowing what else to do, she began running—running straight at the armed men. It felt liberating in a strange way, to just run as fast as she could, and Gala felt her speed picking up with each step until she was almost flying toward the wheat field, leaving her entourage far behind.

One of the small groups of soldiers stepped forward, putting up their shields as though expecting an attack. At the same time, the archers released their arrows, turning the sky black. Even with her mind in turmoil, Gala could estimate the current path of the deadly sticks, could calculate the trajectory adjusted for gravity and wind. She could tell that many arrows would hit her and a few would even reach her friends.

Still running, she felt a growing fury. It exploded out of her in a blast of fire that covered the sky and the ground all around her. The deadly hail of arrows disintegrated, turning to ash in a matter of seconds, but the soldiers remained standing. Their shields were emitting a faint glow that somehow protected the men from the heat as a cloud of ash settled magnificently over the burning field.

Unfazed, Gala kept running. She felt unstoppable, invincible, and when the group of soldiers loomed in front of her, she couldn't slow down. Instead she slammed into them at full speed, not even feeling the impact of the metal shields hitting her body.

The shields and the men holding them flew into the air, as though they were made of straw. Their bodies landed heavily several yards away and lay there in a heap of broken bones and bruised flesh.

The realization of what she had done washed over Gala in a terrible wave, breaking through whatever madness had her in its grip. Stopping in her tracks, she stared in horror at the carnage she had caused.

Before she could begin to process it all, she heard a deep, harsh voice barking out orders, and she turned just in time to see a soldier running at her, his sword raised.

"Stop," Gala whispered, holding out her hand, palm out. "Please stop . . ."

But he didn't. Instead, he came at Gala, his weapon swinging in a deadly arc.

She jumped back, missing the blade by a hair.

He swung again, and she dodged this, too. His movements were like a strange dance, and she matched him as she would a dancing partner. He swung at her elbow, and she moved back her arm; he swung at her neck, and she dropped down to the ground before springing up again. He moved his foot forward; she moved hers back. He started moving faster, stabbing and slashing at her with lightning speed, and she felt her body adjusting, responding to his speed with increasing quickness of her own. Out of the corner of her eye, she could see more soldiers approaching, though they were still a distance away.

It didn't seem real, any of it, and Gala could feel her mind going into a new kind of mode. Now it was as though she was watching herself from a distance. Rather than just reacting to the soldier's movements, it was almost like she was predicting what he would do based on the subtle movements of his muscles and minute changes in his facial expressions.

Still caught up in her deadly dance, she sensed someone approaching her from the back. It was there in the dilation of her opponent's pupils and a flash of reflection in his eyes. And just as the other soldier took a swing at her, she bent in time to feel the sword swishing through the air where her head had been just a second ago.

Now she was up against two attackers, but it didn't seem to matter. She was still able to dodge their swords. One swung at her arm and the other at her thigh, and her body contorted in a way she'd never had it bend before. It was uncomfortable for a moment, but effective—the soldiers' swords missed her again.

That was when she heard the first growl and a scream. A lion jumped at the soldiers, and she felt its agony as some soldier's sword pierced its paw. At the same time, she heard the pained cry of the soldier whose throat got ripped out by the lion's sharp teeth.

Yet another soldier joined Gala's opponents. Now she was up against three, but she was learning their movements and the dance was becoming easier, not harder. It seemed like she could move like them, only better and faster. More efficient.

More lions pounced at the soldiers. Without even knowing how, Gala could feel the animals' movements. It was as though a strange link was forming between her and the beasts, and suddenly, impossibly, some part of Gala's brain seemed to be correcting the lions' movements, making them dodge the soldiers' swords just as Gala was dodging the attacks that came her way. At the same time, she was keeping the lions contained, preventing them from tearing at the soldiers' flesh as the animals hungered to do.

Filled with bloodlust, the lions fought her control, and she felt the link between them weakening as more soldiers joined in the fight. She was now dodging five attacks at once. A sword reached one of the lions, brutally slicing through its back, and Gala felt renewed fury—only she couldn't tell if it was her own or the lion's.

And at that moment, she heard Maya and Esther screaming in fear.

Her mind exploded with rage.

Gala was through with mere defense.

As the next soldier made his move, she grabbed his sword, wrenching it out of his hand with one swift motion and burying it in his chest. Pulling it out, she dodged the swing of her second attacker, and the sword in her hand went for his throat. She synchronized her deadly movements in such a way that when she dodged the third attacker's blow, his sword arm continued on, slicing open the shoulder of his comrade. And before the wounded soldier could even scream, Gala caught his falling sword, swinging both weapons in a fatal arc.

Two headless bodies fell to the ground as Gala remained standing, her mind still clouded by white-hot fury. Somewhere out there was a lion in its death throes, its agony maddening her further.

More soldiers attacked, and Gala's swords sliced through them with brutal precision. She didn't consciously control how her hands and body were moving; instead, it was almost as if she was someone else. Parry, thrust, slice, dodge—everything blended together as she fought to get to the animal whose pain she could feel. Men fell all around her, dropping like flies, and the ground turned red with blood.

Then four large soldiers loomed in front of her, moving with a speed unlike anyone else she had encountered thus far.

The biggest of them had a pendant around his neck.

CHAPTER FORTY-ONE

✳ BARSON ✳

Nothing was going according to plan. Barson watched incredulously as the beautiful young woman hacked her way through his men, fighting with superhuman strength and skill.

When he had first seen her appear out of thin air with her strange companions, he had known that the rumors were true—that she was a powerful sorceress indeed. Teleporting so many was an achievement that few, if any, members of the Council could match. How had a young woman he'd never heard of before managed such a feat?

For a moment, he'd hesitated, wondering if he was doing the right thing. To destroy something so beautiful would be a shame, yet he'd made a promise to Augusta—and he needed his lover on his side. Coming to a decision, he had ordered his men to attack.

They were already prepared for a different kind of battle; no army had met a sorcerer this way since the time of the Revolution. Of course, back then, nobody had developed the strategy he was about to test.

Instead of clustering together, he had his soldiers separate into small groups to minimize the chances of any one particular spell working on them all. He would never forget how easily Augusta had decimated the peasants' army, and he had no intention of letting his men meet the same fate. Unlike those poor souls, his army had protection from elemental spells and detailed instructions on how to handle unusual movements of the earth. Thus, when the girl had unleashed the most powerful fire spell he had ever seen, they had been spared.

What he had not counted on was encountering a master swordsman. Because that's what the girl had to be, despite her delicate appearance. She fought like a man possessed, like a demon of old fairy tales, with a skill and agility that possibly superseded his own— a skill that increased with every moment that passed. How was she learning so fast? What was she? There was a kind of calculated precision to her graceful movements that seemed almost . . . inhuman.

He noticed only one weakness. She seemed to get distracted when the lions and the old women were in danger. And as distasteful as it was, Barson knew what he had to do.

Giving the order to set the beasts on fire, he moved forward decisively with his best men.

She met them without even a hint of fear. Within

moments, Barson and his men were fighting for their lives. The girl was working two swords in her hands, thrusting at any hint of an opening, parrying every blow that came her way. The worst thing of all, however, was that she was adapting with every strike, getting faster and more efficient as the fight went on. If he hadn't been in mortal danger, Barson would have given anything to study her technique—because at this point, she was perfection itself, a virtuoso with a blade, her every move imbued with deadly purpose.

The first blood in this frantic confrontation came from a strike at Kiam's shoulder. A minute later, Larn was bleeding from his thigh. Furious, Barson put all his strength into a last desperate assault—and then he smelled the acrid odor of burning lion fur.

The girl shuddered, her concentration broken, and Barson finally saw an opening in her defense. One quick lunge, and his sword sliced open her belly, leaving behind a deep, gushing wound.

She screamed, dropping her weapons and clutching at her stomach.

Barson and his men moved in for the kill.

CHAPTER FORTY-TWO

※ GALA ※

Gala had experienced pain before, but nothing had prepared her for this.

The agony was debilitating. The man with the pendant—the man who seemed to fight like no other—had sliced her open.

Clutching her stomach, she could feel the warm flow of blood trickling through her fingers, and for the first time, she was struck by the realization that she could actually cease to exist.

No. Gala could not, would not accept that possibility.

Time seemed to slow. In the distance, she could hear the lions roaring and feel the pain of their burning flesh. She could also see the soldiers' blades moving ever so slowly toward her, ready to end her life.

In that brief moment of time, a million thoughts

ran through her mind. The pain in her wounded flesh was terrible, and the realization that she'd hurt the soldiers in a similar way added to her turmoil. Would she die now? Could she die? Thus far, her body did not behave as that of a regular woman, but it still had to be bound by some rules that were at least somewhat based on how human bodies worked. She got tired; she ate and slept. She got scared and happy, felt heat and cold. Would she be killed if those swords that were moving ever so slowly reached her body?

No, Gala decided. She could not risk letting that happen; she could not let them kill her. She loved existing too much. She had too much to see, to experience. She wanted to see Blaise again, to feel his kisses.

She also had the lions, Esther, and Maya to save.

Just as the swords of the four soldiers were about to pierce her flesh, she put all her energy into one last desperate blast. Focusing all her fury on the metal blades that had caused so much pain, she willed them gone with all her might.

And as whatever spell she thus unleashed started working, Gala felt a burst of agony unlike anything she'd known before. The lions roared, and she felt *their* pain and suffering, the screams of the soldiers adding to the chaos.

Through the haze clouding her mind, she understood what happened. She'd made all the swords on the field explode, driving deadly shards of metal through the soldiers' armor and into every bit of exposed flesh. Nobody had escaped unscathed—not the soldiers, not the lions, and not even Gala herself. Only Maya and Esther were sufficiently far away to be safe. Here on the field, the smoldering remnants of grass were covered with blood.

Dazed, Gala stared at the metal shards sticking out of her body. Somehow, seeing them made the pain worse. Falling to her knees, she threw back her head with an agonized scream. As though responding to her agony, the shards of metal came out of her body, hanging for a moment in the air before falling to the ground. All around her, the same thing was happening to the soldiers and the lions.

It didn't help the pain, however. Her vision blurring, Gala struggled to her feet. All she wanted to do now was get away, rise above this terrible field of slaughter before anyone recovered enough to attack her again. And that was when she felt her body slowly floating up from the ground.

Strong hands grabbed her leg as she was rising into the air, and Gala saw the soldier with the pendant—the one who'd wounded her—holding on to her with grim determination. His face and armor were covered in blood, but that didn't seem to stop him. She was far too weak to shake him off, and they floated up together, rising slowly into the air.

Below, Gala could see the battlefield. It was littered with bodies and soaked with blood. She had done this; she had caused all this pain and suffering. The realization was worse than the agony wracking her body.

Lifting her hands up to the sky, Gala watched the bright blue expanse. A sound escaped her throat, a sound that turned into something else. She couldn't stand the feel of blood on her hands; she needed to wash this nightmare away.

She began to cry. Sobs escaped her throat and tears ran down her face, her entire body shaking as it rose higher and higher above the ground. The soldier's hands tightened on her leg, his fingers brutally digging into her skin, but she couldn't bring herself to care, too consumed by her own horror and bitter regret.

A flash of bright light shocked her vision. It was followed by a loud boom and a rapidly darkening sky. Clouds appeared, veiling the sun, and the wind picked up. Another flash of light, another boom, and Gala realized that it was lightning and thunder. A storm was gathering, a weather phenomenon she'd only read about before.

The skies opened and the rain began, huge drops falling on Gala, soaking her to the skin. The cold wetness felt good on her overheated skin, washing away the blood and grime.

The rain also seemed to reinvigorate the big soldier hanging on to her leg. He let go with one hand and pulled out a dagger from somewhere, holding it against her thigh.

"Take us down," he ordered harshly. "Right now."

Gala tried to kick at him, but the dagger dug into her skin, and she could see the murderous intent on the man's face. He was determined to bring them down at any cost—even if doing so meant losing his own life.

Her body still gripped by unbearable pain, Gala instinctively reached out to the storm, feeling its fury deep in her bones.

Suddenly, there was another flash of light and an explosion of pain. Sparks flew, and Gala realized that a lightning bolt had struck the man's dagger, its force traveling into both of their bodies. The soldier's grip on her leg loosened . . . and he plummeted to the ground below.

Shocked and dazed, Gala continued floating for a moment before she found the strength to focus on something other than the pain. Remembering the thief she had healed, she tried to recall the way she felt then—the peace that had permeated every fiber of her being. And then she began to feel it again, the warm sensation that started deep inside her and radiated outward through her outstretched arms, intensifying with every moment that passed, the pain melding into pleasure, into a sense of warmth, light, and happiness.

She wanted to freeze this moment and feel this good forever.

Through the fog of pleasure, she felt unconsciousness slowly creeping in, and she could not fight it anymore.

She would fall into a pleasant dream, Gala thought, and blanked out.

CHAPTER FORTY-THREE

※ AUGUSTA ※

Exiting the Council meeting, Augusta hurried to her room, walking as fast as she could without actually running. During the best of times, Council meetings were far from her favorite activity, but the one today had been particularly intolerable. Jandison had yammered on and on, and all the while Augusta had been sitting there thinking about the fact that, at that very moment, Barson was probably getting rid of Blaise's abomination.

She wasn't afraid for him, exactly. Her lover was a force to be reckoned with on a battlefield, and she had used plenty of protective spells to aid him in his task. It was more that she was anxious to see the creature destroyed, permanently wiped out of existence. For the past two nights, she'd had nightmares, dreams of that thing growing more powerful and the ground turning red with blood from the carnage that it caused. She knew the dreams were just a product of her subconscious mind dwelling on the situation, but they were disturbing nonetheless.

It would be good to know that the issue was taken care of.

Walking into her quarters, Augusta headed straight to the mirror that would show her the battle through Barson's pendant. Sitting down in front of it, she took off the cover.

The image in front of her was that of a battle in progress. Augusta watched with a sense of gratification as the creature unsuccessfully used a fire spell against Barson's army. Augusta's defenses held, as she'd known they would.

However, as the battle continued, Augusta grew increasingly anxious. The thing was moving its body in unnatural ways, learning sword fighting with inhuman speed. Augusta knew of no sorcery that could allow someone to fight like that.

Soon, the battle became a massacre. The creature killed with horrible precision again and again, until all Augusta could see was blood and death. The fact that the monstrosity manifested itself in the form of a delicate young woman made the scene that much more macabre.

As Barson began moving toward the creature, Augusta felt her stomach drop. "No, don't," she whispered at the mirror, beginning to realize how much she'd underestimated this unnatural being.

And then Barson succeeded in wounding it.

Augusta jumped up, yelling in triumph—until she saw the creature perform its most destructive magic yet. Disregarding its own safety, it made all the swords shatter to bits, sending deadly pieces of metal flying everywhere.

"Barson, stop!" Augusta screamed as her lover— bleeding, but alive—grabbed on to the thing, floating upward with it. "Let go! Please, let go!"

He couldn't hear her, of course, and Augusta watched in horrified shock as the storm began and a lightning bolt speared through Barson's body. Her elemental protection spell had likely dampened the full effect of the strike, but the pain must've been unbearable, even for Barson. His hands unclasped, and he began falling to his death.

A few seconds later, the image in the mirror broke into a dozen pieces and went dark.

Letting out a scream of agonized rage, Augusta hit the mirror, over and over, until her hands were bleeding and the mirror lay shattered on the floor.

Sobbing, she sank to her knees.

She had done this. She had caused her own lover's death. If she had gone directly to the Council as soon as she'd learned about the creature, none of this would've happened, and Barson would still be alive. Keening in agony, Augusta rocked back and forth.

She had let her feelings for Blaise cloud her judgment, but she would not make that mistake again. Blaise was now dead to her—as dead as his creature would be when the full power of Koldun's sorcerers got unleashed upon it.

The thing was evil, and evil had to be stopped at all costs.

CHAPTER FORTY-FOUR

※ BLAISE ※

His heart pounding in his chest, Blaise flew as fast as he could. Out there, in the middle of the giant storm, was Gala. She was floating in the air, with a man hanging on to her legs. The ground was covered with bodies of soldiers. Blaise couldn't tell if they were dead or just severely wounded.

His chaise shook as he pushed it to its very limits, trying to go faster and faster. The wind from the storm was hampering his efforts, so he grabbed for his bag, fishing out the Interpreter Stone and a few cards. Frantically adding a few key parameters to the code, he fed the cards into the Stone and waited.

Immediately, a new wind picked up. It was weak compared to the insane forces Blaise assumed Gala had somehow unleashed, but it was blowing in exactly the direction he needed.

Next, Blaise took out a handkerchief. Ignoring the

DIMA ZALES

rain and the lightning, he did a verbal spell. When he was done, the handkerchief began to grow until it was more like a sheet. Another spell, and the sheet was attached to the back of the chaise, becoming an impromptu sail of sorts.

The chaise went faster, helped by the wind.

Lightning kept hitting the ground, and Blaise watched in horror as one bolt hit the man holding on to Gala. In the bright flash that followed, Blaise saw the man's face.

It was Barson, the Captain of the Sorcerer Guard—a man known to be a fighter without equal.

At the lightning strike, Barson's entire body jerked. Then he let go of Gala and began to fall.

A moment later, Blaise began to feel a strange sensation—a blissful warmth that somehow permeated his body despite the wind and rain lashing at his skin. All the tension drained out of him and was replaced with a kind of unusual calmness, a peace unlike anything he had ever experienced before. It was mesmerizing, hypnotic, and Blaise felt himself starting to drift under, his mind clouding with the intense pleasure.

A healing spell, he realized vaguely, his thoughts slow and sluggish, as though he was falling asleep. A healing spell like his mother used to do, only a thousand times more powerful. A healing spell that would make him forget everything if he allowed it.

No, Blaise thought, his nails digging into his skin. He couldn't let himself go under. Reaching for the letter opener he always carried in his bag, he pulled it

312

out and stabbed his palm. The pain was sharp and jarring for a moment, and then his flesh sealed itself, as though nothing had happened. He repeated the action, over and over. The bursts of pain prevented him from getting sucked into that mindless, blissful state.

Up ahead, he saw Gala starting to fall and felt the effects of the healing spell beginning to wane. The lightning and thunder eased, though the rain continued pouring at a steady pace.

Angling his chaise toward the ground, Blaise got underneath Gala's falling body just in time.

She landed on top of him, and Blaise caught her in his arms, pulling her close. She seemed to be unconscious but alive, her slim body soft and warm against his chest. Shaking, Blaise mentally thanked all his teachers, even the bastard Ganir, for encouraging and nurturing his mathematical gifts. Had the angle of his descent been even slightly different, Gala would've plummeted to the ground below.

Looking down at her exquisite face, Blaise bent down and gently kissed her lips, tasting the rain and the unique essence that was Gala. He couldn't believe she was finally here, with him, and he hugged her, trying not to crush her in his arms. Even dressed in a peasant outfit and with dirt marring her cheeks, she was beautiful enough to make him ache.

They descended slowly, and he saw the field fully for the first time. All around them, the soldiers of the Sorcerer Guard were beginning to stir, though many still had shards of metal sticking out of their armor. There were also lions walking around, a sight that would've surprised Blaise more if he hadn't been so overwhelmed with everything else. On the very edge of the field, he could see Maya and Esther. They had their arms around each other and were staring at the field with terrified expressions on their faces.

The chaise touched the ground, and Blaise climbed out, still holding Gala cradled in his arms. She shifted, making a soft noise, and then her eyes fluttered open.

Smiling, Blaise met her gaze.

"Blaise!" Her face lit up with joyous wonder. "You're here!"

"Yes," he said softly. "I'm here, and I am not going anywhere." Bending his head, he kissed her again. Her arms wound around his neck, and she pulled his head down, kissing him back with so much passion that Blaise felt a bolt of heat despite the cold rain that kept coming down. For the first time since Gala left, he felt alive—alive and craving her with every part of his being.

Before he could completely lose his mind, Blaise pulled back. As loath as he was to stop, he needed to take stock of the situation. "What happened here?" he asked, gently placing her on her feet.

Gala blinked, seemingly taken aback for a moment, then frantically looked around. "They're healed," she said in amazement, stepping back and pointing at the lions. "Look, Blaise, they are all healed!"

Blaise looked at the wild beasts that now seemed to be heading toward Maya and Esther. "That's good, I guess," he said, a bit uncertainly. Around them, he could see some of the soldiers slowly starting to get up.

"They're healed, too," Gala said, following his gaze. "I must have done it without meaning to." She sounded relieved, which struck Blaise as odd.

"I thought they were trying to kill you," he said. "What happened here today?"

And as they walked toward Maya and Esther through the field of dazed, but slowly recovering soldiers, Gala told him all about the fight and the incidents at the market and Coliseum.

Blaise listened in awe. He had known she would be powerful, but even he couldn't have imagined some of the things she would do. And she didn't even seem to have control over her powers yet.

"I'm sorry I left," Gala said as they were approaching the two older women. Her voice was filled with bitter regret. "I caused so much havoc and suffering . . . I can't control myself, Blaise. I should've stayed with you and tried to learn sorcery like you wanted me to do, instead of going off to see the world. None of this—" she motioned toward the bloody field, "—should've happened."

Blaise took her hand, squeezing it lightly. "Don't worry," he said quietly. "I will be with you from now on." Her hand felt small and cold within his own, and he realized how fragile she was despite her powers.

Gala nodded, and he could see that some of her earlier exuberance was no longer there. Even though only a few days had passed, she seemed different, more mature somehow. As they walked, he could see tears running down her face, mixing with the raindrops.

"Not all of them are moving," she said, looking at the fallen soldiers. "Blaise, I think I killed some of them." There was a note of poorly concealed horror in her voice.

Blaise again cursed himself for not being there to protect her. "You were defending yourself." He stopped, bringing her to a halt as well. Placing his hands on her wet cheeks, he met her grief-stricken gaze. "Gala, listen to me, this was not your fault."

"Of course it was," she said bitterly. "I did this. I killed those men."

"They were trying to kill you," Blaise said harshly. "They are the ones at fault, not you. If I had been here, I would've killed them all. You, at least, healed the survivors. That's more mercy than they deserve—"

"Gala!" Maya's shriek interrupted the moment, and they both turned toward the sound. The two women were standing a dozen yards away, surrounded by a circle of lions. "Gala, get these man-eating monsters away from us!"

To Blaise's surprise, a tiny smile appeared on Gala's face, and the lions lay down, curling into giant furry balls at Maya and Esther's feet.

"No," Esther said frantically, "don't make them

corner us—just make them go away." Turning to Maya, she said loudly, "And you, don't you realize that yelling at them might make them feel threatened?" The two women went on to bicker, and the lions merely raised their ears from time to time, content to ignore the humans.

"They seem to be fine," Blaise said to Gala when she turned her attention back to him. "You saved them, you know. I don't know what the soldiers would've done to them."

She nodded, her eyes still looking far too shadowed for his liking, and Blaise knew that it was little consolation to her right now, that she would never be able to completely forget the events of this terrible day.

CHAPTER FORTY-FIVE

※ BARSON ※

Barson was plummeting toward the ground when he felt the first wave of ecstasy washing over him. This must be what it feels like to die, he thought, as all pain left his body and a blissful peace took its place. It was unlike anything he had ever experienced before. All his wounds seemed to heal, the remaining shards of metal exiting his body as though pushed out by some invisible force.

Then he slammed into the ground.

The impact knocked all air out of his lungs. Black spots swimming in front of his vision, Barson fought to draw in a breath through the compressed cavity of his chest. He could see the pendant lying on the ground in front of him in pieces. It was right next to his armor-plated arm, which seemed twisted at an odd angle. He had a strange thought that he was broken too, just like the pendant.

Then the pain hit him in one massive wave. It felt like every bone in his body was shattered, every organ bruised and bleeding on the inside. His vision blurred, and hot nausea boiled up in his throat, but he fought the blackness that tried to suck him under. He couldn't, wouldn't allow himself to die like this.

And just as Barson felt that he would lose that fight, the pain began to lessen again, disappearing as miraculously as it did before. He could feel his body healing, mending, and it was the most amazing sensation—until that blissful peace hit again, bathing him in the exquisite warmth.

He couldn't fight the sweetness of the oblivion any longer, and he let the wave of pleasure sweep him under.

CHAPTER FORTY-SIX

※ GALA ※

"I want to leave this place," Gala told Blaise after the lions left Maya and Esther alone, curling up a few yards away instead.

Having Blaise here, with her, made her feel better, but she needed to get away from this field of carnage. Guilt, sharp and terrible, was gnawing at her insides. She had killed people today; she had cut short their existence. It was the worst crime Gala could think of, and she had committed it—not once, but many times today.

The different what-if scenarios kept running through her head. What if she had been able to just make them fall asleep? What if she had made their swords disappear instead of shattering into a thousand pieces? If she had been able to control her powers, she could've defended herself without resorting to murder.

"Yes," Blaise agreed. "We need to go. We might be able to hide in one of the other territories—"

"No," Esther interrupted, coming up to them. "You will be recognized—and now, so will she. No disguise will be able to hide her after this." She motioned toward the field.

Maya approached as well. "Esther is right. Besides, this one—" she pointed at Gala, "—starts doing insane sorcery whenever she's upset."

Gala stared at Maya, struck by the fact that the old woman was right. Her magic—her uncontrollable powers—were very much tied to her emotions. She wanted to kick herself for not making this obvious connection before.

"So what do you suggest instead?" Blaise frowned at Esther. "We can't go back to the village, and Turingrad is out of the question. As soon as the Council hears about this—and they will—they're going to be after us. As powerful as Gala is, the two of us don't stand a chance against the combined might of the Council."

Esther hesitated for a second. "There is one place they wouldn't look," she said slowly. "The mountains. That might be where we need to go."

A silence followed. Gala had read a little bit about the mountains that surrounded Koldun and protected the land from the brutal ocean storms. At no point did the books describe the mountains as a habitable place.

Blaise looked like he was considering the idea. "Well," he said finally, "it is just wilderness, but we might be able to survive there. It won't be comfortable, but I'm sure we'll manage—"

"I'm not sure if it's just wilderness," Maya said, looking frightened. "I've heard rumors."

"What rumors?" Gala asked, her natural curiosity awakening. She could picture herself in the forest with Blaise, surrounded by beautiful plants and animals, and the images were quite appealing. The lions would be happy there, too; she had been wondering how to set the magnificent creatures free without them eating anyone or getting hurt by frightened humans, and this seemed like the perfect solution.

"They say that people live there," Esther said, leaning in as though afraid someone would overhear her words. "They say that those people are free, that they don't belong to any sorcerers."

Blaise appeared surprised. "Why haven't I heard about this?"

"I imagine most sorcerers haven't heard about this," Maya said. "That's why those people are supposedly free. Rumors say many of them are from the northern territories, where the drought is especially bad, but some come from further south."

Gala looked at Blaise and the two women. Going to the mountains meant that she would be far away from the soldiers and anyone else seeking to harm her—and that she would never have to harm anyone else in return. "Let's go there," she said decisively. "Maybe we could help those people in exchange for their hospitality. Blaise, you could enhance their crops, right?"

Her creator gave her a warm smile. "Yes, indeed. Sounds like we have a plan."

* * *

Gala watched in fascination as Blaise worked on a spell to expand his chaise. The goal was to make it big enough to accommodate four people and thirteen lions.

When the enlarged object stood there, almost blocking the inn, they all got on, even the lions. Gala mentally guided the animals onto the object, making sure they didn't panic or growl at Maya and Esther— who were eyeing them quite warily, afraid of having the wild beasts so close. In contrast, Gala liked having the animals near, the proximity of their furry bodies making the chaise feel warm and cozy. Blaise did a quick spell to add a waterproof shield around the chaise, so they were also protected from the steadily falling rain.

As they rose into the air and began heading toward the mountains, Blaise turned to Gala with a strange expression on his face. "Gala," he said softly. "Are you seeing this?"

"Seeing what?" Gala asked. All she could see were the sheets of rain, coming down hard and turning everything grey. The storm was not as violent as before, but it seemed to stretch as far as the eye could see.

"The rain. It's rapidly spreading," Blaise said,

reaching out to take her hand. The look on his face as he gazed at her was tender and reverent. "Gala, I think you might have ended the drought."

SNEAK PEEKS

Thank you for reading! I hope you enjoyed the book. If you did, please mention it to your friends and social media connections. I would also be very grateful if you helped other readers discover the book by leaving a review on Amazon, Goodreads, or other sites.

The story of Gala, Blaise, Augusta, and Barson continues in *The Spell Realm*, which will be available soon. Additional works in progress include *Mind Awakening* and *The Thought Readers*. Please sign up for my newsletter at www.dimazales.com to learn when the next book comes out.

I love to hear from readers, so be sure to:
   -Friend me on Facebook:
   https://www.facebook.com/DimaZales
   -Like my Facebook page:
   https://www.facebook.com/AuthorDimaZales

-Follow me on Twitter:
https://twitter.com/AuthorDimaZales
-Follow me on Google+:
https://www.google.com/+DimaZales
-Friend or follow me on Goodreads:
https://www.goodreads.com/DimaZales

Thank you for your support! I truly appreciate it.

And now, please turn the page for sneak peeks into my upcoming works . . .

THE SORCERY CODE

EXCERPT FROM *MIND AWAKENING*

Author's Note: *Mind Awakening* is a science fiction novel. The excerpt and the description are unedited and subject to change.

* * *

Ethan remembers being shot in the chest. By all rights, he should be dead. Instead, he wakes up in a world that seems like futuristic paradise . . . as someone else.

Who is the real Ethan? The computer scientist he remembers being, or the world-famous genius everyone appears to think he is? And why is someone trying to kill him here, in this peaceful utopian society?

These are some of the questions he'll explore with his psychologist Matilda—a woman as beautiful as she is

327

mysterious. What is her agenda . . . and what is the Mindverse?

* * *

Ethan woke up.

For a moment, he just lay there with his eyes closed, trying to process the fact that he was still alive. He clearly remembered the mugging . . . and being shot. The pain had been awful, like an explosion in his chest. He hadn't known one could survive that kind of agony; he'd been sure the bullet had entered his heart.

But somehow he was still alive. Taking a deep breath, Ethan cautiously moved his arm, wondering why he wasn't feeling any pain now. Surely there had to be a wound, some damage from the shooting?

Yet he felt fine. More than fine, in fact. Even the pain from his rheumatoid arthritis seemed to be gone. They must've given him a hell of a painkiller in the hospital, he thought, finally opening his eyes.

He wasn't in a hospital.

As soon as that fact registered, Ethan shot up in bed, his heartbeat skyrocketing. There wasn't a single nurse or cardiac monitor in the vicinity. Instead, he was in someone's lavish bedroom, sitting on a king-sized bed with a giant padded headboard.

The fact that he could sit up like that was yet another shock. There weren't any tubes or needles sticking out of his body—nothing hampering his movements. He was wearing a stretchy blue T-shirt instead of a hospital gown, and the black pants that he could see under the blanket seemed to be rather comfortable pajamas.

Lifting his arm, Ethan touched his chest, trying to feel where the wound might be. But there was nothing. No pain, not even a hint of sensitivity. All he could feel was smooth, healthy pectoral muscle.

Muscle? Was that his imagination, or did his chest seem more muscular? Ethan was in decent shape, but he was far from a bodybuilder. And yet, as ridiculous as it was, there appeared to be quite a bit of muscle on his chest—and on his forearm, Ethan realized, looking down at his bare arms.

In general, his forearms didn't look like they belonged to him. They were muscular and tan, covered with a light dusting of sandy hair—a far cry from his usual pale limbs.

Trying not to panic, Ethan carefully swung his legs to the side of the bed and stood up. There was no pain associated with his movements, nothing to indicate that something bad might've happened to him. He felt strong and healthy . . . and that scared him even more than waking up in an unfamiliar bedroom.

The room itself was nice, decorated in modern-looking grey and white tones. Ethan had always meant to furnish his bedroom at home to look more like this, but hadn't gotten around to it. There also seemed to be some kind of movie posters on the walls. Upon closer inspection, they were more like theatrical production ads—ads that depicted a stylized, buffer, and better-looking version of himself.

What the hell?

In one of the posters, Ethan's likeness was holding rings on a pencil very close to his face. The rings were linked like a chain, and the image was titled *Insane Illusions by Razum*. In another ad, he was wearing a tuxedo and making a woman float in mid-air.

Was this a dream? If so, it had to be the most vivid dream Ethan had ever experienced—and one from which he couldn't seem to wake up. Ethan's heart was galloping in his chest, and he could feel the beginning of a panic attack.

No, stop it, Ethan. Just breathe. Breathe through it. And utilizing a technique he'd learned long ago to manage stress, Ethan focused on taking deep, even breaths.

After a couple of minutes, he felt calmer and more able to think rationally. Could this possibly be his house? Perhaps he'd suffered some kind of brain damage after being shot and was now experiencing memory loss. Theoretically, it was possible that he'd gotten a tan and started exercising—even though his rheumatoid arthritis usually prevented him from being particularly active.

His arthritis... That was another weird thing. Why didn't his joints ache like they usually did? Had he been given some wonder drug that healed gunshot wounds and autoimmune disorders? And what about those posters on the walls?

Doing his best to remain calm, Ethan spotted two doors on the opposite ends of the room. Taking one at random, he found himself inside a large, luxurious bathroom. There was a large mirror in front of him, and Ethan stepped closer to it, feeling like he was suffocating from lack of air.

The man reflected there was both familiar and different. Like his arms, his face was tan and practically glowing with health. Even his teeth seemed whiter somehow. His light brown hair was longer, almost covering his ears, and his skin was perfectly clear and wrinkle-free. Only his eyes were the same grey color that Ethan was used to seeing.

Breathe, Ethan. Breathe through it. There had to be a logical explanation for this. His buff build could be explained by a new exercise program. He could've also gotten a tan on a recent vacation—even though he couldn't recall taking one. However, he also looked younger somehow, which made even less sense. Ethan was in his mid-thirties, but the man in the mirror looked like he was maybe twenty-five. Surely he wasn't vain enough to have gotten plastic surgery at such a young age?

Blinking, Ethan stared at himself, then raised his hand and brushed back his hair. Everything felt real, too real for it to be a dream. Could the doctors have done something to him that had this incredible side effect? *Yeah, right, they invented the elixir of immortality and had to use it on me in ER.*

Leaving the bathroom, Ethan approached the wall and looked at another poster. There was a definite resemblance between what he saw in the mirror and the guy on the poster. In fact, he was confident that those posters were of himself—or, at least, of himself as he was right now, in this weird dream that was unlike any other.

Taking the other door, he entered a hallway that was covered with even more posters of his likeness performing various illusions. At the end of the hallway, there was a room. Likely a living room, Ethan decided, even though it was empty aside from a piece of furniture that resembled a couch.

A couch that was somehow floating in the air, as though it was hanging by some invisible thread from the ceiling.

What the...? Swallowing hard, Ethan stepped into the room, trying to see if there was someone playing a joke on him.

There wasn't anyone there. Instead, in one corner of the room, several trophies were floating on top of little pedestals. Seemingly made of gold, the trophy figures were those of men holding a sword. Approaching them carefully, Ethan tried to see how they were able to float in the air like that, but there was no visible mechanism holding them up. *Weird.*

Spotting a large window on the far wall, Ethan walked over to it, needing to look outside and reassure himself that he hadn't gone crazy, that he was still in New York City and not in some strange parallel universe.

And as he looked outside, he froze, paralyzed by shock and disbelief.

* * *

If you'd like to know when *Mind Awakening* comes out, please visit Dima Zales's website at www.dimazales.com and sign up for his new release email list. You can also connect with him on Facebook, Google Plus, Twitter, and Goodreads.

EXCERPT FROM
CLOSE LIAISONS BY ANNA ZAIRES

Author's Note: *Close Liaisons* is Dima Zales' collaboration with Anna Zaires and is the first book in the critically acclaimed erotic sci-fi romance series, the Krinar Chronicles. It contains explicit sexual content and is not intended for readers under 18.

* * *

A dark and edgy romance that will appeal to fans of erotic and turbulent relationships . . .

In the near future, the Krinar rule the Earth. An advanced race from another galaxy, they are still a mystery to us—and we are completely at their mercy.

Shy and innocent, Mia Stalis is a college student in

New York City who has led a very normal life. Like most people, she's never had any interactions with the invaders—until one fateful day in the park changes everything. Having caught Korum's eye, she must now contend with a powerful, dangerously seductive Krinar who wants to possess her and will stop at nothing to make her his own.

How far would you go to regain your freedom? How much would you sacrifice to help your people? What choice will you make when you begin to fall for your enemy?

* * *

The air was crisp and clear as Mia walked briskly down a winding path in Central Park. Signs of spring were everywhere, from tiny buds on still-bare trees to the proliferation of nannies out to enjoy the first warm day with their rambunctious charges.

It was strange how much everything had changed in the last few years, and yet how much remained the same. If anyone had asked Mia ten years ago how she thought life might be after an alien invasion, this would have been nowhere near her imaginings. *Independence Day, The War of the Worlds*—none of these were even close to the reality of encountering a more advanced civilization. There had been no fight, no resistance of any kind on government level—because *they* had not allowed it. In hindsight, it was clear how silly those movies had been. Nuclear weapons, satellites, fighter jets—these were little more than rocks and sticks to an ancient civilization that could cross the universe faster than the speed of light.

Spotting an empty bench near the lake, Mia gratefully headed for it, her shoulders feeling the strain of the backpack filled with her chunky twelve-year-old laptop and old-fashioned paper books. At twenty-one, she sometimes felt old, out of step with the fast-paced new world of razor-slim tablets and cell phones embedded in wristwatches. The pace of technological progress had not slowed since K-Day; if anything, many of the new gadgets had been influenced by what the Krinar had. Not that the Ks had shared any of their precious technology; as far as they were concerned, their little experiment had to continue uninterrupted.

Unzipping her bag, Mia took out her old Mac. The thing was heavy and slow, but it worked—and as a starving college student, Mia could not afford anything better. Logging on, she opened a blank Word document and prepared to start the torturous process of writing her Sociology paper.

Ten minutes and exactly zero words later, she stopped. Who was she kidding? If she really wanted to write the damn thing, she would've never come to the park. As tempting as it was to pretend that she could enjoy the fresh air and be productive at the same time, those two had never been compatible in her experience. A musty old library was a much better setting for anything requiring that kind of brainpower exertion.

Mentally kicking herself for her own laziness, Mia let out a sigh and started looking around instead. People-watching in New York never failed to amuse her.

The tableau was a familiar one, with the requisite homeless person occupying a nearby bench—thank God it wasn't the closest one to her, since he looked like he might smell very ripe—and two nannies chatting with each other in Spanish as they pushed their Bugaboos at a leisurely pace. A girl jogged on a path a little further ahead, her bright pink Reeboks contrasting nicely with her blue leggings. Mia's gaze followed the jogger as she rounded the corner, envying her athleticism. Her own hectic schedule allowed her little time to exercise, and she doubted she could keep up with the girl for even a mile at this point.

To the right, she could see the Bow Bridge over the lake. A man was leaning on the railing, looking out over the water. His face was turned away from Mia, so she could only see part of his profile. Nevertheless, something about him caught her attention.

She wasn't sure what it was. He was definitely tall and seemed well-built under the expensive-looking trench coat he was wearing, but that was only part of the story. Tall, good-looking men were common in model-infested New York City. No, it was something else. Perhaps it was the way he stood—very still, with no extra movements. His hair was dark and glossy under the bright afternoon sun, just long enough in the front to move slightly in the warm spring breeze.

He also stood alone.

That's it, Mia realized. The normally popular and picturesque bridge was completely deserted, except for the man who was standing on it. Everyone appeared to be giving it a wide berth for some unknown reason. In fact, with the exception of herself and her potentially aromatic homeless neighbor, the entire row of benches in the highly desirable waterfront location was empty.

As though sensing her gaze on him, the object of her attention slowly turned his head and looked directly at Mia. Before her conscious brain could even make the connection, she felt her blood turn to ice, leaving her paralyzed in place and helpless to do anything but stare at the predator who now seemed to be examining her with interest.

* * *

Breathe, Mia, breathe. Somewhere in the back of her mind, a small rational voice kept repeating those words. That same oddly objective part of her noted his symmetric face structure, with golden skin stretched tightly over high cheekbones and a firm jaw. Pictures and videos of Ks that she'd seen had hardly done them justice. Standing no more than thirty feet away, the creature was simply stunning.

As she continued staring at him, still frozen in place, he straightened and began walking toward her.

Or rather stalking toward her, she thought stupidly, as his every movement reminded her of a jungle cat sinuously approaching a gazelle. All the while, his eyes never left hers. As he approached, she could make out individual yellow flecks in his light golden eyes and the thick long lashes surrounding them.

She watched in horrified disbelief as he sat down on her bench, less than two feet away from her, and smiled, showing white even teeth. No fangs, she noted with some functioning part of her brain. Not even a hint of them. That used to be another myth about them, like their supposed abhorrence of the sun.

"What's your name?" The creature practically purred the question at her. His voice was low and smooth, completely unaccented. His nostrils flared slightly, as though inhaling her scent.

"Um . . ." Mia swallowed nervously. "M-Mia."

"Mia," he repeated slowly, seemingly savoring her name. "Mia what?"

"Mia Stalis." Oh crap, why did he want to know her name? Why was he here, talking to her? In general, what was he doing in Central Park, so far away from any of the K Centers? *Breathe, Mia, breathe.*

"Relax, Mia Stalis." His smile got wider, exposing a dimple in his left cheek. A dimple? Ks had dimples? "Have you never encountered one of us before?"

"No, I haven't," Mia exhaled sharply, realizing that she was holding her breath. She was proud that her voice didn't sound as shaky as she felt. Should she ask? Did she want to know?

She gathered her courage. "What, um—" Another swallow. "What do you want from me?"

"For now, conversation." He looked like he was about to laugh at her, those gold eyes crinkling slightly at the corners.

Strangely, that pissed her off enough to take the edge off her fear. If there was anything Mia hated, it was being laughed at. With her short, skinny stature and a general lack of social skills that came from an awkward teenage phase involving every girl's nightmare of braces, frizzy hair, and glasses, Mia had more than enough experience being the butt of someone's joke.

She lifted her chin belligerently. "Okay, then, what is *your* name?"

"It's Korum."

"Just Korum?"

"We don't really have last names, not the way you do. My full name is much longer, but you wouldn't be able to pronounce it if I told you."

Okay, that was interesting. She now remembered reading something like that in *The New York Times*. So far, so good. Her legs had nearly stopped shaking, and her breathing was returning to normal. Maybe, just maybe, she would get out of this alive. This conversation business seemed safe enough, although the way he kept staring at her with those unblinking yellowish eyes was unnerving. She decided to keep him talking.

"What are you doing here, Korum?"

"I just told you, making conversation with you, Mia." His voice again held a hint of laughter.

Frustrated, Mia blew out her breath. "I meant, what are you doing here in Central Park? In New York City in general?"

He smiled again, cocking his head slightly to the side. "Maybe I'm hoping to meet a pretty curly-haired girl."

Okay, enough was enough. He was clearly toying with her. Now that she could think a little again, she realized that they were in the middle of Central Park, in full view of about a gazillion spectators. She surreptitiously glanced around to confirm that. Yep, sure enough, although people were obviously steering clear of her bench and its otherworldly occupant, there were a number of brave souls staring their way from further up the path. A couple were even cautiously filming them with their wristwatch cameras. If the K tried anything with her, it would be on YouTube in the blink of an eye, and he had to know it. Of course, he may or may not care about that.

Still, going on the assumption that since she'd never come across any videos of K assaults on college students in the middle of Central Park, she was relatively safe, Mia cautiously reached for her laptop and lifted it to stuff it back into her backpack.

"Let me help you with that, Mia—"

And before she could blink, she felt him take her heavy laptop from her suddenly boneless fingers, gently brushing against her knuckles in the process.

A sensation similar to a mild electric shock shot through Mia at his touch, leaving her nerve endings tingling in its wake.

Reaching for her backpack, he carefully put away the laptop in a smooth, sinuous motion. "There you go, all better now."

Oh God, he had touched her. Maybe her theory about the safety of public locations was bogus. She felt her breathing speeding up again, and her heart rate was probably well into the anaerobic zone at this point.

"I have to go now . . . Bye!"

How she managed to squeeze out those words without hyperventilating, she would never know. Grabbing the strap of the backpack he'd just put down, she jumped to her feet, noting somewhere in the back of her mind that her earlier paralysis seemed to be gone.

"Bye, Mia. I will see you later." His softly mocking voice carried in the clear spring air as she took off, nearly running in her haste to get away.

* * *

If you'd like to find out more, please visit Anna's website at www.annazaires.com. *Close Liaisons* is currently available for free at most retailers.

ABOUT THE AUTHOR

Dima Zales is a science fiction and fantasy author residing in Palm Coast, Florida. Prior to becoming a writer, he worked in the software development industry in New York as both a programmer and an executive. From high-frequency trading software for big banks to mobile apps for popular magazines, Dima has done it all. In 2013, he left the software industry in order to concentrate on his writing career.

Dima holds a Master's degree in Computer Science from NYU and a dual undergraduate degree in Computer Science / Psychology from Brooklyn College. He also has a number of hobbies and interests, the most unusual of which might be professional-level mentalism. He simulates mind-reading on stage and close-up, and has done shows for corporations, wealthy individuals, and friends.

He is also into healthy eating and fitness, so he should live long enough to finish all the book projects he starts. In fact, he very much hopes to catch the technological advancements that might let him live forever (biologically or otherwise). Aside from that, he also enjoys learning about current and future technologies that might enhance our lives, including artificial intelligence, biofeedback, brain-to-computer interfaces, and brain-enhancing implants.

In addition to his own works, Dima has collaborated on a number of romance novels with his wife, Anna Zaires. The Krinar Chronicles, an erotic science fiction series, has been a bestseller in its categories and has been recognized by the likes of *Marie Claire* and *Woman's Day*. If you like erotic romance with a unique plot, please feel free to check it out, especially since the first book in the series (*Close Liaisons*) is available for free everywhere. Keep in mind, though, Dima Zales's books are going to be much less explicit . . . at least that's the plan for now.

Anna Zaires is the love of his life and a huge inspiration in every aspect of his writing. She definitely adds her magic touch to anything Dima creates, and the books would not be the same without her. Dima's fans are strongly encouraged to learn more about Anna and her work at http://www.annazaires.com.